Nos. 1 & 2.

One Penny.

THE

GHOST'S SECRET:

A TALE OF TERROR.

LONDON:

PRINTED AND PUBLISHED AT THE OFFICE, CRANE COURT, FLEET STREET.

THE
GHOST'S SECRET:
A TALE OF TERROR.

I could a tale unfold, whose lightest word
Would harrow up thy soul; freeze thy young blood;
Make thy two eyes, like stars, start from their spheres;
Thy knotted and combined locks to part,
And each particular hair to stand on end
Like quills upon the fretful porcupine.--SHAKSPEARE,

THE GHOST INTERRUPTS A DECLARATION OF LOVE.

CHAPTER I.

THE OLD HALL.

Those once-loved halls! where oft he heedless stray'd,
Cheer'd by a mother's love; where oft his heart
Has leapt at sounds of joy which echoed loud
Beneath the vaulted dome.—STARNO.

On Christmas Eve, in the year 1782, Reginald Dalton found himself beneath the porch of a mansion in Hampshire which had been the family residence of his ancestors—the Daltons—from time immemorial.

It was sadly dilapidated, and being occupied only in part, presented but a cold, dreary, and chilly appearance, at total variance with the gay and animated feelings of the young and handsome Reginald.

Dalton Hall was now inhabited by Colonel Hugh Dalton and his three accomplished daughters.

The family, as may be supposed, was distantly related to Reginald, and he was invited to spend his Christmas by the old Colonel in the latent hope that a nearer and closer connection might thereupon ensue between the cousins. His eldest daughter, Edith, was marriageable at the commencement of our story, and her father had private reasons for knowing that in the event of his brother not marrying and himself dying without male issue, Reginald was heir to a baronetcy and a commensurate fortune; in short, he hoped, by keeping up the acquaintance, to replenish his own exhausted exchequer and to make a good match for his favourite child.

This was the real motive which led to the invitation which Reginald Dalton received, and in the acceptance of which no idea of matrimony had the slightest influence.

In accepting the Colonel's hospitality one incentive prevailed above all others; and that was, a desire which he naturally felt of once against visiting a spot in which he had spent some happy hours and a portion of his boyhood.

Within the walls of Dalton Hall he first saw the light of day; but his father dying soon after that event, he took an aversion to the spot and all connected with it, and the estate passed into the hands of its present owner.

The why and wherefore Reginald could never correctly learn, and at the time when the change of ownership took place he was far too young to institute or make inquiries upon the subject.

Brought up by his paternal uncle, Sir Lionel Dalton, Bart., of Birchington, in the county of Kent, he knew little of his own family history, beyond the fact that he was born at Dalton Hall, and remembering some trifling scenes impressed upon his memory by circumstances which occurred there when he was a mere infant, he was impelled rather by curiosity to visit Colonel Dalton than by any affection or respect.

Let us describe the appearance of the old familiar spot as it met his gaze after an interval of six-and-twenty years.

A stone porch admitted him into a passage stolen from the great entrance hall, from which a small low door opened into a parlour, which was tolerably comfortable, and was evidently more modern than some other parts of the edifice, though the stone window frames and narrow casements seemed to indicate that even this apartment might boast an antiquity coeval with the reign of Elizabeth.

Here Reginald warmed himself before a cheering fire, whilst a servant announced his name as that of the long-expected guest.

The company assembled to welcome the stranger consisted of Colonel Dalton, Mr. Pendril, his legal adviser, Dr. Carmichael, the family physician, Miss Edith Dalton, and her two sisters Felicia and Margaret.

When supper was announced, they were ushered into the dining hall, where a table was spread, profusely decorated with mistletoe and holly, but actually groaning beneath the weight of all the delicate and substantial fare usually consecrated to such a season of mirth and holiday feeling.

May such homage to the season continue for all time, and may Christmas never go out of fashion!

A brightly blazing and exhilarating fire, chiefly composed of wooden logs, in a roomy chimney corner, gave a glow of comfort to the otherwise cold naked walls and chilly stone floor of the apartment. The hall reached to the roof of the house itself, and each window, or rather each tier of windows—for it had the appearance of three or four piled one upon the other, the highest finishing with a Gothic arch—was nearly the height of the hall, defying alike the aid of drapery or shutters to keep out the dim light of the moon, and the stars twinkling in their silvery brightness and frosty splendour.

Though Colonel Dalton regaled his young guest with all the comforts and many of the extravagances which only wealth can procure, yet, as his means were shrouded in mystery, he retained in his family a simplicity of manners which belonged only to persons of humble fortune.

Reginald was surprised, nay, somewhat confounded at finding himself, as well as the other guests, waited upon by the youngest daughter of his entertainer. An excusable vanity prompted him to attribute this attention to his fine clothes, for he wore a coat of the finest scarlet, and the narrow lace that edged his three-cornered hat was no counterfeit, but genuine gold.

Margaret tended him assiduously, but in her duties however, she was greatly assisted by that old appendage to a baronial hall, the buttery hatch, which raised its gigantic but convenient head in the apartment, having escaped the demolishing hand of modern renovation.

Reginald well recollected this hatch, for it had the appearance, when closed, of a large door, but the upper part only opened horizontally, and when let down formed a table accessible alike to the hall or pantry.

On this were placed the dishes which formed the supper of the evening, and this simple contrivance saved many a long and roundabout walk to those who had to place the viands before the assembled guests.

The table itself had a double attraction in the eyes of Reginald.

It brought vividly to his recollection that happy period of his existence, when the most trivial circumstances afforded him pleasure; and he now, when grown a man recollected when a boy he had once jumped from that very table to the ground, to decide a wager between the butler and the house steward.

In addition to this pleasure, he had the gratification of being served by Margaret Dalton, who was continually filling his goblet with the choicest wines, from a sideboard no less antique than the buttery hatch. He observed it was placed in a deep recess, and consisted of a large marble slab, supported by half-a-dozen rampant lions, with lifted claws and growling mouths, which he well remembered his mother had specially ordered to be crammed with mortar and painted over, because they frightened her darling boy.

The supper passed with the usual and commonplace conversation.

The Colonel indulged in bitter sarcasms against his neighbours, in which he was cordially joined by Dr. Carmichael, who had probably more reason to be dissatisfied with them, inasmuch as he had never been professionally called in by any of them upon any occasion; and yet epidemics and contagious fevers had been prevalent at times.

With the Colonel the case was different. From some hidden cause he was disliked by those who ought to have been his associates and friends.

In revenge he gratified a paltry spirit, by detracting from the merits and disparaging the virtues of almost everybody he knew, especially those gentlemen who were his immediate neighbours.

He lived upon vituperation. It was his food. It was easily gorged and poured out. He, in fact, reconciled himself to his own deficiencies by coarsely abusing the foibles and eccentricities of others.

He was a man who kept cold water and ice always at command, sufficient to freeze the most boiling cauldron.

The conversation of such a relation was not particularly agreeable to Reginald, and he really was not sorry when the lawyer and the doctor rose to take their leave.

Their departure caused the family to think of retiring to their separate apartments for the night.

Colonel Dalton apologised to his guest for being compelled to place him in a chamber that was very seldom used, but at the same time assured him that every care had been taken to obviate any danger that could arise to him from damp or cold, by means of good fires and warming stoves.

When the chamber in which it was proposed that he should sleep was first mentioned, Reginald observed great eagerness to speak in one of the Colonel' daughters. The fair and youthful Margaret was stopped, or he fancied so, by a scowl from her father and a significant bend of the head from her eldest sister Edith, as the latter desired the youthful attendant to light a taper and show their guest to his bed.

Margaret did as she was bid.

Reginald followed his beautiful guide and ascended to his chamber.

It was approached by a narrow spiral stone staircase, which almost gave way beneath them as they ascended it.

This surmounted, they wound their way through a variety of long intricate passages, stumbling over an equal number of steps which crossed their path, till they reached the massive door, which opened into the gloomy apartment provided for him.

Reginald nearly stumbled as he gazed at it, for his fair guide would not break the mysterious silence which had been imposed upon her, even to warn him of an abrupt and uneven step which impeded his progress.

The feeble and flickering light of the wax taper which Margaret held in her hand, fell upon a narrow arched door, thickly studded with large decaying rusty nails, and was only opened by a huge iron ring, which, when pulled, admitted them by means of a latch into the dismal interior.

"This, Mr. Dalton, is where you are to sleep to-night," said Margaret, ushering Reginald in, "but a more comfortable apartment shall be got ready for you in the course of to-morrow."

CHAPTER II.

THE HAUNTED CHAMBER.

Agony unmix'd, incessant gall,
Corroding every thought and blasting all.
THOMPSON.

MARGARET and Reginald entered a large, irregular bed-room, the dreariness of which was but slightly relieved by a fire which moodily burned in an old-fashioned chimney, beneath an equally old-fashioned mantle-piece.

Reginald observed that the walls of the chamber were rudely carved with the arms of his forefathers, and embellished with the ever-defiant lion which had caused him so much terror in the days of his childhood.

He instinctively shrank from their contemplation.

The worm-eaten oak mouldings recalled the place to his recollection.

It was the identical chamber in which he had once been confined for an act of juvenile disobedience, for two entire days, by order of his mother.

Whitewash was the cold covering of the chamber walls, and in many parts the wash itself had peeled off, leaving the bare bricks exposed to the gaze of its occupant.

The hangings of a huge oaken square four-post bedstead were of a dingy white, a cheerless, chilling colour at that season of the year, with ugly black velvet valances, cut into hideous curves and scallops, from which the line of ugliness was continued with minute exactness in the grey worsted lace which bound the the edges.

A curiously fashioned toilet, hung with very old but elegant point lace, an equally ancient washing-stand, and six carved oak chairs with high upright cane backs completed the solitary splendour of the room.

Whilst Reginald moodily viewed his resting-place, Margaret placed his taper on the toilet, and casting upon him an unmistakeable glance of pity, hastily wished him a good night, and made her way from the gloomy apartment with so much speed as quite to forget the shutting of the ponderous door.

Reginald fancied he heard his fair conductress sigh heavily as she tripped across the vaulted passage.

He might have been mistaken, but he was confident he could hear her stumbling her way back again, as if the affrighted girl were in too great a hurry to regard the inequalities of her path.

Reginald stood alone in that uncomfortable and cheerless chamber.

He was not superstitious; but there are times and situations in which the boldest among us, who at other periods scorn the idea of anything bordering on superstition, feel its influence, despite of reason and religion; and Reginald felt something very like it the moment Margaret had quitted him, and he found himself the solitary occupant of that solitary chamber.

A description of his very disagreeable sensation is uncalled for, for it must have been felt at some time or another by most persons, though ninety and nine out of every hundred are ashamed to confess it.

The flickering light of the fast dying fire fell upon the brass nails which formed the initial letters M. D. D., on the lid of a large oak chest.

Reginald recollected that chest well. It had originally been the property of Maria Domville Dalton, one of his aunts, and formed the only seat allowed him to sit upon, when doing penance, by command of his mother, for the offence we have before alluded to.

He looked towards that chest with an undefined apprehension of seeing the spectral form of the identical cat, for the torturing of which he had been justly punished by his mother, start from the inside, pounce upon him, and claw him with its talons.

The next moment he smiled at his own folly, and took up the taper to examine the room.

The first thing he recognised was a small arched door, similar to the one through which he had entered, excepting that it was elevated a few steps from the floor.

After a few efforts he succeeded in unfastening the door, when a sudden rush of the incoming wind extinguished his taper; but this he soon relit at the fire, and screening it with his hand, he once more approached the door.

It was some time before he could make his taper burn steadily enough to examine the place which the passage led to. It was altogether new to him, for he had no recollection of it when a boy.

It led, however, to a small turret chamber, crumbling from disuse and greatly dilapidated, with a narrow arched window, through the broken panes of which the clustering ivy had obtruded itself, and was creeping along the interior walls, giving them an air of strange desolation.

Looking through the broken window, Reginald discovered beneath it the roof of a ruined porch, one which he well recollected was the principal entrance to his father's house, for beside it stood a very aged yew tree, to the top of which he had often climbed when a mere boy.

His survey ended, he was glad to close the door again on the dark green foliage, and quit such a neglected portion of the mansion.

He returned to his own room.

When in it he could not entirely divest himself of that awful mysterious feeling which the gloom of his new lodging inspired him with, and as if a mere boy again, he felt a sort of childish safety when he sank into a soft feather-bed, and incontinently wrapped his head in the silken coverlid.

Reginald drooped into a sound slumber, so deep and so sound indeed, that it must have been a loud noise which awakened him, as if from a dream, to a state of nervousness, which made him tremble from head to foot and shook the mansion to its foundation.

He listened. The noise, regular in its recurrence, continued, and seemed to resemble that made by a chair on which some person was rocking an infant to sleep.

Surprised at what he deemed an unwarrantable intrusion in his apartment, Reginald hastily drew back the curtains of his bed, and to his very great astonishment, distinctly saw before the fire, which at that moment flashed into a bright blaze, the back of a woman of very singular appearance, with an infant on her lap.

Every now and then the rocking of the chair stopped, and the motion of the stranger's elbows indicated her to be performing some other offices which pertained to the duties of a fond and doting nurse.

She would stretch out her own hands to the fire. Then she would rub the feet and limbs of the infant briskly, her stiff satin robe rustling as she moved her arms up and down to produce the friction necessary to impart warmth.

Reginald spoke, but received no answer.

He spoke again, and rather angrily.

"Who is it that dares to disturb me at this early hour of the morning."

No answer.

"I repeat, who are you who dares thus impudently intrude in a private chamber ? "

Still silence.

Reginald spoke a third time, and louder than he had done before.

The rocking of the old highbacked chair was the only sound he heard.

He now got seriously angered, and with an oath commanded the intruder to quit the apartment.

When his own voice, loud and violent as it had been, died away to a fearful silence, he stepped out of bed, determined to expel the intruder by manual force, if requisite.

But Reginald was awed !

He walked cautiously and timidly round, to have a more perfect view of the mysterious being who annoyed him.

He was not asleep.

He was not dreaming.

He was awake and sensible.

He perfectly well remembered striking his foot against the huge iron fender which encircled the ancient fire-place, but despite the acute pain occasioned by the accident, he was determined to look the intruder full in the face.

It could be no menial of the establishment who would dare to take that liberty which he now rose to resent.

Reginald was amazed !

He was spell-bound !

He was thunderstruck !

His mother stood before him in the very habit she wore when he himself used to climb her knee, and crave her blessing !

She appeared to him as young and as beautiful as ever ; but for the livid hue of her lips and the deadly whiteness of her cheeks, she sat a living angel.

Her eyes were, however, chill and lustreless, and the parched lip appeared to be quivering with the cold.

The infant's hands and fingers were of the same icy hue, and seemed paralysed with cold.

Endeavouring to infuse warmth into the child's limbs his mother dislodged the swathing band which encased its features.

Reginald was astonished ; and well he might be, for in that infant he beheld a perfect facsimile of himself, as he appeared in a miniature painting which was still preserved, and which, taken soon after his birth, was being handed down as an heirloom to the family.

The picture was in the possession of Sir Lionel Dalton, and is still hanging up at Bodmin Hall, in the Isle of Thanet.

Reginald stood gazing upon himself, the original of that picture, as in infancy he swayed to and fro in his mother's lap.

Though it was but a moment that such a vision was given to his view, he had a perfectly clear and most distinct remembrance of his own appearance and of his mother's dress.

His mother was clothed in a gown of stiff satin, made high about the neck, surmounted by a ruff, the quillings of which looked like carved work ; a single row of closely set studs, confined it close to the chest till it met the stomacher, which was terminated by a bow of blue and black ribbon; her sleeves were made tight to her arms in the fashion of the times, and finished at the wrists by cuffs of point lace bound back in the form of a mitre. Her hair was strained back from her forehead, and on it she wore a black coif, bordered with large pearls.

Reginald's infant self had likewise his tiny body made shapely by a formal stomacher; his plain borderless cap, bib and cuffs being of stiffened lawn, crimped and pinched into a kind of miniature fretwork.

Every particular was too deeply impressed upon Reginald to be forgotten, though brief was the space allowed him to gaze upon the phantoms.

Suddenly the rayless eyes of the dead mother were fixed upon the living Reginald.

They kindled to a look of terror, as, rising from her high-backed chair, she closely pressed the infant form of his second self to her bosom, and uttering a wild and piercing shriek, as if in recognition, exclaimed, "Reginald, you come to avenge me !"

Though terrified beyond the powers of description, Reginald Dalton stood calm and collected before the shadow of his beloved mother, and inspired almost with supernatural courage, he dropped on one knee, and looking up in the face of her shadow, answered—

"If man or woman hath done thee wrong, mother, I will avenge you."

"Swear to do so Reginald !"

"My word, mother, is my bond—both to the living and the dead. Believe me, I will see justice done to you !"

"Swear it !"

"By my bright hopes of an eternal hereafter, I swear never to enjoy one minute's peace on earth till I have avenged you."

"Good, Reginald ! Obedience is the tie of filial love. I shall now have rest in my grave, since I have extorted this promise to avenge a foul and coward murder."

"Murder ?"

"Yes, Reginald, covert and cruel—cowardly in the extreme."

"By whom? and how, mother ?"

"Subtle poison passed in a loving cup, which left no dregs to betray the hand which gave it."

"And that hand quailed not ?"

"Steady and cool as adamant."

"Whose was it ? Who is the butcher that could slay in cold blood the best of mothers, the dearest of wives and the kindest of friends ?"

The spirit pointed with its thin and bony finger in the direction of the turret, and in a sepulchral voice answered—"Reginald, my son! It was —— "

But Reginald was not destined to learn that night the murderer's name from the appealing lips of his mother's ghost ; for the crowing of chanticleer was heard in the distance, and the grey streaks of a dull and sombre morning shed a dim light as they poured in at the windows.

The spectre melted into indistinctness, and was prevented from fully divulging its dreadful secret even to the ears of him who was missioned to avenge it.

But the reprisal will come anon.

Reginald stared upon the vacuity which the spectre left long after the phantom itself was seen no more.

The fire, which had blazed up with a blue sulphurous and supernatural brightness before, flickered and spent itself out as the forms of the mother and the child became obliterated and lost in vapour.

It may appear somewhat strange, but it is nevertheless true, that with the disappearance of the spectre Reginald's superstitious terror died away.

When the ghost had mysteriously melted from his

...ight, he sat for a considerable time on the oaken chest ...uminating over what he had seen, but without tha ...ndescribable awe which had pervaded his mind when ...e first took possession of the chamber.

He could only account for this stoicism on the prin-...iple that apprehension, having no limits, is less bear-...ble than the certainty of the greatest calamity.

Comforting himself with this reflection, he returned ...o his bed, if not quite free from terror, totally unawed ...y the dreadful tidings which had been imparted to ...im.

He could not rid himself, however, from thinking of them, and they kept him awake for the residue of that eventful night.

CHAPTER III.

REGINALD SEEKS AN EXPLANATION, BUT IS REPULSED·

His tongue was envenomed, and venom did its work.
FENELON.

IN the morning Reginald Dalton made his way to the parlour, where a bright coal fire speedily dispelled the gloomy recollection of the horrors he had encountered in the night.

He determined to keep all knowledge of what he had witnessed from his host or any of the family, but when Margaret appeared to preside at the morning meal he detained her from her more useful occupation, first by the common salutations of the morning, and then by cunningly turning the conversation to the antiquity of the house, and expressing, in a careless off-handed sort of manner, his wonder if there was any legend attached to the Old Hall.

Margaret smiled, and told him that it was well that he had not inquired for such stories the night before, as the gratification of his curiosity might have interfered with his repose.

Would she be good enough to oblige him with any bit of romance connected with the place that she could possibly remember ?

Her father, she was certain, would give him every information upon that subject, but she had been ex-pressly forbidden by him to allude to it in any way or shape whatever.

At breakfast Reginald did not beat about the bush but boldly struck into the thicket at once.

"Colonel, do you believe in ghosts and supernatural appearances ? "

"I do not, Mr. Dalton ; and, moreover, I think that man a downright fool who gives credit to anything of the kind."

"The dead are not permitted to revisit the earth, then ? "

" Certainly not."

" Therefore we must take as fictitious the many extraordinary tales, ancient and modern, which are handed down to us about these sort of things ? "

"They are all perfectly absurd. Ha ! ha ! ha ! "

"You have great courage, Colonel, to laugh at a subject upon which even the most learned of men and the wisest of divines are sceptical ! "

"Perhaps I have good reasons to laugh at such non-sense."

"If you will not allow it possible for the spirit to return to earth after it has once left the body, Colonel, you will, at least. admit that the contemplation of the body itself after death in any way is terrible to those who witness it, and must be much more so to those who have caused death."

"The terrors of death are no terrors to the good ; he that commits no evil has nothing to fear."

"I quite agree with you, Colonel, but solitude, you know, will beget terror ; darkness even engenders it, and the silent hour of midnight will sometimes predis-pose the stoutest heart."

"No sensible man, Mr. Dalton will give way to fear. It is beneath the dignity of a being who calls himself rational. Fear, when it gains an ascendancy over the mind, renders life a burden. It debases our nature, poisons all our comforts, and make us despicable in the eyes of others. In battle the brave soldier is in less danger than the coward : in less danger even of death and of wounds, because better prepared to defend him-self. But why have you touched upon this topic, my young friend ?—did you not sleep well ?'

As this was the cue which Reginald wanted, he candidly confessed that he had not slept well, and was about to enter upon an explanation of the mysterious cause, when the Colonel turned sharply round upon him and said,—

"I would rather not hear any particulars of this kind in the presence of my girls ; they are timid enough at the best of times, and if your dream, or your fancy, or whatever it may be, borders on the marvellous, I shall have them refuse to fetch me my dressing-gown from upstairs at dusk, or walk in the garden after dark. See, they are already sitting nearer to one another, we will, therefore, with your permission, defer this discussion until we are alone."

"Tea or coffee, Mr. Dalton?" asked Edith.

"Tea, I thank you," replied Reginald ; and seeing that the Colonel was not to be drawn into anything like a conversation upon the subject, he turned to address a few commonplace observations to Margaret.

He observed that the sweet girl turned deadly pale.

"Oh, father," said she, "I am certain that my cousin has seen you know what, and that uncle John did not invent the story after all."

" Be silent Margaret. You are a little coward, and I am surprised to hear you mention such a ridiculous subject when you know I have over and over again forbidden you to allude to it, or anything of the kind in my presence."

"If Miss Dalton has heard anything which can—"

"Excuse me for interrupting you Mr. Dalton, but I must beg you will not, in this house, at least, continue a topic personally disagreeable to its master."

Reginald was too well bred to persevere.

Apologizing to the Colonel for what he termed mere idle curiosity, he sipped his cup of tea and munched his toast for a considerable time, deeply lost in thought.

At last he broke the silence by inquiring after the health of some old friends of his father's, and asked among other questions, whether any persons of position and consideration had lately come to reside in the neighbourhood of the old Hall.

"None that I know of " said the Colonel.

"Pray who is the present possessor of the Grange at Romsey."

"A person of the name of Hardcastle."

"Jeremiah Hardcastle ?"

"Yes."

"Is he a pleasant neighbour ? "

"Decidedly otherwise."

"I am sorry to hear it."

"I wish he had continued to live at Southampton, for he is likely to do little good here."

"I regret much to hear so ; what do you object to in him ? "

"He differs with me in politics."

"What else ? "

"Runs down the game laws."

"I dont blame him for that. They are oppressive and iniquitous. What say you, Miss Edith ?"

The young lady appealed to dared not to venture an opinion at variance with her father's and so declared that she knew nothing about politics or the game laws either.

"Well Colonel, putting aside these obnoxious im-positions, what other objection have you to Mr. Hardcastle ?"

" He is mean to a degree."

" Indeed !"

" And narrow-minded."

"How does he show it ?"

"He keeps no establishment."

"Perhaps he spends the expense of one in acts of private benevolence?"

"I don't believe it. I sent one of my own labourers, who met with a sad accident, to him, expecting that he would subscribe to a little petition, but all he said was that he would look into the matter."

"And did he look into it?"

"I cannot say."

"Then it is rather illiberal to infer that he did not."

"Oh! but he is so exceedingly unneighbourly that I cannot help disliking him."

"How, unneighbourly ?"

"Why, I took a liking to one of his spirited horses the other day, and bid him a good price for it. Would you believe it ?—he was so churlish as actually to refuse my money. They tell me that rather than sell it to me he sent it to Romsey fair. Then there's my Edith, you must know she is passionately fond of flowers. Passing his garden, the silly girl saw an uncommon plant, and begged a small cutting from it."

"Which, of course, the young lady immediately obtained."

"Indeed not. She was disappointed. Our gardener mentioned her wish, but instead of obliging my daughter, Mr. Hardcastle was rude enough to give positive orders that the plant should not be touched."

"I am rather surprised, for this very same Mr. Hardcastle is called the pink of politeness in London."

"I am equally surprised to hear you say so, for I do assure you that I don't believe he has one single characteristic of the gentleman about him."

Reginald was quite astonished to hear the Colonel's opinion.

Mr. Hardcastle was a very old friend of his father's, but he concealed his chagrin, confident that the true character of the gentleman would develope itself in time, and that his real motives would presently appear.

Nor was he deceived.

Scarcely had the breakfast things been removed, when the labouring man, before alluded to, and who carried his arm in a sling, begged permission to speak to the Colonel.

The ladies having retired to their several household duties, he was admitted.

"Well, Jonathan, how did you get on ? Did Mr Hardcastle perform his promise ? Did he give you anything ? I am sure he did not, for I had but faint hopes for you when you said he promised to look into it."

"But he has looked into it, sir ! God bless him ! He made some inquiries about me. and when I waited upon him yesterday afternoon, he said he had taken some pains in my case, and finding that I bore a tolerable good character, he had interested himself amongst his neighbours and friends, and had succeeded in collecting the sum of thirty pounds for me."

"Thirty pounds ?"

"Yes, sir."

"That's pretty well, Colonel, for a churlish old neighbour," dryly remarked Reginald, as he stirred up the tea in his cup.

The Colonel bit his lip.

But his humiliation was not yet complete.

Presently Mr. Meadows, Mr. Hardcastle's gardener, made his appearance with the very cuttings which Miss Edith so much admired, and which he had now transmitted to her most carefully, and with a note, stating good and sufficient reasons why the seedling had not been disturbed before the proper season.

Colonel Dalton was too proud a man to admit an error, though flagrant to everybody else.

The moment the gardener's back was turned he coolly observed that Mr. Hardcastle was a shrewd man, and doubtless felt that he owed him, the Colonel, a little amends for not sooner cultivating his acquaintance.

But Reginald did not see his conduct exactly in that light.

He insisted upon it that the delicate way in which the gift had been conveyed, resounded in the highest degree to the credit and honor of the donor.

The gardener had scarcely taken his leave when the Colonel perceiving his neighbour's groom to be passing, and wishing still to have a fling at him, called out to the man to come to him from the window, and when the man approached it he sarcastically asked him how much more cash he had really got for his master's horse than what he had been offered.

"Lor bless you, sir, I sold him for one-half of what you would have given. I sold him to the coaching people, and they'll break him on his vicious tricks, I'll be sworn."

"There, do you hear that, Mr. Dalton ? "

"But why did you sell him so very cheap, my good man," asked Reginald, crushing a rebellious lump of sugar at the bottom of his cup with a spoon.

"Why you see, your honor, it were so very vicious and so very likely to kill its rider one of these days, that I was ordered to take whatever sum the coach owners offered for him. I might have sold him better, I know that, but master wouldn't let I, for he said, said he, the horrid critter shan't kill any people with my consent."

"That is the sole reason why the animal was not sold to my friend here ? "

"It is, sir ? "

"Colonel, you really ought to be highly obliged to this man's master."

"I must admit it was rather polite on his part."

"Polite, Colonel ! I think it was something more than mere politeness. It was downright real goodness of heart !"

"You are inclined to be disputatious this morning Mr. Dalton, We will, if you please, drop the subject."

"Mr. Hardcastle is —— "

"Mr. Hardcastle is, I dare say, a marvellous proper man in some person's opinion, but let him be what he may, I will never condescend to make his acquaintance."

Short-sighted Colonel !

He little dreamt at the time he uttered this supercilious and egotistical exclamation, of the dreadful manner in which he would be introduced to Mr. Hardcastle's notice in after years.

CHAPTER IV.

THE GHOST INTERRUPTS A DECLARATION OF LOVE.

See where it comes again !—HAMLET.

THERE was something so irresistibly fascinating in the beauty and candour of the young Margaret, that Reginald was captivated with her even before he was aware of it.

Colonel Hugh Dalton being called suddenly to London a few days after Reginald's arrival at the hall, on business of an urgent nature, he had ample opportunities of being alone with his fair cousin, and of fully learning her temper and disposition.

Oh! this love !

It is a very wonderful and unaccountable passion.

It is of such a power in its operation that it has often taken the diadem from kings and queens, and made them stoop to those of obscure birth and mean fortune.

It arrests the sword out of the conqueror's hand, and makes him captive to his slave.

Love is the great instrument of nature; the bond and cement of society; the spirit and spring of the universe, and without it chaos is come again.

Love is such an affection as cannot so properly be said to be in the soul, as the soul to be in it; it is the whole man wrapped up into one desire.

It is now necessary to state that, true to her promise,

Margaret did not allow Reginald to sleep a second time in a chamber which had so much alarmed him.

He had now been comfortably reposing for more than a fortnight in a small and convenient apartment, neatly fitted up for him near the Colonel's library, and as Reginald was an early reader, it afforded him many and frequent opportunities of a little private converse with Margaret, who was ever eager to take down from the shelves the particular book he required.

Though burning to do so, as yet he had not summoned sufficient courage to allude to the apparition of his dead mother.

He longed to speak, but at the same time he would rather that the ice should be broken by his fair cousin.

Margaret and Reginald were much together.

The other sisters, either dreading to be interrogated on the subject of the haunted chamber, or seeing the impression which Margaret had already created in the breast of their father's guest, were jealous and uneasy in the presence of both, and only favoured their relative with their company at meals, or on other occasions which civility demanded.

Her cousin had not been more than a fortnight at Dalton Hall, when Margaret conceived a passion for him which was daily increasing, and which she was afraid he would but too soon perceive.

Reginald was exactly in the same situation as regarded himself.

He not only saw in her a disposition to acquaint him one day or another with the full details of the mystery he desired to solve, but also every attribute of a woman of the greatest virtue, and the most amiable qualities.

He found that it was not in his power to stifle a passion he was no longer master of.

He well weighed their relative positions, and was not slow to perceive that the merit, the virtue, the beauty, the courage, and the generosity of Margaret preponderated over all other reflections.

To put the poor girl's affections to a severe test, he determined upon a very old expedient.

Having received an unimportant letter from his uncle, Sir Lionel Dalton, he pretended to her that he was called away suddenly and on very urgent family matters, and that it was imperative that he should set off on the instant.

Using a conventional expression, when the lover communicated this intelligence to his fair one we may be permitted to say that she turned all manner of colours.

Reginald and Margaret were both perplexed.

Margaret would have fainted, but Edith entering the room, her coming at a time which seemed rather *mal apropos* in truth was disagreeable to neither, as they were both at a loss what to say, and the interruption afforded breathing time.

Reginald recovered his self-possession the moment Edith had withdrawn.

"I greatly thank you," said he, " for the many favours you have conferred upon me, and must ask for your permission to run home on rather important business."

"You are in a great hurry! Do you think that after having been here whilst father was at home we ought to be deprived of your company now that he is away—and we so dull and lonely?"

"It is very unfortunate, but "——

"I'll hear no excuses. I know you are too polite to leave us alone."

At any other time he would be but too happy—too honoured.

As he pronounced words to this effect, he fancied he saw a tear starting into the eye of his cousin, and the sight completely unmanned him. He burst out into a rhapsody of endearing words.

"No, Margaret," said he, "I will not go; we will never be separated from each other. My life shall be entirely devoted to you, for my heart is not able to

testify so much as you deserve, the holy love I bear you. I adore you, and if you will accept me, such as I am, I shall esteem myself the happiest of men."

"I have shown you too much regard already," replied Margaret, " to prevent me from concealing the fact, Mr. Dalton, that I esteem you sufficiently well to be proud of such a declaration."

"Do I hear right ? Is my passion reciprocated ? Am I regarded ?"

"Blame me not for the seeming freedom I may have taken in making you acquainted with my feelings by this natural confession ; but time will let you see that to the purity of my intentions there are joined a constancy and devotedness which nothing will change."

It would take volumes of printed matter to narrate all that Margaret and Reginald said to each other, or to describe one hundredth part of the tender, sweet, affectionate endearments which passed between them, and seemed diffused through their souls.

It is impossible to represent to the reader those looks, those airs and those eyes, which tell better than words can express, and which a perfect and happy love alone knows how to spread itself on those it inflames ; whoever has thoroughly loved will easily conceive it, but nothing can inform the uninitiated.

The shadows of the evening were fast falling upon the walls of the apartment as Reginald ratified his formal proposal by an affectionate salute on the fair cheek of Margaret.

It was the first he had ever ventured to bestow on the object of his affection, and she was pressed to his bosom with all the ardour and in all the ecstasy of an honourable and regarded love, when suddenly a cold hand seemed to be passing itself across his forehead.

His whole frame shook violently.

"Dearest Reginald, are you ill, why do you gaze so intently on my father's portrait," asked Margaret.

But it was not upon the Colonel's likeness he gazed.

A more startling object met his view.

His mother stood before him, not in the satin attire in which he had last seen her, but in the shroud and sear cloth of the grave, and looking just as he remembered she did look, when he ventured to take his last sad glimpse of her stretched in her coffin, a cold and pallid corpse, ere that frail tenement in which she was to repose for ever was soldered down.

"Margaret ! My beloved Margaret ! See there ?"

"What Reginald ? What ?"

"Do you not see her ?"

"See who ?"

"My mother ! She beckons me."

"Reginald, I see nothing, yet all there is, I see !"

"Hush ! She still beckons. She is about to speak ! "

And the spectre, for it was the ghost of his murdered parent, approached him with an involuntary movement of her lips, as if in the act of addressing him.

Margaret, alarmed by the wild and excited appearance of her lover, hastily disengaged herself from his clutch and rang for a servant.

The sound of the bell, as it audibly vibrated throughout the different passages of the mansion from the violence with which it had been pulled, disturbed its spectral visitor, and when a servant entered, bearing the table lamp ready lighted for the night, it vanished altogether.

Had Margaret seen that appalling apparition ?

We shall learn in a future chapter.

CHAPTER V.

AN EPISODE IN THE DRAMA—SOME ACCOUNT OF THE DALTONS.

Too many lovers will puzzle a maid.—OLD SONG.

LET us now look into the antecedents of the Dalton's, as every member of that family forms an important link in the chain which is to connect their history with the revelations of *The Ghost's Secret.*

On the borders of the New Forest, and near to the picturesque and pretty village of Ringwood, resided a wealthy farmer, named Lascelles, who, being in thriving circumstances and exceedingly well to do in the world, spared no pains or expense on the education of his only child—a daughter.

Mary Lascelles grew up a lovely woman, and lacking neither beauty of person or accomplishments of mind, had various suitors.

Amongst the latter she numbered three brothers of the name of Dalton.

The first was Lionel Dalton, who succeeded to a baronetcy on the death of his uncle, Sir Hepworth Dalton, and who was undoubtedly the richest of the three.

The next was his second brother, Hugh Dalton, brought up to no profession whatever, but originally intended for the church, though after the death of his father he bought himself a commission in the army.

The third was the youngest of the trio, Reginald Dalton, a fine, handsome, open-hearted young Englishman, who wooed and won Mary Lascelles, as we shall see in the sequel.

Reginald being a younger brother met with but little favour in the eyes of Mr. Lascelles, and in all human probability would have been banished from the presence of his idol, but for the fact that whenever he visited the farm he was accompanied by his brother, Sir Lionel Dalton, and the ambitious father indulged in hopes that the latter might " dazzle the eyes and bewilder the brain " of Mary.

It was his ambition, and his hope that he might live to hear his child called Lady Dalton. He would then die happy.

But he died before the accomplishment of his wish, and Mary being freed from parental restriction, was at liberty to choose for herself.

Grief for the loss of a father, whom she loved with an unfeigned tenderness, preyed upon her spirits for a time, and made it necessary for her to pause before she gave the final " Yes " or " No " to either of her suitors.

The majority of these were abandoned at once, and the Daltons only remained as habitual visitors to divert her melancholy.

The aim and object of the brothers were alike, but in their operations how different !

Lionel endeavoured to amuse her mind by costly presents and frivolous amusements.

Hugh sought to pervert her understanding, by which means he hoped to succeed in a nefarious scheme touching her property.

Reginald soothed her sorrows, and whilst he never alluded to his own passion, he created an endurable one in the breast of the being he was solacing.

The nature and dispositions of the three brothers were so exceedingly opposite, that they must have particular mention.

Lionel had a great deal of levity in his composition, but with all his follies, he possessed many virtues ; charity, humanity, and benevolence, were practised by him to an uncommon degree.

Hugh on the contrary, was selfish, self-willed and self-sufficient. Having displayed some little ability, his father sent him when he was quite young to Eton, from thence to Cambridge, and soon after he came from the University, he left England on his travels.

Whilst on the Continent he committed a crime which was but too fashionable at the time.

He called out the brother of a woman he had betrayed and shot him dead, because he had taken umbrage at his conduct.

We confess to a " fearful bias on the subject of duels," but as Hugh Dalton was exceedingly young at the time he fought one, and might have been provoked beyond all endurance by the epithets bestowed upon him by his antagonist, we let the black curtain of oblivion and secrecy fall upon him as to that adventure, and proceed with our history.

After her father's decease and burial, Miss Lascelles thought it prudent and proper to invite a female relative to reside with her.

Mrs. Hornby was the favoured individual ; but the former was not to be complimented on her choice of a companion.

The lady pretended greatly to commiserate the lonely condition of her dear young friend, but it was merely the affectation of feeling, for her sensibility on any point was never so likely as when herself was concerned, and a habitual weakness of constitution made her think lightly of the sufferings of others.

Her mind was vacant, her manners childish, and the early indulgence of a fond husband gave rise to caprices, ridiculous and wearisome.

If a door shut unusually loud an hysterical fit ensued.

If the wind shook the casement, palpitations and tremors were the consequence.

If a child cried in her hearing, or a dog barked in her presence, she was sure to have a nervous headache for the remainder of the day.

Her husband had been the slave of her whims, though his understanding condemned what his good nature yielded to—prejudice. By over fondness he saw not her faults till it was too late to amend them.

Trifles alone occupied her notice, and worldly grandeur was the greatest desire of her soul.

Mary Lascelles, though not fearful of her own contamination, divulged but little of the secrets of her heart to her companion, and studiously avoided any conversation with Mrs. Hornby, when the latter endeavoured to descant upon the future prospects of her dear friend.

Mary successfully parried her attempts to draw her into a controversy on the subject for some time, but the wily visitor contrived one day to draw from its hiding-place a secret which had been locked up for weeks.

The tact she displayed was worthy of a diplomatist. She would thus talk.

" Not marry, indeed ! You'll marry, my dear, and sooner than you imagine. Strange changes happen in this eventful world. I shall see the once gay, beautiful Mary Lascelles metamorphosed into a baronet's lady, sitting in her plain morning dress, with a huge morning cap, vigilantly rocking the cot of a son, who will be born, I hope, to inherit the virtues and honours of his father, Sir Lionel Dalton."

" Sir Lionel Dalton ! There you are in error, Mrs. Hornby, for if I am to marry, Sir Lionel Dalton would be the last person I should think of."

" Nonsense ! Sir Lionel's the man. There, don't blush ! I am sure I am right, so confess it at once."

Mary shook her head, but made no verbal reply.

" Well then, I suppose, it's his scholarly brother, Mr. Hugh. What a tame creature that man will make of you. All your jewels will be laid aside ; your sweet, rattling voice will be confined to half whispers, and when you want to take a stroll in your own garden, you will be compelled to ask his permission."

" Mrs. Hornby——"

" Oh ! I mean it. Mrs. Templeton called on me the other day, and said that she had heard from some person to whom you had divulged it with your own lips, that you were actually engaged to Mr. Dalton."

" I am engaged to Mr. Dalton, my dear madam, but not to the Mr. Dalton you suppose."

" You don't mean to say you are going to throw yourself away—that you are about to bestow your hand upon poor little Reginald, do you ? "

Mary blushed and smiled.

" Well I never ! Did you ever ! The intelligence shocks me greatly ; and when I go to my bed to-night will fervently pray that you may escape such a dreadful fate as that."

THE GHOST AT THE GRAVE.

"Why so?"

"Reginald Dalton has not a shilling—he's the poorest of the lot. You'll excuse me, dear, won't you? but he's little better than a mere beggar."

"Admitted, but I have plenty of money: and what I have Mr. Dalton is heartily welcome to."

"Well, if it is to be, I suppose it will be; but my dear girl, my sweet Mary, I hope you will take care to have your fortune settled entirely upon yourself."

"I shall do no such thing, Mrs. Hornby. Such a course would imply distrust and doubt of my husband."

"Just so, Mary, that's so like you; but if Mr. Lascelles had been alive, such a marriage would have broken his heart."

"Mrs. Hornby, I beg you will change this conversation."

"Certainly, certainly, since you desire it; but I hope that I shall live to see you change your mind. There, it's out, and I cannot help it."

Mrs. Hornby was not destined, however, to see her friend change her mind.

A suitable time being dedicated to the memory of her father, though not so long a period as she could have wished, Mary bestowed her hand upon Reginald, and formally installed him in Dalton Hall (for so the farm was in future to be called), and made him master of her fortune and her person.

The marriage ceremony was performed in the village church, and Mary supported herself with a dignity and firmness that surprised Mrs. Hornby, who, notwithstanding the hopes she had expressed, that her friend's mind would change, condescended to superintend all the little delicate preliminaries of the wedding breakfast and the wedding dinner. The favours were even made by her own hands, too, and all the arrangements carried out under her own personal superintendance.

The congratulatory visits paid by Sir Lionel Dalton and Mr. Hugh Dalton at first amused her, but circumstances occurred subsequently in connection with the latter most seriously to alarm her; and it was many months after she was married to his brother before she acquired a tolerable degree of cheerfulness.

CHAPTER VI.

FRATERNAL AFFECTION—LIBERALITY OF SIR LIONEL DALTON.

When shall we three meet again?—MACBETH.

SIR LIONEL DALTON, who confessed himself cleverly distanced in the race of matrimony by his youngest brother, speedily made up his mind to leave the conqueror in full possession of the field, and retire to his seat at Birchington.

Before doing so, the baronet demanded a private meeting with his brother Hugh.

At this conference his better feelings came out, and the following conversation ensued:—

"In this matrimonial and delicate business we have unavoidably run counter to each other, my dear Hugh."

"So it appears."

"Well, then, since Reginald has planned his operations with more success than we did, and made sure of the lady's hand, we must bow to his superior talent and abscond. I suppose you'll leave him in quiet possession of the field?"

"Certainly, certainly, but what was the very particular business for which you summoned me so abruptly into your presence, Sir Lionel?"

"Right, Hugh; there is no time to be lost. I will come to the point at once."

"Do; I hate procrastination."

"Poor Reginald is not rich."

"But he will be soon."

"I do not see it."

"How about his marriage settlement?"

"That is too delicate a subject for me to have questioned him about."

"Well, I hear the young ass has actually settled every shilling of his wife's fortune upon herself."

"It was entirely her own, was it not?"

"Would any man in his position, except a positive fool, tie himself up in such a manner to a woman for life as to be compelled to ask her for his very bread and butter?"

"Not so bad as that, I hope."

"A baronet's son, and the brother of a baronet, with a baronetcy itself in the prospective, actually indebted to a farmer's daughter for breakfast, dinner, tea, and supper, ha! ha!"

"No trifling, Hugh; what is sport to you may be death to him."

"How do you mean?"

"He has quite as sensitive feelings as yourself. I must say we ought to have thought of his position in this respect long ago."

"You are enigmatical."

"Not at all. This is the time when we ought to take his future prospects into our most serious consideration."

"What do you propose?"

"That we start him in life, and each make him a present of £5,000."

"Of course, Sir Lionel, I am not the almoner of your house, and therefore cannot control your liberality as far as you are personally concerned, but for myself, I tell you candidly, I shall not agree to give him a penny."

"Stuff, my dear Hugh, you will think better of it in the course of the week, so I'll give you till Monday before I move in the matter."

"Lionel! you know I am no weathercock to be shifted about at every change of the wind. So far from giving more money to Reginald, I shall give orders to stop my share of the annuity we have allowed him up to this period. I do this without reluctance, as he has now obtained a rich wife."

"The sum which I propose we should conjointly give him is really so small, I am truly surprised to hear you hesitate."

"Ten thousand pounds a small sum! Where the deuce is the money to come from, Sir Lionel?"

"As executors of our late father—Sir Oliver Dalton—we are empowered to do what we please in a matter of this kind."

"Exactly so. I am pleased to refuse him a fraction."

"He is left entirely dependent on his brothers."

"That was not a fault of mine."

"I do not say it was."

"I will incur no responsibility on Reginald's account, I wash my hands of him entirely."

"You will not consent to my giving him the sum I have mentioned?"

"Decidedly not."

"Let me beg——"

"I repeat I have washed my hands of him entirely. I cast him off from our house entirely."

"From your own you may, but rest assured I will receive him into mine. Listen to what I am now about to say, Hugh!"

"I am all attention."

The obdurate brother whistled a tune, keeping time with his finger nails on a pane of glass in the window, in the door of the apartment which stood conveniently open.

"He must have ten thousand pounds, for I have half promised him that sum."

"As you please, brother. But distinctly understand that I do not mean to contribute any portion of it."

"I will not call upon you to do so. I will sell out sufficient stock on my return to London. He shall have it from my own exchequer, and if a boy is born to him of this marriage, that son shall be my heir."

This announcement rather staggered Hugh.

He seemed suddenly inspired to alter his fraternal determination, and was about to address Sir Lionel with that intention.

But Sir Lionel Dalton had vanished.

The brothers did not again meet for many years.

CHAPTER VII.

THE TRIALS AND AFFLICTIONS OF A YOUNG WIDOW.

Hark! the hoarse-voiced, hungry rook
Now croaks aloud.
What means it?—HILL.

WITHIN one year of their happy alliance, Mary Dalton gratified her beloved husband by presenting him with that upon which he had fixed his mind—a male heir to his own name and his mother's estates.

In a few months the delighted parents discovered so much beauty, vivasity, and spirit in their little son, that they fondly believed no child could ever be half so amiable and engaging.

His smile was sweet, and his little countenance intelligent.

He would make desperate efforts to clutch at everything within his reach that he could lay his tiny hands upon, and looked so archly when playing in the nurse's lap, that both his father and his mother would hang over him in mute and joyous rapture.

Before he was two years old one of those diseases which all children of a tender age undergo, seized him.

What anxious moments were endured by little Reginald's parents during the crisis of the disorder.

His cot was removed from the nursery to the sitting parlour, the bells were muffled, and straw strewed over all the stony approaches and avenues to the hall.

All the household prayed for the quick recovery of the young heir.

The father, as he entered the sick house, would lift the iron latch with studied caution, and close the door after him quick and silently, as though the slightest sound or breath of air would disturb his darling child.

Reginald would advance with stealthy step and whisper his inquiries to his beloved Mary, who sat half drowned in tears, with her firstborn in her lap, pressing his feverish lips from time to time to her own, and watching for the return of that glow upon his infant cheek which would be the harbinger of convalescence.

Mary Dalton prayed fervently, both day and night, for the recovery of her boy.

Heaven heard her prayers, for the child soon regained its strength, and was once more able to totter about the house.

But Mary had yet a heavier blow to sustain than the temporary illness of the young Reginald.

It was the will of the father of all to deprive this truly good and excellent wife, of her equally amiable husband.

Mary Dalton bowed and bent her head.

She saw but one link of the mighty chain of events which runs through eternity, and she was too true a Christian to presume to reason on the dispensations of the Infinite One.

Faith taught her to say, "thy will be done on earth," and though stricken down by the weight of the affliction it had pleased the Almighty to shower down upon her, she did not give way to idle and useless repinings.

A few nights before her husband shuffled off his mortal coil, he addressed a letter to his elder brother, Sir Lionel Dalton, begging him to accept the guardianship of his dear boy, Reginald, and in case of anything happening to his mother to look after him and protect his orphan years.

Sir Lionel agreed to accept the sacred trust, and set off at once from his own residence, to assure his brother in person that he was willing to do so.

Travelling in those days not being quite so expeditious as it is at present, nearly a week passed before Sir Lionel reached Dalton Hall, and when he did arrive he found that his brother had ceased to exist.

After the last sad rites had been performed, the amiable baronet showed Mrs. Dalton her late husband's letter, and asked her if it would be with her sanction that he took upon himself the onerous duties of a guardian to her offspring.

The widowed mother was but too confident that her brother-in-law would discharge such a trust better than any one else in the world.

She candidly admitted to Sir Lionel at once that she could not better provide for the future care and comfort of her helpless boy than by entrusting him when arrived at a suitable and proper age to one who was so closely allied to her, and one for whom the boy himself appeared to have a fondness second only to a father's.

After some particular instructions as to the system of education which was to be put in practice until Reginald became twelve years of age, Sir Lionel Dalton took his leave, and it was arranged that when the nephew entered his teens, he was to take up his residence at Bodmin Castle, under the especial care of his kind uncle and future guardian.

CHAPTER VIII.

THE INTRIGUE OF A HEARTLESS WOMAN—ITS PENALTY.

Him who loves only *one* why should they call
More constant than the man who loves them *all?*
COWLEY.

AMONG the first persons who flew to offer their condolements to the widow, was Hugh Dalton, and Mary, taking his asseverations of extreme sorrow at her severe bereavement to be genuine, was pleased and gratified by his daily visits and attentions.

The vicinity of their habitations, gave Hugh Dalton frequent opportunities of visiting his brother's widow.

But his libertine principles having rather singularly developed themselves, a coolness ensued on the part of Mrs. Dalton towards him, and she was at last compelled absolutely to forbid him the Hall.

The occurrence was as follows:

Being again compelled to have a female friend near her to make her solitude more endurable, Mrs. Hornby was invited to resume the position she formally held at the Hall.

The lady had not been Mary's guest more than a week or two, when one afternoon, as Mary was reading a favourite author in her library, she heard the well known heavy step of Hugh Dalton coming towards it.

Caprice, a whim, or some sudden womanly impulse impelled her to hide behind the curtains which hung before the windows, in order that he might have a little more trouble than was usual in finding her.

Hugh bounced gaily into the room, looked about it in every direction, and not seeing Mrs. Dalton, he asked Mrs. Hornby who ushered him in, where her friend was.

Mrs. Hornby told him that she thought she was in an arbour, at the bottom of the garden, and that she would immediately acquaint her with his arrival.

"No! No!" said Hugh. "My dear madam, I have long waited for this opportunity; let us profit by a happy and unexpected moment, which heaven alone has sent us. Come, my dearest life! Come into the arms of a man who loves and adores you more than anybody in the whole world."

The anxious visitor was about to place the giddy and unthinking woman on his knee, but she seated herself by his side and began to reproach him for the manner he had conducted himself towards the widow, and particularly for attending too much to some things which concerned Mary alone.

"This is jealousy, you gipsy," said Hugh to her; "mere jealousy. You are my soul, my idol, my very existence."

"Then why did you not keep the appointment which you made to meet me in the Green Lane last Sunday, saucebox?"

Hugh stammered out a something like an apology, and impudently said he was too closely watched by Mrs. Dalton to risk a meeting of the kind, at least on that particular night.

"Fie! fie! you Don Giovanni. I don't believe a word of it. I've watched your attentions to Mrs. Dalton."

"My attentions, love?"

"Yes. Did'nt I see you devour an orange with avidity which the pert creature peeled yesterday, although I had expressly forbidden you to do it the night before."

"If I had refused my dear Mrs. Hornby, it would have been but too palpable to your friend. Dissimulation I abhor, but I assure you I was compelled to have recourse to it, or we have might been detected."

"You know what I have done for you, and the condition into which you have brought me," sobbed Mrs. Hornby.

What this condition was it is impossible to say; but the lady burst into a flood of tears, and Hugh extricated himself as well as he could from the volley of reproaches she had cast upon him.

He kissed her cheek a thousand times, and swore with execrable oaths that he, from his soul, loved her infinitely better than the stuck-up doll who was laying her snares to intrap him into marriage.

The indelicate and ill-deserved allusion which Hugh made to her benefactress, caused Mrs. Hornby to laugh outright; and Mary burned with indignation and disgust to resent it.

Unable to bear the disgraceful and immodest scene any longer, Mrs. Dalton made a rustling behind the curtain, which Hugh no sooner heard than he snatched up his hat and withdrew.

Mrs. Hornby had the assurance to open the curtain, and seeing Mary behind it, poured forth such an unlady-like string of invectives, that it was some time before Mrs. Dalton could speak, such an effect upon her had surprise and anger.

The scene was altogether new and painful to Mary.

She speedily withdrew from it; determining in her own mind to desire Mrs. Hornby to quit the Hall the first thing in the morning.

The lady wisely made her escape in the night, and avoided a lecture she knew too well she deserved.

During the time Hugh Dalton was permitted to visit the fair widow, he ascertained, and made himself minutely acquainted with many of her customs and domestic habits.

He found that she indulged herself with a nap in the afternoon, and took it on a sofa in what used to be her husband's studio.

As she was one day reclining upon this sofa, preparatory to her usual afternoon's sleep, she was disturbed by the abrupt entrance of her brother-in-law, who quietly closed the door after him, and locked it into the bargain.

Mrs. Dalton was terribly alarmed when she found Hugh approach her, roughly seize her by her arms, and endeavour to stop her mouth with his silk handkerchief.

"She attempted to scream out, but he paid no attention to her cries except by renewed efforts to stifle them.

Having, as he thought, safely secured his victim, he was proceeding to extremes, with all the *sang froid* of an accomplished libertine, and as though he was privileged to divert himself with the unfortunate lady quivering beneath his colossal grasp.

His base and wanton behaviour made Mrs. Dalton struggle the more to free herself from his loathsome embraces.

By almost superhuman exertion she succeeded in bursting from him, and flinging such a rude assailant a considerable distance from her.

Looking at her for some time without saying a word, he was going to speak, but he knew not how, or where to begin.

However, without the least compunction or seeming shame for his audacity, he very coolly made a bungling preamble, and asked pardon for what he had previously done under her roof, and was then doing.

Ashamed to make her servants acquainted with the shock her modesty had sustained, Mrs. Dalton refrained from alarming them, and Hugh, taking courage from this and her continued silence, gave her to understand that it was merely for want of opportunity that he had not explained himself more fully before.

Mrs. Dalton did not condescend to reply.

He then endeavoured to assure her that he intended every respect in the world, and that if she would accompany him to where he wanted to convey her, she should be far happier than she could ever be, lonely and desolate as she was, in her own dull house.

Mrs. Dalton declared she would not listen to anything he had to say—indeed, was determined by every means in her power to alarm her household, unless he unlocked the door and quitted the apartment immediately, and for ever.

The intruder declared his passion, and offered to verify its truth by marriage, if she would accept him.

He had no doubt of being able to satisfy her of the regard he had always entertained for her, and that after marriage he would let her see, by the most inviolable friendship and the greatest submission, that he wished nothing so ardently as to repair the faults for which he had given her such just reason to be offended.

She told him that his contrition, if sincere, might, in part, remove the bad opinion she had entertained of him, but as for marrying him, that was prevented by her own disinclination and the laws of her country.

Her conduct and heroic confession had but one effect upon Hugh Dalton.

He gnashed his teeth and clenched his fist.

Striking the latter violently on the mahogany table which stood before him, he exclaimed, "By heaven, madam, I will break this stubborn spirit."

"No," replied Mrs. Dalton, "you never can."

"Do not force me again to use violence when I wish to treat you with lenity."

His words were as a prediction of what was to follow.

Hugh Dalton now threw off all restraint, and springing upon Mary with the fury of a roused lion, succeeded in gagging her mouth with the handkerchief he had endeavoured previously to use for the same purpose.

In vain she struggled and made an effort to call out.

His fiery eyes soon informed her of the wicked determination of his heart, and he boldly told her that if she attempted the least resistance to prevent him from accomplishing the sole purpose for which alone he sought her, and for the gratifying of which he was prepared to risk his life, he would not hesitate to stab her to the heart.

He then attempted to lift her up in his arms, with the intention of carrying her towards the sofa, but it was the will of Heaven to furnish her with surprising vigour.

She gazed upon the treacherous villain with so much indignation that he quailed beneath her looks, and was obliged to keep his eyes on the ground.

Nevertheless, he never released his hold; and having Herculean strength at his command, it was an easy task to fling his poor victim at full length upon the sofa.

In falling, Mrs. Dalton's head came in contact with her work basket.

Its contents were strewed about in all directions, and a bright pair of scissors catching her eye as they fell near her head upon the pillow of the sofa, she dexterously armed herself with them, and pierced his back so suddenly and forcibly, that the villain was compelled to let go his hold.

Mrs. Dalton was speedily released from the danger she was in and the indignities she had undergone.

Without one effort at retaliation, and without uttering one word of reproach, her cowardly assailant unlocked the door, and left the house, and immediately proceeded to Dr. Carmichael's to have his wound dressed.

Fortunately for him it turned out a mere scratch, as the point of the scissors glanced against one of the buttons of his braces, and blunted much of the force with which it had been directed.

Finding that he had been more frightened than hurt by the adventure, he invented some idle excuse in explanation of the real cause, and attributing it to a slight accident, he paid Dr. Carmichael his fee, and returned in no very pleasant mood to his own residence.

CHAPTER IX.

HUGH DALTON IS CONFOUNDED BY AN ALARMING INTIMATION—THE TABLES ARE TURNED.

> —— Tho' under hope
> Of heavenly grace, and all proclaiming peace,
> Men live in hatred, enmity and strife
> Among themselves.—MILTON.

IN less than a week from the event narrated in the preceding chapter, a tall dark-looking man, wrapped within the folds of a huge cloth travelling cloak, stopped at the door of a gloomy house in Lincolns-Inn-Fields, to the outer door of which was affixed a brass plate, informing the British public that the place belonged to "Edghill, Potter and Pendril, Solicitors," whose offices were on the ground floor.

The tall dark looking man was Hugh Dalton.

He set off to London to consult his legal adviser, as to the best way of satiating his revenge, the moment he discovered that he was unhurt.

He rang the office bell.

The inner door opened almost simultaneously of its own accord.

"Well, Mr. Dalton, to what are we indebted for the honor of this unexpected visit?" said Mr. Edghill as his client took his seat at the desk before him.

"Business of a serious import, Mr. Edghill."

"Doubtless. The expulsion of a refractory tenant, eh?"

"Nothing of that kind."

"I see—you are about to repudiate a promise of marriage, and wish us to defend you?"

"Guess again."

"You wish us to enter an action for trespass?"

Hugh smiled.

"In the excitement of the season some neighbour killed a pheasant in your preserves?"

"Nothing of that sort. Guess a second time."

"Well, really dear, Mr. Dalton, I can't go on guessing all day. The small charge of six shillings and eight pence which is entered in our book against you for this interview, will not compensate me for my loss of time; but to oblige you, I'll make one more guess, and I'll be shot if it does not prove a correct one."

"Do."

"You have forgotten yourself with your cook."

Hugh laughed, but shook his head, as much as to imply that he could not possibly forget himself.

"Well, the nurse-maid—your position will be the same."

"To put you out of all suspense, Mr. Edghill, I do not want your firm to defend or bring a civil action for me of any kind. I wish to prosecute an infuriated woman for half-killing me."

"Bless me, bless me, what do I hear? Well you don't much look like a half-killed man. But such prosecutions come under the criminal department of our practice, and that is confided to the management of my partner, Mr. Pendril, to whom I will refer you. Here, Jenkins, show this gentleman up-stairs into Mr. Pendril's room."

In the presence of such a very learned pundit as Mr. Erasmus Pendril, Hugh was, if possible, less at ease than when consulting his partner, the erratic Mr. Edghill.

The introduction over, Mr. Pendril took a pinch of snuff, wiped his spectacles with a hankerchief, placed them across his nose, and looking his future client full in the face, said, "And what is it, sir, you wish our firm to do for you?"

"Justice!"

"And what is it that, in the general acceptation of the word, but the virtue by which we render to heaven, our neighbour, and ourselves that which is their due?"

"Oh! certainly, certainly," replied Hugh, although he did not exactly comprehend the meaning of what he heard.

"Justice, sir, is of two kinds, communicate and distributive. The first enforces fair dealing between man and man, the second is that by which the differences of mankind are decided according to the rules of equity: the former is the justice of private individuals, the latter of princes and magistrates. To which of these does your visit appertain?"

The gentleman addressed was completely in a fog caused by this learned disquisition on the relative merits of justice, and he could only grope his way out of it by means of a vulgarism. He observed, "I am not a grandmother come hither to be initiated into a method of sucking eggs. I come to propitiate justice, and I am sincere—and most sincere—in my determination."

"Good, very good, my dear sir. The effect of sincerity is mutual confidence; therefore, when you have communicated all the items of your particular ailment, I will propose a remedy."

"I have been injured, and I wish to avail myself of some signal means of revenge."

"Whoever arrogates to himself the right of vengeance shows how little he is qualified to decide his own case, since he demands what he would think unfit to be granted to another. Pray, sir, on whom do you meditate mischief, and for what?"

"For the greatest wrong which one person can do to another—an attempt to take my life."

"One of two courses is open to you: either to give the accused party into the custody of a constable, or proceed against them by indictment at common law. By the way, the quarter sessions commence on Monday in your county, so that you have no time to lose. State clearly, concisely, and collectively when, where, and how you have been assaulted. Recollect that a passionate and revengeful temper renders a man unfit for advice, deprives him of his reason, robs him of all that is great and noble in his nature, disqualifies him for argument, destroys confidence, changes justice into cruelty, turns order into confusion, and upsets that gravity which is required for a clear consideration of a wrong. Now state your case."

Mr. Hugh Dalton did as he was bid, and having finished his version of his affair, offered then and there to strip himself to his shirt and show his legal adviser the murderous wound which had been inflicted upon him by the hand of his sister-in-law.

But Mr. Pendril was not curious in these matters.

Mr. Pendril begged his client to rebutton his waistcoat, which he had begun to unloosen, and gravely stroking his chin with his thumb and fingers, asked if Mr. Dalton had ever done the lady any harm, as there were three kinds of return for injuries:—abject submission, contemptuous disregard, and severe retaliation. The lady in question evidently had had recourse to the last.

The wily lawyer then began a cross-examination, which elicited the real facts, and to which he was before an entire stranger.

"Am I to understand you never took the slightest liberty in your life with Mrs. What's-her name?"

"I don't say that. By way of joke, I might have attempted a kiss."

"Against her will?"

"Possibly against her will."

"And yet you are surprised that she should make a reprisal?"

"Such a savage and inhuman one!"

"Did you ever attempt greater freedom than a mere salute? If you have done so, pray don't conceal it from me. I have heard a great deal about you and your amours, Mr. Dalton."

"My amours?"

"I know, my dear sir, that I am far from obliging you by alluding to any of the monstrous *liasons* I have heard about you in this way, and that in mentioning them I may become an object of your aversion and resentment; but I am nothing if not critical."

Hugh begged Mr. Pendril to disabuse his mind on that head, and declared he quite gloried in hearing him speak so unreservedly.

He proceeded.

"Now, come, be candid. You say you threw the lady on the sofa, when she seized hold of the instrument with which she inflicted the injury of which you complain. Did you do this?"

"I admit that I did."

"What, pray, was your intention towards her?"

This was a home question, and Hugh was silent.

"Most men are afraid to divulge evil intentions. Your silence is natural. I will spare you the recital of yours. Mrs. Dalton stabbed you in defence of her own honour. That's it, isn't it?"

Hugh continued silent, and looked rather foolish.

"If she had killed you, Mr. Dalton, and a coroner's inquest had set upon your body, what would the verdict of the jury have been, think you?"

"Wilful murder."

"Nothing of the kind."

"What would it have been, then?"

"'Justifiable homicide,' Mr. Dalton, which, I must tell you, is tantamount to 'serve him right,' in the legal interpretation of its meaning."

"Have I no remedy against such a dangerous woman?"

"In the course of my legal experience I have always

found that none more impatiently suffer injuries than those who are most forward in doing them."

"By which I am to infer you think me the most guilty of the two."

"I don't say that. By the humanity of the law, a man is always presumed to be innocent till he is found guilty."

"Mr. Pendril, you cannot suspect me of——"

"I suspect nothing.—I accuse nobody ; but I tell you that if this Mrs. Thingamy turns the tables upon you, I should be called upon to defend a very nefarious piece of business, and I fear, with all my logic and all my knowledge of the law, I could not get you off."

"What do you mean?"

"The 'offence' is a capital one."

"But it was only contemplated, not committed."

"That makes no difference in the eye of the law. The attempt to commit is the same thing."

"Well, and what could they do to me under such circumstances ?"

"HANG YOU !"

"Hang me?"

"To a dead certainty. Clever as I reckon myself in such cases, all the chicanery in the world could not save you."

Hugh shuddered.

"I have observed lately, Mr. Dalton," said the precise old lawyer, "and I call your serious attention to the circumstance, that, whenever the recorder makes his report to the King in council of persons under sentence of death in Newgate, the black mark is put against the names of all who make these sort of attacks upon women, and that which you confess to have done is not a shade removed from the worst among them ; therefore, if Mr. Hugh Dalton happened to be amongst such a list, the papers, the next day in giving the names of the criminals and the offences committed, would go on to say, 'all of whom his Majesty was greatly pleased to respite except Hugh Dalton, upon whom the law is left to take its course, and he is ordered for execution on Monday.'"

Hugh was no fool. Prudence required him to weigh well his actions in the balance of reason, and to judge the proportion between the hazard run and the end proposed.

He found that he had nothing to gain but everything to lose, if he ventured to prosecute Mrs. Dalton, even for a common assault.

Thanking Mr. Pendril for his opinion, he agreed to let the matter drop, and took his departure homewards.

A long stage-coach journey gave him time for some very unpleasant reflections.

What if Mary Dalton prosecuted him instead of him prosecuting her?

There were plenty of lawyers who would take her case up.

He might be apprehended on a criminal charge.

He would be exposed.

He might be tried for his life !

He would be certain to be found guilty !

He might be HANGED !

These and similar predictions haunted his imagination throughout the whole of his journey.

Arrived at home, he determined in his own mind to prevent the possibility of any such horrible results.

A man who was haughtily insolent to his inferiors but a few days previously, was now forced to cringe servilely to the meanest being in his employment.

It was palpably evident to his servants that their imperious master, although a proud man and of a good estate, had a secret fear of something dreadful hovering over him, which divested him of his general hauteur and tyranny.

The prying eyes of his own menials already detected that he scrupulously kept from paying his usual visits to Mrs. Dalton.

They did not scruple to descant in the butler's room and the servant's pantry on the harsh and cruel nature of his fraternal feelings.

It was apparent to them that he thought it beneath him to offer comfort to his sister-in-law, or to give himself the least trouble concerning her little son, his nephew, but left them both to the will of Providence ; though the sex of the one and the tender age of the other would, in such circumstances, have almost inspired a barbarian with sympathy and humanity.

But after all Mrs. Dalton's was the most enviable situation of the two.

It is far better to be of the number of those who need consolation, than of those who want hearts to give it.

CHAPTER. X.

MARY DALTON IS SPURNED BY HER FRIENDS.—THE EFFECTS OF SCANDAL.

Behold, how calmly, like an infant wave,
Flows the clear current of her private life !
While the more public stream, by tempests toss'd,
Of every changing wind's the sport or slave.—AKENSIDE.

MRS. DALTON having rid herself of the objectionable Mrs. Hornby, and barred the door against the future approaches of a libertine brother-in-law, now turned her serious attention to the education of her only child.

Notwithstanding she was one of the tenderest of mothers, yet she always exerted her maternal authority in such a manner as excited in her little one the greatest alacrity to execute her commands, whilst at the same time his infant bosom was impressed with the deepest reverence and respect for his mother.

Mrs. Dalton well knew that one of the greatest causes of depravity in youth is owing to its being habituated in infancy to have every caprice and every childish fancy gratified without control.

Nor less strenuous were her endeavours to imbibe in the youthful Reginald true principles of religion and virtue, and to polish him by every kind of literature which was suitable to his juvenile mind.

Nor was her success unequal to the vigour of her attempt, for the boy himself was a noble generous spirited fellow, and beloved by everybody.

But alas ! poor Reginald ! how unstable ! how transitory was his happiness.

His father had not been dead very long, ere Mary's spirit appeared completely broken, and it was evident to those about her that she was suffering from hidden grief.

The facts were these.

Before quitting the neighbourhood of Dalton Hall, Mrs. Hornby took care to circulate her version of the extraordinary scene, which had caused her expulsion from the hospitable residence of her friend.

Mrs. Templeton (mentioned in a previous chapter.) called upon the rector of the parish, the Rev. Mr. Crespigny, and who had performed the matrimonial ceremony between Mary and her husband.

This busybody made such a representation of the affair to the rector's daughters, that the young ladies were expressly forbidden by their parents to pay visits to, or receive them from, Mrs. Dalton.

Mrs. Templeton gave her version of the scandal and related the adventure in such a manner, either from malice or inadvertence, that her friends imagined the young widow so rudely treated by Mr. Hugh Dalton had brought such rudeness upon herself by the forwardness of her own behaviour ; adding :—

"It is quite evident that there must have been something between them, or he never would have dared to take such liberties."

This cruel supposition was greedily received, and carried, in the course of a few days, as a piece of amusing gossip and intelligence to all the families of any note in the neighbourhood, and the consequence was that the virtuous and truly excellent widow became shunned as a pestilence.

When Mrs. Dalton first became aware of the unpleasant rumours current amongst her friends, she smiled at the annoyance, confident of her own rectitude, and therefore took no trouble to set at rest or contradict the rumours which were hourly damaging her fair name and reputation.

There is, however, something due to the opinions and customs of the world, and all who declare themselves above them are sure to be cut off from the society of it, which, without much injustice, we may venture to affirm, is the furthest from their real wish.

How galling, then, must it have been to poor Mary, when, one Sunday morning, returning from church with little Reginald, and coming in direct contact with the Misses Crespigny, face to face, she found that a polite and ingenuous bend of recognition on her side was not returned on the others' part, but that Ellen and Julia Crespigny passed on without taking the least notice of her, as if she was the greatest stranger in the world.

Had she not leaned upon the shoulder of little Reginald she must have sunk to the earth.

Greater indignities even than this were thrust upon her, with painfully humiliating and oppressive celerity.

Chiding one of her female domestics for not returning to the Hall till long after the appointed hour she had promised on the day allotted to her for usual holiday, the pert creature had the impudence to say she had been detained longer than she expected by the ostler at the Blue Lion, who had entertained her with full particulars of her mistress's amour with Squire Dalton.

This was not all.

Her name was expunged from the list of the lady patronesses of the assize ball.

She was also continually annoyed by the receipt of anonymous letters, containing all sorts of sneers and disgraceful accusations.

The spirit of Mrs. Dalton was not indomitable. It was completely broken by the persecutions pursued towards her.

No wonder that she ultimately sank under them.

One attached friend, out of many female acquaintances, alone remained true to her.

This was Mrs. Dove, the curate's wife, who, as Angelina De Courcy, had been her schoolfellow, and who now, in womanhood, still loved her, and took especial pains to rebut the foul and atrocious shafts of calumny levelled at Mary, and who was ready, as she emphatically expressed herself, "to stake her very existence on the purity of her friend Mrs. Dalton."

Mary, therefore, for the present, no longer continued friendless, pensive, or alone.

Her sorrowing breast would have shunned the commiseration of less sensitive souls, and she gratefully availed herself of her friend's aid and sympathy to soothe many of the lingering hours of her pain.

CHAPTER XI.

THE DEATH BED.

The nearest ease, since we must suffer still,
Are they who dare be patient under ill.—POPE.

THE gig in which Doctor Carmichael was wont to drive about to visit his patients was now regularly seen twice a-day waiting outside the porch of Dalton Hall.

Mrs. Dove was then at the bed-side of his patient.

Mary slept occasionally; she slept, indeed, but the burning cheek, parched lip, half opened eye, and convulsive movements, terrified Angelina.

She saw in these the harbingers of that event which was so soon to follow.

She, however, took her place at the bed-side of the sufferer, and never left it through the different gradations of her long and fatal illness.

Fled was the rosy light of joy, and faded the brow of that once beautiful and beloved woman.

Dark shades were gathering over her once sweet and placid features, and the approach of death was stamped visibly on her face.

And yet she lingered.

By fits and starts a brief reviving beam, in melancholy beauty would flit across her cheeks—a gleam which failed not to cheat even Mrs Dove herself, into a transient belief that perchance the two friends were not to part.

In one of those intervals of hope, Mrs. Dalton raised herself in bed, as thoughts of tenderness and love crept around, momentarily assuaging her pain.

"Angelina! will you make me a promise?"

Mrs. Dove took her pale and clammy hand, pressed it to her lips, but could not speak for weeping.

"I know you will, your silence gives me an assurance that you will, and I shall die content."

"Yes, dear! I will do anything that you ask me, but first take this medicine. Dr. Carmichael made me pledge my word that I would give it to you regularly."

"No, not this nasty bitter draught."

But that bitter draught being tendered in all kindness, it was swallowed by the sufferer without another word of repugnance."

"Angelina, dear, open the top drawer and bring me what you will find in it, carefully wrapped up in tissue paper."

"Why, I declare, it is a rose!"

It was a rose, but so crisp and withered, as scarcely to be recognisable.

Mrs. Dalton eagerly clasped it in her hand, and ever and anon affectionately pressed it to her slowly beating bosom.

"Mary, you seem to prize that rose."

"Yes! Its fading leaves and its dear withered stem are sacred to poor Mary. They tell me of hours of peace and well remembered love. It was a fair and bright rose on the morning of my boy's birth, and Reginald, knowing that I was fond of roses, placed this one beside me here, on this very pillow, a few hours before I became a happy mother."

As the minstrels of old, ere they flung aside their beloved harps for the night, would touch with a gentle hand the trembling strings that seemed to wail the dying close of day, and wring from them strains of peace and love, so Mary kept pressing the dear but withered flowers to her lips.

It seemed the keynote to her troubled thoughts, and stilled their restlessness beneath its sway.

Mary had often expressed a wish that she might not die in winter, but that she might sigh her last sigh in the pleasant summer months.

Yes, in the summer time, when the new blown roses were unfolding their delicious sweetness, and the bright winged butterflies—all emblems of a fairer world—should be glancing beneath an azure sky.

Mary had her wish.

It was on a calm and beautiful evening in the month of June that Doctor Carmichael found her still reclining upon that bed from which she was destined never more to rise.

The hand of her little darling but weeping Reginald was clasped in one of hers, and at her feet, in deep but silent sorrow, stood her own attached and devoted friend Angelina.

Many knew that she was dying; yet there played upon her pale features a smile, to which the setting sun, as he flung his golden beams into the chamber, imparted an almost supernatural radiance, as if a foretaste of a blissful eternity had been vouchsafed to smoothe her passage from a world, to which, with all its troubles, she was bound by the tenderest of all ties—maternal affection.

Her smile was one of thankfulness and confidence; of thankfulness for the strength given to her in that hour of trial; and of confidence, that a great and good Being would not desert her Reginald when the hands that reared him were cold and humbled in the dust.

She had the further consolation of knowing that Angelina had solemnly promised to be as a mother to Reginald when she was gone, and, under heaven, would guide him in that path into which it had been her chief care to direct his infant mind.

The scene soon closed.

The last struggle between the aspirations of the soul and the lingering infirmities of mortality being over, Doctor Carmichael placed a seal upon the most valuable of Mrs. Dalton's effects, and removed her infant son to his own residence, there to await the will and pleasure of his guardian, Sir Lionel Dalton, to whom he wrote off by the same night's post, acquainting him with the melancholy though not unexpected event.

So far all that the doctor did was conformable to propriety and rule.

But there was one thing which very much surprised Angelina and her worthy husband, and against which they warmly entered a protest.

This was, the very sudden and almost indecent haste with which he took upon himself to order the remains of Mrs. Dalton to be buried.

The curate wished the funeral to be delayed until the arrival of the relations to whom the doctor had written, expressing his belief that the baronet would come to Dalton Hall and personally superintend the ceremony of interment.

But Dr. Carmichael was inflexible.

His patient, he said, had died of a disease which rendered it absolutely necessary that her remains should be committed to the earth as soon as possible, and therefore he took upon himself the responsibility of ordering her immediate burial.

Mr. and Mrs. Dove remonstrated against such precipitancy, but he at once silenced their objections, by observing that it was the duty of everybody to think of the living as well as of the dead.

CHAPTER XII.

THE GHOST AT THE GRAVE.

There are more things in heaven and earth,
Horatio, than are dream't of in our philosophy.
                                    SHAKSPEARE.

"You will be sure, Jabez," said Carmichael to a grey-headed but portly old man, for whom he had sent, and who stood deferentially before him, with his hat in his hand, as the doctor sat in his study ; "you will be sure to dig the grave eighteen feet deep, at least, and come and tell me when it is ready, that I may look at it, and personally see that all is correct and proper."

'Eighteen feet be main deep, doctor, but I suppose you have heard the rumours as well as I, that resurrection chaps be about in these parts, and you very properly are determined that the poor dear lady's body shall be placed out of the reach of danger."

"I know nothing about that, Jabez, but I have good and sufficient reasons for ordering you to follow my directions in every respect."

"I dare say you have sir, but, strict as you undoubtedly are—I hope no offence in saying so—these body-snatchers may outwit you."

Carmichael said nothing, but proceeded to write out the requisite instructions for the interment, and again commanded the old gravedigger to follow them to the very letter.

"Pray, doctor, may I be permitted to ask of what this here lady died ?"

Doctor Carmichael, nettled at the curiosity of the man, sharply replied, "What's that to you ?" and continued writing at his desk.

"Beg pardon, doctor, but as we havn't had a corpse buried in the old churchyard for many months, I'm certainly a leetle bit curious to learn why Mrs. Dalton

—peace rest her soul—ain't agoing to be laid alongside her husband in the brick vaults beneath th church."

"She'll repose far more comfortably in the spot have selected for her. Besides, Jabez Brown, you are ol enough to know as well as I do that it matters littl where our dust is deposited after we are dead."

"Amen to that," said the gravedigger.

"Have a glass of my strong cognac to give yo strength for your arduous task, Brown; which, by-the by, I wish you to commence at once."

Jabez thanked the doctor for his condescension, an after swallowing with extreme gusto and avidity th proffered brandy he inquired when the funeral was t take place.

"To-morrow afternoon," said the doctor.

"Why bless me," returned the astonished gravedigge "I shall never be able to finish it in time. I've bee sexton of this parish—man and boy—now a matte of sixty odd years, and this is first time in my life was ever called upon to perform its duties in such very expeditious manner."

"Well, if you are incapable of doing it, old man, g assistance, and I'll pay for it. Doctor Carmichael ha no wish that you should be overworked, at your time (life."

But Mr. Jabez Brown would not hear anything abou assistance. He had buried three generations of th parish in his time, and he was not going to have hi spede wrested from him by a stranger. Not he.

"Well, then, I suppose you'll make an effort to g it ready, by three o'clock, at the very latest," sai Doctor Carmichael.

"I will, sir."

"Thank you, Jabez."

"I must work all night to do it—but I'll do it, an doubtless, you will bear in mind—not that I a timorous or childish—it's far from pleasant work diggin away by moonlight in the solitude of the lonely churc yard, and perhaps disturbing the rats and moles, i a grave eighteen feet deep in the earth."

The very thought of it appeared to make the ol man hot and uncomfortable.

He kept wiping huge drops of perspiration from o his bald forehead with a ragged cotton handkerchie which every minute went in and came out of th crown of his old worn-out and greasy hat.

The doctor at last discovered his drift, and throwin a handful of silver to him across the table, bade hi pick the coins up and be off about his business.

Within half-an-hour from this interview, Jabez Brow had his foot upon his spade, and was turning the fir shovelful of earth over the long and beautiful virgi grass, which encompassed the secluded spot selected b the doctor for the grave of his late patient.

It was past midnight before the venerable sexton ha accomplished even six feet of the required depth.

It struck one by the old church clock, when his plun met told him that he had digged to the depth of eigl feet.

Ten more remained to be excavated.

He lit his pipe, and rested awhile from his labours.

Whiff after whiff ascended in light blue flakes abo his head, and gave a volcanic appearance to the hole l had so far dug.

The light so emitted guided and directed his old wi to that precise spot in the churchyard where she wou find Jabez.

He sprung out of his earthy prison at her well-know approach, and gratefully demolished the buttered toas and greedily swallowed the contents of a jug of indi ferent tea which the considerate creature brought wit her, even at that early hour, to refresh and comfort hi in his laborious work.

When good Mrs. Brown had hobbled out of th churchyard, on her return to their cottage, Jabez r commenced his work.

THE GHOST AT THE BED-SIDE

He could not have penetrated into more than one foot beneath the surface of the earth he was disturbing, when suddenly his ears were assailed by the sounds of music.

" Come, none of that, youngster," said Jabez, thinking it was his grandson Nicodemus, who, having commenced to learn the violin, had made a remarkable proficiency on that popular instrument, and in the pride of his young heart had seized upon that extraordinary and romantic hour of the morning to give his grandsire a proof of his ability.

But it was no such thing.

Nicodemus Brown was fast asleep and snoring in his bed over the henroost, in the garden of the grave-digger's cottage on the high Romsey road.

The sounds continued, and were of a heavenly description.

Jabez was so enraptured by them that he threw aside his mattock and his spade, and sat cross-legged over some boards of a coffin he had accidentally displaced, in order to listen to them.

The music was so sweet and fascinating that, although somewhat struck with awe at the supernatural sounds he was induced to get out of the grave and look about him.

But Jabez Brown had better have continued within the narrow limits of the resting place and last home he was preparing for its cold and insensible tenant.

Suddenly the whole churchyard was illuminated up by a red glare of light. So red and vivid was it, that he could clearly distinguish the small hands of the turret clock in the belfry, which now pointed to the exact time —five minutes past one, which was the precise period at which the extraordinary event we are now narrating took place.

At first Jabez Brown thought that some wicked incendiary had fired a farmer's haystack, and he was for quitting the churchyard and giving instant alarm, but the glare of light changed from its original crimson colour to a palish blue.

The grave-digger was now terribly alarmed.

His whole body trembled; what remained of his

decayed teeth shattered audibly in his equally decayed gums.

His legs knocked together, and refusing their usual office brought him on his knees to the ground.

Looking up towards the outside walls of the venerable church, he dimly discerned the form of a female peering at him from the inside of the vaults beneath them.

The form was that of a lady, elegantly arrayed in floating drapery, but he could not exactly discern her features, as she wore a thick veil and was at a considerable distance from him.

Suddenly she appeared to wrench out the irons or bars of the grating, which prevented a free and uninterrupted passage towards him, and emerging from the charnel house she darted her cold and bony fingers upon the collar of his working jacket, shaking him with violence and with amazing strength from head to foot all the time.

Jabez was as a man pilloried.

He could neither turn his palsied head to the right nor to the left.

He made a feeble attempt to elude the woman's grip, but she only held him the faster.

The veil fell from her face, and then Jabez for the first time discovered that it was Mary Dalton, or her spectre, with whom he was in contact.

There sat a wondrous paleness upon her brow, yet it was not sad, and there was, too, a more than common fire in the expression of her eye.

"Jabez," said the ghost, "thou hast entered into an unholy contract. This night is the third of the moon. Is it not written, 'Cursed be they who part man and wife?' In life we were united, so in death we will not be divided."

Jabez groaned audibly.

"Place my mortal remains side by side with Reginald, and do what you can to avenge my murder!"

"Murder!" screeched out the affrighted gravedigger. "Mur——"

"Yes, murder, Jabez Brown."

"When, how, where, and by whom?" said the gravedigger, for in her life-time he respected her, having on divers many times been the recipient of her bounty.

"By——" but the solemn chimes of the church dial telling the hour, and denoting two in the morning, the spirit began gradually to vanish from the presence of the spell-bound grave-digger.

The grey streaks of daylight summoned it away, and Jabez himself, sank, paralysed and insensible, to the bottom of the half-made grave he had been digging, as the music recommenced and the spirit was wafted into space and air.

*   *   *   *   *

Some labourers passing through the churchyard at six o'clock in the morning to their accustomed work in the vicinity, discovered the dead body of poor Jabez, and reported his death accordingly to his dame and the parochial authorities.

His death was, of course, attributed to over-exertion in extreme old age.

A younger and more stalwart hand was called in to finish the work the poor fellow had commenced, and the secret of what Jabez Brown had witnessed in that churchyard remained unknown for the present.

CHAPTER XIII.

LAST SAD RITES—THE GHOST AT THE BEDSIDE.

A gentle sweetness and attractive grace
Dwelt in her form and beautified her face;
Modest, without reserve, from affectation free,
Wise without pride and generous was she.—SHAW.

THE next day at the appointed hour the remains of poor Mary were conveyed to their last resting-place.

It was a sad and melancholy sight to see the modest and unostentatious group winding slowly its way through the village churchyard.

The simple but touching melody of the funeral anthem was floating on the summer breeze, and was infinitely more solemn and affecting than if it had been chaunted by burly white-robed choristers over the grave of ennobled greatness, and vibrating on the ears of aristocratic listeners in the long-drawn aisles of a cathedral.

Mr. Dove performed the ritual, and it was remarked that as the deceased had been an early and attached friend of his own wife, in delivering the solemn service, he moved even to tears the majority of those present.

His allusions to our frail and perishable nature, and his touching verification of the truism that " in the midst of life we are in death," was forcibly illustrated by an eloquent and feeling allusion to the melancholy death of the sexton, cut off so suddenly from earth when in the very act of preparing a grave for their beloved sister.

There was one among the mourners who grieved with a sincerity too apparent to be assumed, too real to be doubted.

This was Angelina.

Her sobs vibrated audibly inside the church, and were the subject of marked observation by all who stood uncovered at that grave.

Her husband's melancholy duties being over, Mrs. Dove returned with him to the vicarage, there to seek consolation from the holy volume whose light she hoped had guided Mary Dalton through the dark valley of the shadow of death, to that eternal region where the tears are wiped from all mourners.

She was restless and uneasy, and half choked by incessant sobbing.

Angelina in vain turned over the sacred pages, and when Mr. Dove took his seat in his neat and snug library with the intention of writing out his homily or sermons for the morning and afternoon service of the succeeding Sabbath, he found his wife still deluged in tears.

The volume of Holy Writ lay closed on the table before her, and little Reginald Dalton was vainly endeavouring to chase away the copious and pearly drops which fell ever and anon from the eyes of his mother's best friend.

His tiny kerchief was used in vain. She still kept weeping, as if her heart would break.

"Angelina," said Mr. Dove, "this is not as it should be. I call your attention to it as a man and a Christian."

"I cannot help my feelings, Edward. She was so good, and so kind, and she suffered so much, that it is in vain I try to get her out of my thoughts."

"This, my dear, is as much as to say that you do not forgive Him for taking her from you."

Mr. Dove pointed upwards as he spoke.

"Oh! but she was so patient under suffering and so beautiful, nobody could look on her without being kind to her. Poor, dear, Mary Dalton!"

"Recollect, Angelina, I lost my dear friend Harry Somers about this time last year, and he was dearer to me than half the race of mankind beside. Did I then give way to such unseemly grief?"

Angelina still kept sobbing, until her replies became absolutely hysterical.

"No, I bowed my heart at the time with submission to His will. Let me beg of you to do the same in this your present bereavement."

His wife made an effort to carry out her husband's wishes.

She endeavoured to rally herself and appear cheerful.

She directed that Reginald, who had been staying with them all day, should be carefully wrapped up and carried in the arms of a domestic to the house of

Doctor Carmichael, who had undertaken his safe custody until the arrival of Sir Lionel Dalton.

The boy gone, she kissed the forehead of her husband, wished him good night, and retired to the solitude of her own thoughts for the usual couple of hours which would of necessity elapse before Mr. Dove could join her.

What Mrs. Dove witnessed in this brief interval she never dared to mention to her husband, for two sufficient reasons.

First, she knew but too well the ridicule with which he always greeted such topics, and his utter disbelief in the theory of them.

Mrs. Dove had been in bed, as she conceived, little more than half-an-hour.

She was quietly dozing off to sleep, after returning thanks to her Creator for all his goodness to her.

Suddenly she fancied she heard the white curtains of her bed, upon which she was lying, move.

At first she imagined the rustling sound which accompanied the movement of the bed curtains was made by her husband, who, having finished his weekly task rather earlier than usual, had crept up quietly to bed in order that he might not disturb his sorrowing wife.

She addressed him, "Is that you, Edward?"

She received no answer.

Being a little deaf she supposed he had not heard what she said, and therefore she repeated the interrogatory in a louder key.

Still getting no answer, she hastily drew aside the curtains and sat up in bed.

Mrs. Dove turned deadly pale. As she was speaking, as she thought, to her husband, the shades of darkness were suspended on a sudden, and a light diffused itself around her like the flash of mid-day. She looked up and gave an involuntary start.

What could it be which caused her to do so?

That which would appal the stoutest heart.

In a chair by her side sat Mrs. Dalton, enveloped in her shroud.

That very shroud in which Angelina had assisted to enwrap her.

Six hours had not elapsed—for it was scarcely ten o'clock—since Mrs. Dove saw with her own eyes her friend committed to the earth, and had silently reiterated her husband's solemn words, "Ashes to ashes, and dust to dust," as he slowly and cautiously dropped a handful upon her coffin.

Angelina essayed to speak, and did.

"Mary, for what purpose do you pursue me?"

Waiting her reply, Angelina endeavoured to look her spiritual visitor full in the face.

"To stop thy weeping, Angelina. I cannot rest in my grave if you will persist in these useless childish lamentations. My shroud is yet wet with your tears, and it will never dry whilst they continue to fall thus upon me. See."

And the spectre seized the affrighted hand of the alarmed Angelina, and placed it upon the frill of her shroud.

The latter started convulsively as one of her heated and feverish fingers was forcibly made to touch what appeared to Angelina to be a wetted cloth.

By a vigorous effort Mrs. Dove withdrew her hand and with much self-possession desired to know of her spectral visitor why and for what purpose she revisited earth, and her friend, Angelina, before others.

In a sweet and clear voice the phantom answered, "To impart to you a secret, Angelina, and one of dreadful import."

All sense of fear or alarm suddenly left the latter, as she felt an unconquerable and irresistible desire clearly to hear and understand words so awfully addressed to her.

Repeating a portion of the ghostly words, she asked the spectre what secret she could possibly wish to impart to her.

She held her breath, awaiting a ghostly intimation.

The spectre proceeded: "Yes, a secret, Angelina, and whilst it remains unrevealed to you, who are dearest to my heart and memory, I am unavenged. Angelina, I shall know no rest till retribution overtakes him."

"Him? Who?"

"Attend!"

The spectral friend bent her head towards the pillow, in the direction of Angelina's ear, as if in the act of whispering to the cool and collected being who sat upright in bed to listen to her. The sudden opening of the chamber door dispelled the vision, and the spirit fled.

Mrs. Dove shrieked aloud.

"Why Angelina, my dear, what is the matter with you. Still thinking of your departed friend, or, having dozed off to sleep, have you been dreaming of her?" said her husband, as he entered the bed room and placed his candlestick on the dressing table.

Mrs. Dove did not dare to inform the curate of what she had been an eye-witness, but taking her cue from the hint he himself gave her about a dream, attributed her great alarm to one which she said she had just experienced, and in which Mary had appeared to in her shroud.

The good curate had but little rest that night.

Angelina would ever and anon clutch him by the arm and declare that somebody was in the room.

Three times was Mr. Dove compelled to get out of bed that night to satisfy his wife that the chamber door was locked on the outside, and that not even a cat could have entered into the apartment without his knowledge.

It was late at night, or rather, early the next morning, when Angelina dropped into a slumber.

At breakfast following, Mrs. Dove could not resist the very natural impulse she felt to communicate to her husband what she had seen before falling asleep the night previously.

But Mr. Dove bit his lip and rebuked her.

"Why did you retire to your bed so early, Angelina," said he, "reason or common sense should have induced you, who are apprehensive of chimerical danger, to have remained with a husband who is ever ready to protect or assist you. But as my guidance is utterly abandoned, and an otherwise intelligent woman follows a meteor light, born of a diseased imagination and nursed in the gloom of superstition, I must endeavour to check your infatuation."

It was the first time in his life that her clerical husband had ventured to rebuke her, and the reproof went to her very heart.

She had no means of convincing Edward that she really had held converse with the spirit of her departed friend, and therefore, as she hoped it would never again be permitted by an all wise Creator to disturb her, she said no more upon the subject.

In a few days her mind was diverted by other events.

Sir Lionel Dalton arrived at the Hall, and his nephew was quickly transferred to Bodmin Castle, the baronet's seat in Kent.

The servants of the household were paid or pensioned off, and the Hall itself, being partly dismantled of all the modern furniture, with which the good taste of his brother had adorned it in his life time, was handed over to the care of the emissaries of Hugh Dalton, who attended to take possession of it in his name, he having, in a most unaccountable whim, commissioned the firm of Edghill, Potter and Pendril to employ an agent to purchase the title deeds of the old Hall and its adjacent grounds, for his own occupation at some future period.

CHAPTER XIV.

THE ATTACK BY THE HIGHWAYMAN.

Now to rifle—rob and plunder.—OLD SONG.

DURING some years, no written communication was received from Hugh Dalton by his brother; and, from the circumstances of his previous conduct, none were made by the baronet to him.

Affairs stood much in the same position as usual, when Sir Lionel Dalton read in the county newspaper the intelligence that his brother Hugh had purchased a commission in the army, and was about to depart for India, as the colonel of a regiment ordered on immediate active service.

The next gazette corroborated the paragraph.

The fact was that the libertine propensities of the roué had made sad encroachments upon his constitution; added to this, he rather imagined that he was occasionally cut by the more solid and respectable of his acquaintances.

Truth must out.

Hugh Dalton was no fool.

He felt his own degradation.

He was sensible of his own crimes, and felt in all its bitterness the hollowness and miserable folly of his licentiousness, and he was therefore anxious to quit England, only to return to it when his misdeeds were forgotten.

He could not very comfortably continue in the land of his fathers much longer.

Very respectable people, when they saw him afar off, passed over on the other side.

Even the very women with whom he had intrigued laughed in his face.

Mrs. Hornby had already cast him off from her affections, and had turned away to seek some wealthier keeper.

He was shunned as an evil thing.

All this he saw, but his heart was hardened, and he did not tremble before that dread tribunal, the laws of which he had so shamefully violated.

He merely shifted the scenes and plans of operation.

Behold him now in the assumed rôle of a soldier and a gentleman.

Will he long support the latter character?

Hugh was born to be a bad man, but in the earlier portion of his life he had given no very great indication of it, beyond being a remarkably rough-spoken boy, and distinguished for a proneness to "barrings out," playing truant, and robbing orchards of their superfluous fruit.

Yet he was a rascal at heart from his very cradle, and as he grew up, rascality was the main pivot upon which all his actions turned.

Like Punch, however, he was clever—exceedingly clever, and could make a noose for another man's neck.

His acquaintanceship with Doctor Carmichael commenced under singular circumstances, and will fully illustrate the foregoing assertions.

Before proceeding in our accounts of his exploits it is necessary to state how and where he became acquainted with the doctor.

On an autumnal evening in the month of October, but at a period many years antecedent to the commencement of the present history, and when the evening was just closing in, a gentleman on horseback stopped at a small inn on the extreme margin of a road which led from the city of Canterbury to the little village of Birchington, and ere the landlord of the "Travellers' Rest," for so it was called, was aware of it, the stranger himself had dismounted and was chucking a handsome young barmaid under the chin, who made her appearance in the hope to receive his orders for a costly supper.

"What a dreadful night we are going to have of it," said John Cutts, the landlord, to his wife who was within the bar, but loud enough for their guest to hear.

"Of course, the good gentleman would not think of proceeding any further on such a night as this," replied his hostess, taking up the thread of her husband's previous remark; "he would be a courageous man, indeed, if he did."

"Why, what is there to fear?"

"Alas!" interposed Mrs. Cutts, "hasn't your honour heard about the poor dear gentleman who was shot dead by a highwayman a few nights ago on the Margate road."

"Whereabouts on the Margate road, my good woman?"

"By the finger-post, your honour; just to your left as you leave Birchington."

"I know it well. Let me ask, was the murdered man on foot or on horseback, Mrs. Cutts?"

"On foot, your honour. He was used to collect the rents for my Lord Darnley, and was supposed to have a large sum about him when attacked—foolhardy man as he was, to attempt that road on such a night."

"Well, it appears the rent collector had but two legs to carry him out of danger's way; I have four."

And the stranger laughed at his own fancied security, looking first at himself and eyeing his sleek mare with satisfaction.

"The road is very bad," persisted Mrs. Cutts; "so bad, indeed, sir, it must be a good animal that will carry your honour without tripping."

"Ah, you may well say tripping," observed John Cutts, "the mail itself was overturned last night."

"You don't say so!"

"If I were a conjuror I should say we should have a heavy fall of snow before the moon rises," continued the landlord.

"And if the moon does rise, I know I shall be all right. I thank you for the information that Madam Cynthia is going to favour me with her company on the road."

The stranger quickly swallowed his hot brandy and water, being in a sudden hurry to get off.

"Only to think, now, if the gentleman should be waylaid," said Mrs. Cutts, "and that beautiful gold watch in his possession."

Hugh Dalton, for it was no other person than he, had been looking at his repeater to ascertain the correct time.

"By Jove, I have overstayed my time, and danger or no danger, I must reach Bodmin Castle before twelve, or shall find all my father's servants gone to bed and fast asleep."

"Heaven grant that a son of Sir Oliver Dalton may reach his home unmolested!"

"I have no fear—not in the least."

"We trust, however, sir, that you carry but little value about you?"

"A roll or two of bank-notes—nothing but what I could well afford to spare."

The supercilious and ostentatious nature of this foolish remark was commented upon in the kitchen of the inn, in which a suspicious group of men were enjoying a bowl of punch, for the purchase of which each had clubbed his share.

"It's a hundred to one," said the chairman of the carousing party, "but the gentleman has his throat cut before he gets a couple of miles from the 'Travellers' Rest.'"

"He'll be pinked," said another.

"Shot, to a dead certainty, as I'm a living man," observed a third. "Before this time to-morrow night he'll have as many holes in his lavender-scented carcase as a culander."

"Ha, ha, ha!"

The room rang with their merriment.

But Hugh was not within hearing of any of the prophetic jests.

At parting with his host and hostess he had observed "the highwayman was not yet born who could rob me," and with this egotistical and defiant remark he vaulted into his saddle, and was soon out of sight.

Onward he galloped, utterly regardless of the well-intentioned admonitory cautions of Mr. and Mrs. Cutts.

He felt himself the only hero of that lonely road.

But truth must out—Hugh Dalton had little of the romantic in his composition.

Though young, he was a matter-of-fact citizen of the world—a young cosmopolite, and he neither cared nor felt for any person but himself.

He had ridden about half his allotted distance without having heard the threatened and ominous words—"Stand and deliver!"

He was no knight-errant, no crusader of old, nor was he wending his way to his "lady-love," though bent on reaching the castle in which he meant to repose for the night as quickly as ever he could.

It began to rain.

Suddenly he fancied he heard a horseman behind him.

Despite the pattering of the rain, the well-known tramp of a quick rider fell upon his ear as he closely followed him through the drizzling mist.

Some one was fast gaining on him in a soft, chalky road.

He turned his head back, and saw a person, well mounted on horseback, evidently trying, by a brisk trot to come up with him.

To expedite his own speed was useless.

The stranger was on a bit of blood quite as good as his own.

In a moment Hugh's pocket pistol was pulled from its resting place. It was quickly cocked and in his hand, duly levelled and ready for the anticipated mischief.

The pursuer, nothing daunted by what he saw, rode up to his side and addressed him with rather a tremulous voice.

His words were :—

"May I be permitted to say a few words to you, sir ?"

"Say your say, and be off with you, or I fire !"

"I am no thief, sir. Turn aside your weapon and hear me—for the love of God, hear me !"

This was not the usual salutation of a knight of the road.

It was so unlike what would have fallen from the lips of Dick Turpin, or Tom King, that the person addressed put aside his weapon of defence and told him to speak out at once.

"I have a small silver watch," replied the young man. "See, here it is—will you give me forty pounds for it?"

The applicant drew from his fob a watch and held it up to the gaze of Hugh.

"Forty pounds for that bit of pinchbeck ! Do you think me mad or drunk, my fine fellow ?"

"It is of silver, keeps time and goes well."

"I dare say ; but let me tell you that if it was made of gold and twice the present size, I have no need of it. There can be no deal, so perhaps you'll be good enough to look for a customer elsewhere."

"I must have forty pounds for it."

"Must is a strong word. But using your own phraseology, I must decline the purchase."

"You won't buy it?"

"Certainly not."

"No, no ! Then lend me the money and keep the watch till I redeem it."

"I am no pawnbroker."

"I did not say you were ; but such is my condition. I must not be trifled with. There's no use in bandying words ; do you mean to accommodate a poor wretch or not ?"

"Well, if it's the same to you, perhaps you'll take no for your answer, and leave go of my reins."

In the agitation of the moment, the young man had seized hold of Hugh's bridle with one hand, whilst he was feeling in his pocket as if for something with the other.

He's feeling for a pistol, thought Hugh.

He felt for his own in its usual place—the side pocket of his outer coat.

It had vanished.

He had dropped it on the road, instead of replacing it in his pocket, a few minutes before.

He endeavoured to conceal a knowledge of this accident from the stranger.

Presenting the knob at the end of his whip to the face of the man, he shouted, "If you do not ride off on the instant, I shall fire !"

"You may as well, sir," returned the other, "fire away at once, for without forty pounds I can never face her again."

"You are not quite up to the mark in your avocation," said Hugh, looking at the stranger with a feeling of interest, "you might have killed a dozen men within the time you have been talking to me."

"God forbid," nervously replied the young man, "She has suffered enough already on my account. It would break her heart entirely. I may be a robber, but, for her sake, I will not be an assassin."

A knowledge of the fact that there was a woman in the case, by the spontaneous admission of the stranger, aroused the curiosity of Hugh, and with a feeling of interest which he could not resist, he drew forth his pocket-book, and taking out a large roll of bank notes, he handed them over to his assailant, bidding him help himself.

To his astonishment, the would-be highwayman returned the notes, untouched, to Hugh, saying, "Your generosity unmans me. No—no. I merely want you to buy this watch. I beseech you to do so. Give or lend me the sum I crave—it's only forty pounds, whilst in your pocket-book there must be more than a hundred."

"Quite an amateur Sixteen-String Jack," thought Dalton to himself, as he keenly surveyed the supposed robber, and recovering his usual spirits from the very novelty of the incident, he proceeded to say, "Well, I see, we are to have a deal, after all."

He counted out eight five-pound notes, one by one, from the roll, before he replaced the bulk in his own pocket.

"There," said he, handing them over to the stranger, "You are but a bungler at your trade, after all. Well, I won't upbraid you. Some artful gipsy may have brought you to this. Hand over the watch and be off in search of a more honest calling."

The miserable being joyfully clutched the bank notes, and with a hurried "God bless you, sir," clapped spurs to his horse, turned sharply round, and was out of sight in a moment.

When Hugh had partly recovered from his surprise, he exclaimed "D——n the fellow ! I should vastly like to know the necessity which has driven him to levy contributions in this way upon his Majesty's subjects."

Hugh pursued his journey.

At the first hostelry he came to he stopped to examine the value of the pledge upon which he had advanced so large a sum.

It was an old-fashioned silver watch, almost worn out, and could not originally have cost its owner more than a couple of pounds.

At that particular time, and evidently after years of long service, it might possibly be worth about ten shillings—no more.

It had no maker's name, no crest or inscription or initial letter, or any thing else, by which a discovery might be effected as to the whereabouts of the rightful owner.

Nevertheless, the mode and manner by which it came into the possession of its new owner were so very remarkable that he determined to keep it as a memorial, with the consolation of quietly repeating to himself the well-known and trite adage—"A fool and his money are soon parted."

A short time afterwards Hugh Dalton left England on the grand tour mentioned in preceding pages.

CHAPTER XV.

A RECOGNITION IN THE CHEMIST'S SHOP.

The face was familiar to him. He was even positive he had seen it before. Where could it have been?—JONATHAN WILD.

AFTER viewing the principal cities of Europe, and spending a vast amount of cash, Hugh returned to England, much in the same condition as the monkey who had seen the world.

Business called him to Lincoln's Inn-fields on a visit to Edghill, Potter, and Pendril's office.

He was passing through Fleet-street on that occasion, one morning in the month of July, marking the astonishing improvements which had been effected even in those days during his short absence.

Various, as may be supposed, were the many changes he noticed in his perambulations.

New habitations had sprung up in the place of old ones.

Men who had been assistants to or previous partners in houses of business to which he had occasion to repair before he left the metropolis, now figured away as the head of these firms themselves.

The oppressive heat of the weather—for it had been a hot, sultry day—had caused him to have a severe headache.

The pain being almost intolerable, he looked out for a chemist's shop at which he might buy something to relieve him.

On the opposite side of the way to that on which he stood was a very handsome druggist's shop.

It had a plate-glass front.

A large gilded pestle and mortar was placed over the centre shop-door to denote the nature of the pharmaceutical business carried on within its portals.

The rays of the sun reflecting the blue, red, yellow, and purple colours which gleamed from the show bottles in the magnificent window almost dazzled him.

He looked up for the name of the fortunate and evidently well-to-do dispenser of drugs.

He saw in fine bright gilded letters the following announcement :—

"CARMICHAEL, CHEMIST AND DRUGGIST."

Somebody, whom he saw, happening to pass by at the time, and seeing him staring so very hardly across the way, naturally enough asked him what he was gazing at.

"At the alteration in that doctor's shop, Mr. King."

"What, Carmichael's?"

"Yes! When I left London it had but one small window-front, and was kept by a common-councilman, one Peter Andrews. I suppose Peter has been called to his last account?"

"Not he."

"Has he retired?"

"Yes, after being made an alderman."

"I am surprised to hear of his elevation. How came he to give up business?"

"He thought it was quite beneath an alderman's dignity to wield the spatula, so he adopted a cruel alternative."

"What did he do?"

"He threw physic to the dogs the year before they made him Lord Mayor."

"Yes."

It is now kept by a lucky fellow one George Carmichael. He was apprenticed to the alderman. They say the great painter, Mr. Hogarth, took him for his model in his last grand series of pictures. There cer-

tainly is a strong resemblance to Carmichael in the painter's "Idle and Industrious Apprentices."

"Well, it's better to be born lucky than rich."

"The coincidence is singular, for the once humble apprentice is going to be married to the Alderman's daughter in a day or so."

"Dear me! Quite a dramatic incident."

"Nevertheless, it is true."

"Is the dutiful apprentice the choice of a personable creature?"

Hugh Dalton could not not refrain from putting this question, for he was very inquisitive on every point where a woman was concerned.

"Beautiful as an angel."

"Dark or fair?"

"Fair."

"Tall or short?"

"Of an average height."

"How high?"

"About five feet."

"Thin or stout?"

"Rather inclined to be stout."

"My style of woman, to a nicety. Give me Venus with a good pound of flesh upon her. I hate your lath and plaster beauties."

"I must say she is passable."

"Gad, your description has driven my headache clean away. I should like to get a peep at her."

"You can easily do so."

"How?"

"Step across to the shop, and under pretence of imbibing a cooling draught, look about you. She's frequently in it."

Dalton stepped over to the shop.

For some minutes he endeavoured to get a peep into its inside gratuitously.

He leered through the large and handsome plate glass, seemingly at the pink and white lozenges, which were arrayed in diamond-cut forms on a showboard in the window ; but, in reality, to feast his eyes upon the alderman's fair daughter.

He admired the small blue stone smelling bottles, with silver tops, on a tray.

The deuce a bit of a petticoat could he discern.

Hugh did not like much trouble, and was giving up the chase.

On second thoughts he determined to enter boldly, and expend a few shillings in some useful articles for his toilet.

Carmichael, seeing a stranger about to enter his shop politely rushed forward and pulled the door open for him.

But instead of entering the shop, Hugh turned abruptly on his heel and walked off quietly towards Temple Bar.

He could not have been more astonished had he seen the evil one.

Hogarth's model apprentice was the identical young fellow who had defrauded him on the Canterbury road of forty pounds, good and lawful money, in exchange for a worthless watch.

The happy apprentice who had arrived at the high honour of marrying a Lord Mayor's daughter was a common cheat.

Innately revengeful, Hugh Dalton actually gloated over the reprisal he would now make upon the midnight marauder.

A thousand ways of retaliation started up to his imagination.

Should he walk to Guildhall and procure a warrant against the Lord Mayor's future son-in-law?

What if he gave him into the custody of a passing constable?

On he walked, turning over in his mind a hundred different modes of retaliation.

Suddenly he became a rigid moralist, and thought it was a strict duty which he owed to society not to let successful villany go unpunished.

He would therefore prosecute the scoundrel at the Old Bailey, if it cost him a thousand pounds.

He would invite all his friends to attend the place where he would be hanged.

He would pay for fifty hackney chariots to take them to Tyburn, with pleasure.

After thinking of as many different modes of punishment as there are days in the calendar, Hugh made up his mind to defer putting any of them into execution till he had partaken of a good dinner.

A splendid spread, at a first-rate tavern in the neighbourhood, followed by a bottle or two of excellent madeira, caused him to alter his tactis.

He now was more curious than ever about such a singular and most unaccountable young highwayman.

So curious indeed was he on the subject, that he could not help seizing a waiter, who was attending upon him, by a button of his coat, as he placed a dish of walnuts on the table.

Hugh asked him if he knew Mr. Carmichael, the druggist.

"I do, sir, I am proud to say. He is chairman of a club of politicians, who hold their weekly meetings in this very house."

"What sort of a character does he bear?"

"Unexceptionable in every respect, sir. He's a great friend of our worthy vicar's, and bears a high 'karacter as a religionist sort of gentleman."

"Is he about to get married?"

"Not as I know's on, sir."

"Waiter, we live in a queer world."

"We do, sir, werry queer."

"One man gets hanged, and another laughs at him."

"I should say he was an uncommon unfeeling wretch who would laugh at a poor fellow creature in that dreadful situation, sir."

"Yes: but one man may steal a horse whilst another must not look into a stable. What say you waiter?"

"I don't understand the law of horse stealing, so, please, sir, excuse my giving an opinion."

"No equivocation waiter. I desire to know if that scoundrel is considered as an upright man."

The waiter, who, by this time, had quite forgotten the name of the person his guest meant, begged to ask to whom the gentleman alluded.

Hugh Dalton repeated the name, deliberately spelling it, and afterwards muttering the words "scoundrel," "highwayman," "rascal," and "swindler."

Seizing an empty decanter, and dashing it on the mahogany table, as he delivered his invectives against the chemist and druggist, he delivered himself with so much force, that he shivered the brittle vessel into a thousand fragments.

The waiter ran to his master and declared there was a gentleman so "tossicated" in box No. 2, that unless the watchman was called in, he would inevitably smash every bottle he could lay his hands upon.

The landlord making his appearance, followed by several elderly gentlemen who hastened to see what was the matter, Hugh recovered his equanimity, and calling for his bill, paid the full damage and staggered home to his lodgings.

At breakfast in the morning, Hugh was himself again.

Soda water and lemonade had done their office, and he sat calmly ruminating on the odd event of the last afternoon.

Strange to say, he was not half so desperately inclined towards the midnight marauder as on the previous day.

He put this and he put that together, and before he had finished his bohea arrived at a different conclusion.

Although the young man had held in his hand Hugh's pocket-book, which actually contained more than five hundred pounds in bank notes, he only took forty pounds—nay, he did not even do that, for it was himself who counted them out and handed them over to him.

Altogether, Mr. Hugh Dalton was puzzled what course to pursue.

He determined, however, to do something, for he started off to Fleet-street with that laudable intention.

Arrived at his place of destination, he peeped into the shop, and gazed for full ten minutes on its master before he entered.

It was the highwayman, sure enough.

Mr. Hugh Dalton stalked into the shop.

The master advanced to meet him.

"What can I have the pleasure to serve you with?" said he, bowing low to the ground, in the presence of a presumed customer.

"I don't want to buy any of your drugs, Mr. Carmichael, but having unfortunately come out without money this morning, I wan't you to lend me a few pounds."

The chemist and druggist stared at him.

"If I had the honour of knowing you, sir, I should not hesitate for a moment, but, as we are entire strangers, you must really excuse me from complying with your request."

"Do I understand you rightly? You refuse to lend me a pound or two, do you?"

"I regret to say I must adhere to one strict rule of business, but as you appear to be a gentleman, and have come out, as you state, in a hurry, and may be inconvenienced by temporaray want——"

"Well?"

"As far as a few shillings go, they are heartily at your service."

"D——n you, and your shillings into the bargain."

"Sir. This language——"

"May be emphatic, but not inexpressive. I want ten pounds, and if you'll lend them to me, I will leave this pocket-book with you as a guarantee for the return of the money to-morrow morning."

Hugh Dalton threw down on the counter an old worn-out red morocco memorandum book, which happened, to be in the pockets of his great coat.

"This pocket-book, sir, is not worth twopence."

"Well, here's something else. I've a valuable watch in my fob, what do you say to *this?* Ten years ago, though no pawnbroker, I advanced a young gentleman forty pounds upon it."

Carmichael turned deadly pale, and fell down on his knees in an agony of supplication.

"Now you atrocious villain, you, what have you to say to that?"

Carmichael clasped his hands together, as he continued on his knees in supplication, and exclaimed—

"Do not crush me, sir, whoever you are. It was my first and only crime. I was driven to it to save the home of a widowed mother, as you shall hear, if you will kindly and generously consent to give me a quiet *private* hearing.

"Be candid, then, and let me know the full particulars."

"I will, sir, if you will let me wait upon you, or give me a call, the day after to-morrow. You shall know all, and I err indeed in my knowledge of a truly good man, if you do not pity as well as forgive me. Believe me, I have had little peace since that most dreadful night."

"But why do you beg so earnestly that I should call the day after to-morrow? Why not to-morrow—why not to-night?"

Carmichael turned deadly pale, and dreading lest any other persons might hear what he had to say, leant over the counter and meekly said,—

"Because—because, sir, I am to be married to-morrow, sir. You alone have the power to prevent me; but I hope you will not; nay, on my knees I would implore you not."

He was about to descend to this humiliating position, when Hugh bade him be of good courage, and promised to wait upon him for the appointed interview on the day after the morrow.

Hugh was quitting the shop, when the druggist called him back, saying the money was at hand, and begging permission to hand it over to him, principal and interest, that very moment.

Hugh Dalton took the money, for it was an article he was very fond of; but, at the same time, he kept possession of the battered silver watch, for purposes of his own.

Before quitting the shop, he turned to Carmichael and addressed him.

"Mind, twelve o'clock on Friday, I shall be punctual. You need not distress yourself on my account. Keep your own counsel, and I will keep mine. Your secret is unknown to the world: whether I divulge it, depends upon your future conduct."

He then departed.

The giant figures, which formerly formed a subject of great curiosity to "the young man from the country" were striking the hour of twelve with their clubs upon bells above the church clock of St. Dunstan, when Hugh Dalton, punctual to his appointment, made his appearance at the shop.

Mr. Carmichael ushered him into his private surgery, and locked the door after him, that their privacy might not be disturbed.

He told the touching and simple story of the real motive which led him to commit the dreadful act which had placed him irrevocably in Hugh Dalton's power.

His mother, who lived in a cottage in Kent, near the city of Canterbury, had become bail for a relation, in the sum of forty pounds. The man absconded, and the person to whom the money was owing, being vindictive, threatened his mother, who was confined to her bed and ill at the time, to throw her into prison if the debt and costs were not paid forthwith.

Had she sold off everything she possessed in the world she could not have made up half the money.

In her distress, she wrote to London a detail of her distresses and sent it to her son. He set off immediately on the receipt of this letter from his mother, which informed him of the facts, but he only arrived in sufficient time to find his parent in the company of bailiffs, who had taken her in custody for the amount, and were in the act of carrying her off to prison.

The scene was heartrending.

By dint of great persuasion and some bribes, the bailiffs were induced to let the poor mother remain in their custody for that night, whilst the son made an endeavour to raise the money.

They gave him until the next morning for that purpose.

If he did not return with it by that time, Mrs. Carmichael was to be taken off to the county prison.

Almost beside himself, with not sufficient money even to carry him back again to London if he failed, the broken-hearted Carmichael succeeded in borrowing a horse, under pretence of riding some miles to beg the money from a rich relative, who lived at Canterbury.

What took place on the road leading to that city has already been described.

We will now return to the interview.

A good office done harshly, has been justly compared to a stony piece of bread: it is for him that is hungry to receive it; but it almost chokes him in the going down.

This was exactly poor Carmichael's case.

It will be shown by the following short conversation, which ensued after the offender had declared his sincere contrition and had begged mercy at the hands of Hugh.

"I hear you have married a young and beautiful wife."

"Yes, sir, and one who is quite as good as she is beautiful."

"You would not like me then to make her acquaint with your crime?"

Carmichael shuddered.

"Nor to acquaint my Lord Mayor with the doubtful character of his son-in-law."

Carmichael sighed heavily. He seemed gasping for breath, but contrived at last to articulate—

"Oh! sir, you are far too good, I am sure, to blast my future prospects in life by such exposure."

Hugh pretended not to hear the appeal. He proceeded.

"It would be a terrible thing for one in your position to be hurled to the ground and pointed at by his former companions as a man who——"

"Spare me, for mercy's sake, spare me, sir! The very walls may have ears. For God's sake do not talk so loud."

But Hugh talked still louder.

"I can only consent to keep your diabolical secret upon one condition."

"Oh, name it—name it! I feel confident you are far too kind and generous to extort anything from me incompatible with honour and integrity."

"Your notions of honour and integrity, differ from my own, but I won't upbraid you if you'll promise to do whatever I may require of you at any future period."

Carmichael seemed to hesitate.

"My question requires but little reflection. Simply yes or no. To you, acquiescence is everything to me it makes not the slightest difference. Recollect at the time you so shamefully plundered me——"

Hugh kept raising his voice still louder every time he addressed the transgressor.

His craftiness had its due effect.

Carmichael promised to do whatever might be requested.

"But you must swear it, and I have less repugnance in asking you do so, since the robbery you so basely committed——"

The trembling wretch he was addressing shook in every limb.

The fiend in human form, who was torturing him, took up a small Bible, which was opportunely on a table near him, and giving it into his victim's hands, called upon him to kiss it and swear by its contents to do his bidding.

Having extorted the required oath, Hugh Dalton left the shop.

CHAPTER XVI.

LIFE IN INDIA—THE WILL ON THE SPUR OF THE MOMENT—DALTON'S LUCK.

Ambition is the dropsy of the soul:
A thirst we must not yield to, but control.
DRYDEN.

WE must now recur to a period in Hugh Dalton's career subsequent to his purchasing into the army.

To his astonishment, after he had done so, his regiment was ordered off, at a moment's notice, on actual service.

His destination was India.

The commands came from high quarters, and he had bought in too recently to sell out again.

To do him justice, he had no wish of the kind.

He was naturally ambitious.

He hoped one day to be favourably mentioned by the commander-in-chief of the British forces in India or in the government despatches from the hottest of all climates.

Hot in a double sense he found it.

He was continually exposed to the fire of the enemy and the amazing heat of the weather.

The combined effects of these made considerable encroachments upon his health.

Within six months after he first began to traverse the plains of India, he was greatly altered.

THE SPECTRE WARNS MRS. SOMERS.

Hugh entered the army, fired by a natural impulse—ambition.

It may be remarked that no passion has produced more baneful effects than this one, and yet ambition is not a vice, except in a vicious mind.

Hugh was ambitious of forming rich and influential acquaintances, and he was successful beyond his most sanguine wishes.

Amongst his bosom companions was a Major Durrant, of the Bengal cavalry.

This major was known to be rich.

Hugh courted his acquaintance, engratiated himself into the old soldier's good opinion, and ultimately became his constant companion day and night.

Major Durrant was exceedingly fond of good living, and at the table of his friend Colonel Dalton he was always sure of a well-made curry.

Major Durrant had a niece in England, and so favourably impressed was he by the accounts he heard of the beauty and amiability of his sister's child, that he was frequently despatching hints, if not distinct promises, to both mother and daughter, that the latter should inherit his fortune.

Within the first month of his acquaintance with Durrant, Hugh had wormed this secret out of him.

He played his cards accordingly.

His first grand *coup* was to ascertain the precise amount of the fortune itself.

He found it to be quite as much as would suit his purpose, and rather more than he expected.

A clear estate of two thousand a year without incumbrances was worth trying for.

Hugh set his best wits to work to obtain it.

He attacked the rich old uncle on his vulnerable point.

He flattered him.

So pleased was the erratic major with the "food of fools," that he found he could not eat or drink at any meal if Colonel Hugh Dalton was absent from it.

Hugh was constantly telling him that he knew all about his gallant actions.

He could not close his ears.

He was always being told of the major's prowess

since the first moment the brave major himself drew a sword or took up arms in India.

That the subjection of this fort, the blowing up of that particular mine, and the glorious termination of some clever *coup-de-main*, were all brought about by his superior tactics, skill, and military manœuvring.

Major Durrant greedily swallowed this sort of poison, and it insidiously worked its way to his heart.

He began to idolize the colonel.

One day at tiffin, over a bottle, he declared that if ever he returned safely to England he would introduce his friend to his beautiful niece Felicia Somers.

Nay, what was more, if the lady liked him he should be proud of the alliance.

Hugh was a lucky dog.

A second bottle led him to disclose an important secret.

Hugh was luckier still.

Within his own mind he was certain that his niece would like the colonel.

A third bottle had a more potent effect.

Like or not like, she should never have any other husband with his consent.

More luck. Hugh was now a made man.

A fourth bottle completely did the business.

And this observation will show how.

"This very night, my good friend, I will make my will, and put it out of her power to refuse you."

"My dear major, I will not hear of such a thing. What! fetter the affections of a young and guileless girl?"

"Your sentiments do you honour, Colonel Dalton—great honour; but I am determined."

It was now time for Hugh to commence operations, and make his way through the breach so opportunely opened.

He called his usual cunning to his aid.

He would appear quite indifferent about the matter.

"Strong as is my belief, my dear major," said he, "in female perfection, I am too old a soldier already to fall down and worship the first idol whose glittering surface is to be mistaken for gold. No; when I marry, I marry a woman for herself alone. I don't care a brass farthing for money."

"Dalton, my boy, they ought to have made a parson of you; you are wasting your time here among sepoys and nabobs."

"You flatter me, major, you do."

"Not a bit. If I had been brought up to the church, with a tithe of your talent, I should have become an archbishop by this time."

"I am certain you would," drily observed Hugh, as he replenished the major's empty goblet with a magnum of sparkling madeira.

The wine did its office.

"Pens, ink, and paper!" shouted the major, almost upsetting the dessert before him in order to reach his writing-desk.

Major-General Durrant would insist upon making a last will and testament.

And it was written.

It was very short, but fully to the purpose.

The major left every shilling he had in the world to his niece, Felicia Somers, upon condition that the said niece married his dear friend, Hugh Dalton.

What if she refused to marry the colonel?

That was cleverly provided for by Hugh Dalton, who seized the golden chance, and clinched it by suggesting the introduction of a codicil himself, which settled the business.

If she did not marry the aforesaid Hugh Dalton, the whole of the property was to revert to the aforesaid Hugh Dalton himself.

Other stipulations were introduced into the document, against which the major was either too infatuated or too drunk to take an exception.

The most important one was that in case of the wife's death the whole of the property should be at the absolute disposal of the surviving husband.

Hugh Dalton was called upon to witness this precious document; but, with pretended modesty, accompanied by a vulgar oath, he swore that he would be no party to inflicting such restrictions upon one of the fair sex.

He rose, however, from his seat on the settee and called in the necessary and impartial persons, who were required to attach their signatures to the bit of paper to make it a legal document.

After the will had been duly witnessed, Hugh was asked if he would undertake the safe custody of it.

This was the very thing he wanted.

He again pretended to be reluctant.

He would rather it should be supposed that he knew nothing about the matter.

This time, however, the major's earnest entreaties were successful.

Hugh Dalton pocketed the will.

He was ever side by side with the major, and as constantly plying him with his favourite madeira.

The burning atmosphere of India and the madeira did their work.

Major Durrant, of the Bengal Cavalry, was a dead man within ten weeks after signing the will.

Scarcely was the breath out of his body than Colonel Hugh Dalton determined to depart for England the first opportunity.

After he had seen the sad remains of his friend decently interred, he turned all that friend's available assets into ready money ; and a temporary peace fortunately occurring, he set sail for England on his new matrimonial project.

CHAPTER XVII.

LOVE AT FIRST SIGHT—ITS FOLLY AND ITS CONSE-QUENCES.

> By thee deceived, the flatter'd fair,
> Prepar'd not for the artful snare,
> Against her fortune basely plann'd,
> To ruin gives her hasty hand.—COWLEY.

In the pleasant vale of Llangollen in North Wales, resided Mrs. Somers and her daughter. If not in affluent circumstances, they were tolerably comfortable.

They seemed to be passing the meridian of their days in the sweetest of vales, surrounded by the love and respect of many highly esteemed friends.

Perhaps the respect shown to the widow and her daughter was not a little owing to the rumour current amongst their neighbours that the latter was heiress to a rich uncle.

Felicia indulged no anticipations on the subject.

She might or she might not one of these days come into possession of a trifle.

It was admitted by her, however, if her Indian relative should recollect her, she would be bound in common gratitude not to forget him.

It was on the morning of her mother's birthday when the village post-master sent round to their cottage to say that he had a most important packet for Miss Felicia, and that, thinking it might be a remittance of money from India, he did not care to entrust it to the boy who usually went round with the letters.

Curiosity prompted her to go at once to the post-office and put an end to her suspense.

She received a very large packet.

It was a ship letter, enclosed in a big envelope, bordered with black, and sealed with black wax.

The deep black edging of the letter, which was addressed to herself—and not, as previous letters from India had been, to her mother—could not but excite a little curiosity.

Felicia hastily opened the letter to ascertain the contents. She did this at the post-office, and almost at the very same moment it was delivered to her.

She did not tremble as she opened it ; for though the messenger of death is always awful, she had no particular anticipation on the subject.

Miss Somers knew so little of her uncle in India, that the assumption of grief for his loss would have been hypocritical.

The letter itself was an official notification from certain bankers at Calcutta, relative to her relation's death, and informing her of a small sum still remaining in the hands of the firm, to which she was entitled under the will of her uncle, and waiting her pleasure as to its disposal.

The latter intimation was far from an unpleasant one to her ; and being an exciting piece of intelligence she hastened back to her mother for the purpose of communicating the news.

The afternoon's post brought her a far more startling letter than that which communicated to her the intelligence of the death of her uncle.

It was as follows :—

CASTLE BODMIN, KENT,
May 3rd, ——

MADAM:

I scarcely know how now to introduce the very delicate matter to which I have the honour to call your serious attention.

I am recently arrived in England from India, and am bearer to you of the distressing, not to say heartbreaking, intelligence, of the death of the brave Major Durrant.

Brevity will be pardonable upon an occasion like the present.

By your uncle's will you succeed to the bulk of his fortune, upon a most singular condition, and one which I had preferred should have been communicated to you by a third party, but in pursuance of a solemn duty I must communicate it myself.

The condition named by Major Durrant is, that within a certain period stipulated by my lamented friend you are to accept me for a husband.

I trust, prior to the immediate interview I now solicit, you will acquit me of exercising any influence over Major Durrant as to the disposition of his property in my favour, and I feel assured you will, when I inform you, madam, that I never knew of his extraordinary bias in my favour until his representatives placed his last will and testament for safe keeping in my hands.

I do assure you, madam, I had as much expectation of such a decision in my favour, as being crowned king of England.

I had no claims upon his bounty, and I repudiate any acts of friendship on my part towards him, except an interchange of mutual civilities.

We were brother officers ; we fought and bled in the same field together; and it will not be disagreeable to you, as his near and dearest relative, to learn that a braver soldier or kindlier man never breathed the breath of life.

The only way in which I can possibly account for the flattering manner in which he has chosen to consider me in his will, is the gratifying fact that I once successfully defended him from the attacks of a marauding party, who ensnared him into their meshes. He was pleased to say that I was the means of saving his life. He much overrated my poor service, in ascribing his salvation to the timely aid I was fortunately able to afford when such a dear friend was in imminent danger.

My interference was solely humane, without the expectation of benefit to myself, and prompted by the commonest feelings of a Christian, without the slightest wish or hope of personal aggrandisement.

Soliciting the distinguished honour of an early permission to wait upon you,

I am, madam,
Most devotedly yours,
MISS FELICIA SOMERS,   HUGH DALTON.
Harper's Cottage, Llangollen, N. Wales.

The first of these epistles caused little emotion.

The second had a different effect.

Felicia burst into tears.

Every feeling of womanly pride, dignity, and delicacy revolted against the writer.

She felt his letter a mockery and an insult.

Was she to be handed over to the tender mercies of a complete stranger by the insane stipulations of a mad relation ?

She did not understand much about law, but she felt convinced that such a monstrous will could be upset.

Mrs. Somers was indignant at the idea of her brother's folly.

She was enraged—greatly enraged ; but in spite of her anger, she could not help feeling a degree of curiosity to see and converse with the "lucky wretch," as she called Hugh, to whom her child was so cavalierly bequeathed.

Woman, thou art a riddle !

How shall we unravel the sex ?

Now that Mrs. Somers found that she was entirely excluded from all mention in her brother's will, by a strange perverseness of nature, she viewed the affair on its best side, and even before her daughter had seen the gallant knight coming to demand her hand, she began to propitiate Felicia in his favour.

"Fifty thousand pounds !" exclaimed Mrs. Somers ; "why, my dear Felicia, with such a sum you may endure a husband if he's blind, lame, and halt."

But Felicia kept thinking of the abominable condition attached to the legacy, and went to bed that night vowing that if there was not another husband to be got in the whole world, she would not be coerced into matrimony under any such shameful circumstances.

Felicia went on at a fine rate whilst preparing to undress in her chamber.

She was certain she should not get a wink of sleep all night.

Her bitter invectives against Major Durrant roused the indignation of his sister, who was assisting to undress her.

"Felicia, I must beg of you to suspend your judgment. Do not persist in railing so much against this Dalton. I declare, from the style of his letter, he must be a very charming, not to say elegant, fellow—a little blunt, perhaps, but all soldiers are ; besides, he lives in a castle, and is a colonel too."

Felicia sighed.

"There, give your mother a kiss, my love, and in the morning, like a dear, good girl as you are, sit down and write an answer without delay."

"What sort of an answer ?" asked Miss Somers, pausing, and looking archly at her mother, before she engulphed herself in the downy abyss waiting to receive her.

"What sort of answer, child ? Why, an evasive one, to be sure. Name our dinner hour, invite him to join us, and leave him to come or let it alone, just as he pleases."

A rather long altercation ensued, which wound up by a declaration of the young heiress that people might do as they pleased, but rather than be clogged with such a rib, and under such conditions, she would at once relinquish her fortune.

Felicia sank on her pillow, and was in her first sleep when the door of her chamber was reopened by Mrs. Somers, on going up-stairs an hour later to her own bed.

She spoke, and these were her words:—

"Felicia, my dear, I hope by to-morrow morning you will have come to your senses. With fifty thousand pounds you may do something for your poor mother."

But Felicia heard her not, for she was asleep and dreaming of sudden riches.

At the breakfast table on the following morning, the conversation of the previous night was renewed.

"Believe me, dearest Felicia," said Mrs. Somers, "I sigh with you for the shock your feelings have received; but, as we cannot go against our destiny, I hope you will make a generous effort——"

"To do what, mother?"

"To accept the hand of the man, whatever he may be, and bring down the uplifted finger of scorn, should it be pointed at us, by the weight of the money bags he will bring you."

"Then he has a fortune of his own, I suppose."

"His pay in the army of course, my love, and I dare be sworn it is considerable."

Felicia kept ruminating in her own mind what the yearly stipend of a colonel in the army could possibly be; so, after a long pause, she said, "I'll think about it."

"Procrastination, Felicia, will give room for disadvantageous reports against you; and the only way to preserve yourself from them is to write and say you will abide by the conditions of the major's will."

"My dear mother, how you talk! I know nothing about this colonel. He may, or may not, be a good man. I don't say that he is a bad one, but the union of two lovers without equal dispositions is not love; it is an odious association, by which they become partners in vice and accomplices in each other's crimes."

"Quite a sermon, I declare," said Mrs. Somers.

"I wonder what sort of a man he really is? I shall absolutely hate him if he is of a grave or serious demeanour."

"Nonsense; grave men are most constant."

"Then I shall pray he turn out to be a most potent, grave, and reverend seignor," jocularly observed Felicia.

There is something charming in the idea of being really loved.

Felicia thought so, and was about to say as much when her mother suddenly exclaimed—

"Your uncle's wish must not be thwarted. He evidently relied on my concurrence, and acquiescence on your part is due to his memory. I desire you immediately to invite Colonel Dalton to the Cottage; and if it is necessary to make you obey me, and I must use my authority, I *order* you to write to the gentleman immediately."

Felicia looked astonished.

She said nothing, for she knew that her mother's dictum resembled the laws of the Medes and the Persians.

It was imperative.

A letter containing an acknowledgment of the honour intended her, with an invitation to dine at Harper's Cottage on the following Monday, was sent off by that night's post.

The epistle was carefully read over to Mrs. Somers before being dropped into the letter-box of the village post-office, and that lady approved of every word.

No time was to be lost.

She commenced at once to make extensive preparations for the reception of her future son in-law.

In the interval which elapsed before his arrival, the fair inmates of the cottage passed their time in conjecturing what sort of a person he could most resemble.

Mrs. Somers could not get rid of the idea that he was a perfect angel.

She could depose on oath that he would turn out an accomplished gentleman.

Miss Somers had strange misgivings that after residing so long in India he must of necessity be like the generality of Oriental lovers, and turn out very yellow-looking, and very bilious.

Mrs. Somers bade her not anticipate.

She was certain Felicia would find in him all she desired.

"I hope," said the latter, "he will also find me, if not the pink of perfection, at least so far passable as not to need any fault-finding, scolding, or teaching."

On returning in the afternoon from a visit at a friend's in the neighbourhood, Mrs. Somers called her daughter immediately into her presence.

"My dear," says she, "what do you think I have just heard?"

"Good gracious! how can I guess?

"Has Conway Castle been fired?

"Is the good town of Shrewsbury up in arms at a threatened invasion?

"Is uncle Thomas again laid up with the gout?"

"Something more agreeable."

"Don't tantalise me—out with it."

"Your newly expected lover is own brother to a baronet, and may become a baronet himself one of these days."

"Indeed! I am so glad!" cried Felicia, clapping her hands, "it is so delightful, you know, to have proposals made to you by scions of the aristocracy."

"Yes, my dear. Colonel Hugh Dalton is brother to the Sir Lionel Dalton who stood for Carnarvonshire last year, and was returned by a majority of a hundred and three over his opponent."

"Mother, pray answer me one question."

"Yes, dear."

"Did your informant give you any intelligence respecting the honourable member's brother? Have you heard what sort of a man he is?"

Mrs. Somers had heard, but she did not repeat the exact description given to her.

It perhaps would have been better if she had.

All she said was that Colonel Dalton had travelled much, and for his age and station he was a man that had seen a great deal of the world.

This certainly was not saying much.

The period soon arrived when the young lady was enabled to judge for herself.

Monday brought Colonel Hugh Dalton in an elegant post-chaise-and-four to Harper's Cottage.

The rattling of the carriage and the noise of the postilions gave timely notice to Felicia of his approach, and she was able to take a sly peep at him before he beheld her, as she looked at him through the muslin curtains of her bed-chamber window.

The single glance she got of his face and figure sufficed to convince her she had formed a wrong and erroneous opinion of him.

Instead of the hideous looking, not to say woebegone lover she had been led to expect, she saw at once that he was a tall and elegant man, and but slightly sun-burnt.

She made this discovery as he was shaking hands at the door of their cottage with her mother.

The embarrassing interview and a hurried but elegant dinner over, Mrs. Somers left the Colonel and her daughter to themselves.

Prudes may affirm that the lady's kindness was indiscreet.

Under the circumstances it was the only course she could pursue.

Hugh saw in a moment that he had created a favourable impression on the mother as well as on the daughter.

To cement that impression and to make it indelible in the breast of the latter, he had recourse to his usual *finesse* and duplicity.

He would appear disinterested and generous in the eyes of his mistress, to begin with.

"Miss Dalton," said he, "I fear I must look like a perfect hobgoblin or some such horrible creature in your eyes—a very vampire, commissioned by your late uncle to devour you; and if that is the case, or if such are your thoughts, I at once and without hesitation release you from the disagreeable dilemma in which you are placed, and tell you frankly, if you dismiss me from your presence, I shall not be mean enough to insist upon the penalty of your fortune."

Felicia could scarce believe her ears.

"You need not therefore," he continued, "labour under the slightest fear of being hampered with an unsightly encumbrance, which caprice has attached to its possession."

There appeared something so noble in this manly offer that Felicia looked up in his face and could not help exclaiming—

"Do you mean what you say, Colonel Dalton?"

"I do, upon the word and honour of a gentleman."

"This is singular!"

"Not at all. Bring me ink and paper, and I will give you a written release, which shall free you from any future chance of being annoyed through the means of the eccentric conditions appended to your uncle's will. With this assurance, permit me now to take my leave."

Hugh arose from his chair as if to go away.

The manœuvre was successful.

Felicia blushed, and rising herself, said—

"Bless me! I beg your pardon! I hope you are not going. Pray resume your seat, and favour me with your company a little longer."

"If Miss Somers honours me with such a wish, I shall take it as a command."

And Hugh resumed his seat.

What passed in the course of that interview, artfully protracted by the designing colonel to a very late hour, is very material to our story, for it disclosed the beginning of a deep-laid and most important plot.

The result of the very first meeting had this effect.

Felicia Somers was over head and heels in love with Hugh Dalton.

Alas! poor dupe!

During the hours of courtship Colonel Dalton was so gentle, so respectful, so diffident, and so engaging, that in her heart she was rather glad than sorry that her eccentric uncle had relieved her of the trouble of choosing a husband for herself.

Though stopping at the principal inn at Llanberris, which was a considerable distance from the vale of Llangollen, Colonel Dalton visited Harper's village sometimes twice a day.

In fact, Felicia began to watch for the appointed hours, to distinguish his approaching footstep, and while she did so it was apparent to her mother that her cheeks flushed and her heart throbbed.

Meanwhile, Mrs. Somers was in an ecstasy of delight.

She could scarcely contain her joy.

Her child might be ennobled.

At no very distant period she might have the happiness of calling her Lady Felicia Dalton.

Within a very few weeks from this introduction to each other, Hugh Dalton and Felicia Somers were married.

The wedding was a private one.

There was no fuss or ceremony of any kind.

No lawyer was called in to draw up a marriage settlement.

The union was supposed to be one of pure love and affection.

On the part of the bride it really was so.

Felicia rendered up to her husband the entire control of the money bequeathed to her by her uncle, and made no reserve or stipulation of any kind whatever.

Even her own mother was left dependent upon her husband's bounty.

This annoyed Mrs. Somers, for it re-kindled long-dormant feelings of dependence and was debasing to her self-respect.

One day Mrs. Somers declared her intention of pulling down a wall and throwing two of the rooms into one. What did her daughter think of the proposal?

"Oh, I dare say it will be for the best; but, of course, mother, you will ask Colonel Dalton's permission."

"I shall do no such thing, Felicia—what next?"

"Not a board must be disturbed nor a nail driven in without my husband's consent. I have sworn to obey him."

"Indeed! Be assured if he tells me not to make the alteration I shall disregard the injunction. I have not sworn to obey him."

"Then I cannot entertain your project."

"I am surprised, Felicia—so unlike you."

"I hope, madam," said the young wife, drawing herself up, "I hope that the surprise is not an unpleasant one. You have always favoured me with precepts upon connubial obedience, and you ought to be delighted that I now appreciate them."

"Am I not to do as I like with my own place?"

"Excuse me, mother, it is not your own place any longer. Harper's Cottage is now the property of my husband, Colonel Dalton, and it is in future to have a new name, and be henceforth called Harper's Castle."

"To cut this matter short, Felicia, unless I can make the great improvement in it which I desire, I shall leave it."

"As you please, mother, but you know my disposition towards you. As a guest you can remain beneath its roof as long as you like; but it is only as a *guest* you can be acknowledged when the wife of its owner is present."

Mrs. Somers was petrified.

"Unhappy girl! I am pained beyond all expression."

"What at, mother?"

"To see that you let your present prosperity so far puff you up with pride as to allow you to offer such arrogance to the author of your being."

"Are you angry, mother, that I desire to show I am about to become a dutiful wife?"

"No, Felicia, but I certainly wish you would take the same pains to prove yourself a dutiful daughter. At present you are far too young, even to detect that the place wants altering. You have yet to learn what a good wife should be."

"I trust I am initiated into that secret. A good wife should make the cares of the world sit easy on her husband's brow, and add a sweetness to his pleasures. A good wife is a husband's best companion, and his only friend in adversity."

"Proceed, proceed; I see you are well schooled."

"I can, *ad infinitum*, for I have studied the duties of a wife to her husband. She should be the most careful preserver of his health, and the kindest attendant on his sickness; a faithful adviser in distress; a comforter in affliction; and a discreet manager of his domestic affairs; therefore, I will not allow the apartments to be disturbed without his privity or consent."

Mrs. Somers could not account for the very apparent influence which her son-in-law had already obtained over her daughter.

She had always been so very good and kind to her daughter in early life, that everybody accused her of having spoiled that daughter in her after days.

It is certain that she was more hurt than ever Felicia could be when her father corrected her for any trivial or childish fault.

If there was any excuse for those faults, she was the first to find it, and if there was none she would find one nevertheless.

Sometimes she would reprove the child, but the voice of her anger was so soft that one would have mistaken it for that of love; and when a frown depressed her beautifully arched eyebrows, the eyes beneath still expressed so much tenderness that the pardon was confounded with the menace.

If such was her indulgence when Felicia failed in the execution of her duties, how great and apparent was her joy when she fulfilled them! Pleasure sparkled in her eyes, and if any one spoke to her of her health, and of that complexion which seemed to defy the attacks of time—

"My Felicia," she used to say, "has the gift of making me young again."

She was, in truth, an amiable creature.

Dark was the hour for her when Hugh Dalton assumed a sovereign and despotic sway at Harper's Cottage.

His tyranny brought about a sad change, as will be seen in the sequel.

CHAPTER XVIII.

MRS. SOMERS IS ALARMED BY AN EXTRAORDINARY VISITATION ONE NIGHT AT HARPER'S COTTAGE.

Come like shadows—so depart.—MACBETH.

THREE years rolled on.

During this period Mrs. Dalton brought her husband an equal number of children.

They were all girls.

The first was named after its mother—Felicia.

The second was christened Edith, a romantic cognomen selected by her grandmother.

The third was called Margaret, by desire of her father, and was the sweetest and best tempered girl of the three.

She is the heroine of our tale, and the only being destined to fathom the Ghost's Secret.

Colonel Dalton was not an indulgent father.

A cold and awful severity seemed to be the only remedy on his part for the mischief occasioned by their mother's excessive fondness.

He imposed on himself the painful task of making his children tremble before him.

Their smallest faults were reproved.

The more serious ones were punished.

All that was praiseworthy in them he merely considered as a debt of nature.

The three beautiful girls were persuaded that their father was strictly virtuous and just in all his dealings, but neither of them thought him affectionate or kind.

In her first and earliest years, Margaret's soul obeyed the impulse of two sentiments alone.

The fear of exciting her father's anger, and of affecting her mother's health.

Margaret was the especial pet of her grandmother.

Mrs. Somers would hide her faults, and throw around the infant a shield of protection whenever she was threatened with parental vengeance for youthful indiscretion.

This kindness was construed by the colonel into an improper interference on Mrs. Somers' part with the authority of a father over a disobedient daughter.

He would have overlooked this as a venial fault, but his mother-in-law, as years increased upon her, began to assume, in his opinion, a right to domineer in household matters, which did not belong to her.

The long-cherished idea of throwing the lower apartments of Harper's Cottage into one large room was revived with renewed energy on the part of Mrs. Somers, and she now declared her intention of seeing her wishes carried out.

She assigned this as a reason.

A party being given upon one of the children's birthday, she found that the assembled guests were greatly incommoded from the want of space.

She would now speak her mind—that she would.

Mrs. Somers was, therefore, continually at Colonel Dalton to sanction and approve the contemplated alterations.

He appealed to his wife.

She had given a previous opinion, and had not a word to say upon the subject.

Hugh was left to acquiesce or refuse, just as suited his pleasure or inclination.

He certainly gave the required permission ; but he determined in his own mind no longer to tolerate his mother-in-law's interference with the domestic arrangements of his household.

He would get rid of her at any sacrifice.

He did.

The mode and manner of the dismissal will be afterwards narrated.

All was bustle and confusion at the cottage.

Builders and skilful architects were summoned from London, and the business of renovation—often miscalled improvement—immediately commenced.

The colonel hoped that Mrs. Somers would get quit of the nuisance, as he called it, as soon as ever she could.

She promised.

To effect this, the workmen were compelled to labour day and night.

The superintendence of the repairs was confided to the tradesmanlike skill of Mr. Claridge, a well-known London builder.

He was accommodated with a bed in the cottage, in order to expedite the alterations, and he pledged his word to the colonel that neither himself nor any of his men would be at the house more than a fortnight.

Towards the dusk of evening, one day, when Mr. Claridge was alone, and working away in the process of gilding a ceiling, Mrs. Somers unexpectedly entered the room. She was pale, and very much agitated.

"You have been in this room two hours or more, Mr. Claridge ?" said she.

"I have, madam."

"By yourself ?"

"Yes, madam. I gave the men leave to take some necessary repose before recommencing work, which they are to do at five o'clock in the morning."

"You have been alone then ?"

"Yes, madam."

"Have you seen anybody ?"

"The colonel, madam, looked in, to see how we were progressing, before my people left."

"Anybody else ?"

"Not a soul, madam."

"Did you knock against the walls of the partition ?"

"Not that I am aware of, madam—if I did, it was accidentally."

"Three loud taps, at an interval of about five minutes each."

"I am certain I did not."

"It is as I thought."

"What, madam ?"

"Somebody is about to die."

"You are superstitious, madam."

"Oh ! I'm certain something terrible is about to happen, Mr. Claridge !"

The builder smiled, and went on with his work.

"I speak the painful truth. A spirit, or something of the kind, is wandering up and down this house to warn us of a dreadful, fearful, calamity."

Claridge was sceptical. He doubted the possibility of any such occurrence.

"My brain is fevered, and my mind is occasionally bewildered," said the alarmed lady, "but I am positive I heard it."

Calling her favourite grandchild into the room, she said, "Margaret, Margaret, my love, go to your mother, who is sleeping on the sofa in your father's library—awake her—bid her come to me. Something dreadful, I'm sure, will happen, either to the colonel or to your mother."

But Margaret had been too severely lectured by her father to dare to wake her mother from a nap, at the caprice of her grandmother.

Margaret excused herself, and ran away laughing.

It was not caprice on the part of the unfortunate speaker, for what she had seen was a vision of a most extraordinary kind.

Mr. Claridge was destined to see and hear it likewise.

"Here comes the lady," said Mrs. Somers to the builder, as a supernatural form glided into the apartment and stood between her and the person at work.

"Ask her, good Mr. Claridge, will you, what she means by saying that to-morrow will prove fatal to somebody in this house ?"

The figure she directed his attention to was that of a female dressed in the costume described in the second chapter of our work.

It was the identical spectre.

Claridge, taking the apparition which had entered the apartment so noiselessly to be one of the Colonel's visitors, made a respectful move and got down from the ladder on which he was perched, in order that he might more deferentially answer any question she might feel inclined to put to him.

"What may be your pleasure, my lady ?" said the builder.

The habiliments of the stranger induced a belief in his mind that she was a person of quality.

"I have already told this person that danger threatens either herself or some of her family," replied the form, taking her station between the affrighted two.

"How is she to know your meaning, lady? When is she to anticipate the evil?"

"While the moon, which you see gilding the high tops of yonder trees, shines brightly she is in no danger," said the spirit, solemnly, "but let them beware the morrow!"

Claridge felt rather uncomfortable. He had heard of supernatural appearances, but he had never seen one.

He turned to look at his companion.

Mrs. Somers was deadly pale and leaning for support against the ladder from which he had just descended.

Her eyes were wide open.

She was wildly staring at the intruder, and trembling violently.

Claridge summoned sufficient courage still further to interrogate the mysterious visitor.

"When, lady, are we to look for evil?"

"When that moon assumes a blood-red colour."

"It will be an ill omen?"

"The omen will prognosticate death."

"To whom?"

"That is not for *thee* to know. I have answered; now, go thy way!"

The shade pointed to the entrance.

"Stay, I would ask you one question," said Mr. Claridge, quite coolly and collectedly.

"You promise it shall be but one?"

"I do."

"Then turn thy face towards that moon, and when I have answered you depart from this house of evil, without venturing to look back upon me."

The builder did as he was desired to do, and having turned his back upon the supposed lady, asked:—

"Will you name upon whom this dreadful calamity is to fall?"

There was, however, no response to this question.

Mr. Claridge was about to turn round and catechise the visitor further, when Mrs. Somers, guessing his intention, and perceiving that the spectral intruder had vanished, clasped him by the arm and implored him not to mention what they had seen to anybody in the house.

"The colonel is so violent," said the poor lady, "that I should dread his ridicule. He would only laugh at us, without believing our story."

"And well he might, madam," observed Claridge, as lights were brought in to enable him to resume his work. "Well he might; for you may depend upon it that this is a London trick of one of your servants, and only done to alarm my workpeople."

Mrs. Somers hoped it might turn out so, but she feared the contrary.

She, however, extorted the promise she desired from Mr. Claridge as to silence on the matter, and left him to pursue his work.

It is worthy of remark, as a singular circumstance, that notwithstanding his stout protestations as to entire disbelief in the theory of ghosts, Mr. Claridge left his workpeople to finish the job he had undertaken at Harper's Cottage, feigning to be ill, or that he was summoned away to carry out an important contract connected with his business in the metropolis.

CHAPTER XIX.

FIRST STEP IN CRIME — A LORD MAYOR'S DAUGHTER FALLS—A SCENE IN THE KITCHEN.

Woman! the fountain of all frailty!
What mighty ills have not been done by woman?
OTWAY.

SOME months after Mr. Carmichael's union with Miss Andrews, two persons—a man and a woman—were sitting up for the return home of their master and mistress in the kitchen of a druggist's shop in Fleet-street.

The first was the druggist's assistant.

The second, a female, who came under that description of servant commonly called a maid-of-all-work; for though Mr. Carmichael had courted and fairly won the daughter of his former master, it was arranged that he was to receive no dowry on marrying her, but would have to wait till the death of Mr. Peter Andrews for whatever sum the thrifty alderman and ex-lord mayor might feel disposed to bestow upon his daughter Barbara.

The alderman had noticed certain extravagant inclinations on the part of Miss Andrews, which he knew would be but little abated after matrimony; and as he did not want exactly to see the cash which he had worked so hard and so long for flow in an improper direction, he wisely determined not to supply them with too much money all at once, lest any portion of it might be expended in the superfluities of their married life, such as routs, cards, and dress.

Andrews had declared in common council, had repeated his observations in the court of aldermen, and expressed it as his firm opinion from the civic chair when passing through his mayoralty, that notwithstanding the great outcry directed against the weight of taxes and the dearness of provisions, it was more to be suspected that the complaints of his fellow-citizens had their source in their then extravagant style of dress, and the various means of dissipation which pervaded the different ranks of society in the middle of the eighteenth century.

He well recollected, when he was a boy, such a thing as a tradesman taking a country-house before he finally quitted business was never heard of. But things were lamentably altered. Now, a merchant, or even a better sort of shopkeeper, has scarcely entered into trade but he must hire a villa and start a vehicle. Nay, to such a pitch of affectation was everything being carried, that the man of business was actually ashamed to eat his own dinner where he traded, and was found, as soon as Change hours were over, hurrying away to Peckham Rye or Camberwell Green, instead of sleeping as formerly in Cateaton-street or Honeylane Market.

He was determined to show the value of his precepts by his own example.

He stuck rigidly to business, he did, until driven out of it by the importunities of his daughter Barbara, who held it to be monstrously ridiculous that her "Pa," who was worth nearly a plum, should descend to wear an apron, and be seen handling a pestle and mortar in Fleet-street.

Such being the disposition of Miss Barbara, it will occasion no surprise that the solitary maid-servant which prudence only allowed, was elevated into the dignity of a lady's-maid, and in order that she might not soil her hands or incapacitate them for the duty of attending her mistress, when that lady was dressing, she was allowed the aid and co-operation of a char-woman for a couple of hours daily.

This decrepid and aged creature did the hard and dirty work of the house, whilst Penelope domineered over the assistant or talked scandal with her mistress.

It was while waiting up one night for Mr. and Mrs. Carmichael, who had gone to the play, that this conversation ensued between the assistant and Penelope,

"I think," said Ghrimes, "there is a quality in this ale which it should not have."

"I think you give yourself a great many airs which you should not have."

"It is bitter. I prefer mild ale, and my master said that was the only description of beverage he kept in his cellar."

"Things are come to a pretty pass when a doctor's assistant has the insolence to find fault with our brewer!

The ale is from the finest malt, and cost us twenty shillings a barrel."

"Cost *your lady* twenty shillings a barrel, you should say—not *us*, Penny."

"Well, you knows what I means. What's the use of *resulting* me by such *infections* ?"

"Curse the ale ! I'll drink no more of it. Mr. Carmichael might make his fortune if he would put this stuff in his shop. It would make a splendid emetic."

"You are always for *preciating* things, if they are ever so *masculate*. You ought to do as I'm compelled to do—put up with anything. Who'd ever think I should be so reduced so low as to condescend to be waiting woman to a doctor's trollope ? "

"A doctor's what ?"

"I knows what I means, and I means what I says." I have acted in a higher *spear* than this. Misfortune makes women, as well as men, acquainted with strange bedfellows."

"But you have no right to call your mistress by such an unwarrantable title. Do you know the meaning of ' trollope'?"

"Perhaps I do and perhaps I don't."

"You ought never to utter a word, however harmonious it may flow, till you have been made acquainted with its import and its meaning."

"You talk finely—just as if you could read the *hiregliffics* on master's bottles in the shop-window yourself."

"Well, we won't quarrel."

"I won't, if you won't," simpered Penelope, sheepishly.

"That wretched mixture of malt and hops has left a most unpleasant taste in my mouth. I prescribe a glass of hot gin-and-water for myself, and to be taken immediately, if you will be so good as to make it for me, my dear Perelope, and then give me your candid opinion of our mistress."

The liquor was set before him, and Penelope, being addressed by the assistant as "my dear," suddenly became exceedingly communicative.

"Why, as to missus, she is very *capericious*. I'm sure she'll never be happy with master—more's the pity. There's worse than him in the world."

"That's gospel—here's his own health in his own gin-and-water."

"Aye, a great deal worser. I've my reasons for saying so."

"He's pretty warm, isn't he ?"

"Yes, the business, they say, is worth a good five hundred a-year to him."

"Well, that will keep the pot boiling."

"Missus would get rid of ten times that amount if it was at her disposal."

"How ?"

"She games."

"What ?"

"Plays devilish deep."

"No !"

"And drinks, she does."

"You don't say so ?"

"Awful !"

"Really ?"

"Now, between you and I and the post, she has some very strange methods of paying what she calls her ' debts of honour.' "

"Why, you would not surely insinuate ——"

"I ain't agoing to *sinnivate* nothing. I agrees with the bird of Avon, Shakspeare, who says, somewhere in his beautiful book, that let you be pure as snow you can't escape *calomel*."

"Calomel ! what do you know about calomel ? It's calumny you mean, I suppose ?"

"Well, if you knows what I means, I say again, where's the use of *disposing* me ? I don't call speaking the truth *calomel*, not I."

"And pray, what is the truth ?"

"This. There's an intrigue going on in this house."

"The devil !"

"There certainly is, and I wonder missus has the *frontery* to let me see what I do see, and that every night of my life."

"Why, they have not been married six months—the honeymoon is scarcely over."

"I always discountenaces such goings on, I do."

"You have some buckram in you, I'll admit."

"Sir ?"

"I say you are tightlaced."

"I believe you have forgot to whom you are addressing yourself ?"

"To a lady's maid—a slave to the whims of a whimsical woman."

"Mrs. Carmichael considers me more in the light of a companion. She reposes all her secrets to my keeping, you low-bred fellow, you !"

"Therefore she is, indeed, a most whimsical woman. But I don't credit a word of what you're telling me."

"Don't you. Who took a rose-coloured note to the Captain ? I mean that Sadgrove, of the Kennington Volunteers ? Who did it on the sly, the evening of the day when missus had her first quarrel with master. Why, I, to be sure ?"

"They quarrel then ?"

"Like cat and dog."

"Alas ! how little can we judge of other's happiness; but they must submit very quietly to each other's temper and disposition, since I have never heard them row."

"The voice of discord ain't often heard below stairs ; it's when they are up-stairs that they goes it, and all about the *voluntary* Captain."

"Am I to infer that your lady is carrying on a clandestine correspondence with Mr. Sadgrove ? "

"Sure as my name's Penelope."

"Shameful !"

"I don't see it. The early blossoms of her love were rudely wrenched from her bosom by the iron hand of connubial tyranny."

"What do you mean?"

"Master's a great deal out, isn't he."

"Business calls him away."

"But business ought not to keep him away. His wife is often alone till two or three o'clock in the morning."

"That's as the case may be."

"She's got her feelings, hasn't she? When her lacerated heart finds itself alone and neglected, under such circumstances, it's natural like she should become callous to the will of her husband."

"Still, as his wife, it is her duty to obey him."

"She won't. Not she."

"He's kind to her, isn't he ?"

"Yes."

"What more can she expect ?"

"A great deal more. I overheard their conversation yesterday morning. I was stationed—"

"At the key-hole of the door eh ?" interrupted Ghrimes.

"No, sir, I was not stationed at the key-hole of the door; I was attending to my duties on the stairs, taking up the carpets, for the man coming to paint the banisters."

"Well."

"Missus asked if master was going to take a country house."

"Is he?"

" ' What,' said Mr. Carmichael, ' take a country house madam ? we have a comfortable house over our heads already. We have an excellent joint on table every day ; we have a superior bottle of wine on Sundays; we keep two servants, besides which, you will have a large fortune when your father dies, and come into all I may leave when it pleases Providence to take me; but, if you think I am to keep a country house and

THE SPECTRE IN THE SURGERY.

carriage out of my present earnings, you must be mad.'"

"I think Mr. Carmichael was right," drily observed his assistant; "doubtless she will conform to her husband's wishes."

"Don't be too sure of that. She will pay him off in his own coin."

By paying him off in his own coin, Penelope meant that Carmichael's home would soon be upset and himself disgraced, if not dishonoured.

Penelope greatly excited the curiosity of Ghrimes, who, knowing that if such a break-up really did happen he would have to look out for another situation, began a system of coaxing and wheedling to squeeze the necessary information out of the lady's maid.

He was politic, too.

He made another and stronger glass of hot gin-and-water.

He would insist upon her partaking of it with him.

She imbibed, and, oh!

It is beyond the power of language to describe the sensations of a heart like that of the sensitive Penelope as, with increasing assiduity, the son of Galen proffered her the crystal goblet; fragrant and foaming with its hot contents, and tendered by his own hand, it seemed of more than nectarian sweetness; whilst at each return of the replenished glass he begged and prayed of her to tell him whether she thought what she had hinted at would be brought home to her mistress.

To get at this Ghrimes flattered her.

Her romantic heart, for the first time, swallowed copious draughts of the pleasing poison.

Unbosoming herself to Ghrimes, she declared that if Mr. George Carmichael was not already a member of a certain club he speedily would be.

"What induces you to suppose so, my dear *Miss* Penelope?" said Ghrimes, endeavouring to impress upon the maid-of-all-work the notion that he had a respect for her and considered her superior to the situation she was then filling.

Penelope inelegantly placed her finger upon the side of her nose, and said :—

"Catch a weasel asleep. I've watched them."

Desirous of learning the most minute particulars of an amour, which was evidently carried on through the medium and with the assistance of Penelope, he plied his fair communicant with another glass of gin and water, and promised if she would tell him the full particulars, he would " hear all, see all, and say nothing."

But that gin-and-water defeated his wishes.

From the moment Penelope swallowed her share of the second glass all was illusion.

The blue plates and dishes on the dresser appeared to dance in duplicates around her.

Ghrimes and his glass assumed a topsy-turvy appearance.

Ghrimes was below—the glass was above.

The tea-kettle, which was kept on the hob with its water boiling, sent forth its orchestral harmony much after the fashion of modern steam-engines, and the whizzing sounds rushed on her ear in unintelligible chaos.

When she was summoned by a terrific rat-tat-tat to ascend the kitchen stairs to open the door for her master and mistress, her tottering knees refused their wonted office.

Supported on one side by the convenient rails of the kitchen stairs, and on the other by the busy, inquisitive gentleman to whom her new emotions owed their birth, she contrived to open the door, but gave a mortal offence to both her master and her mistress by an unmistakable hiccup that saluted them in their faces. Nor were matters mended when she caught hold of her mistress by her shawl as she was ascending the stairs and exclaimed,

"I say, marm, I've another love-letter for you from Captain Sadgrove !"

Oh, Geneva, such is thy work !

CHAPTER XX.

THE ELOPEMENT.—FLIGHT OF BARBARA.—THE MYSTERIOUS LETTER.—A HUSBAND IN A FIX.

By suffering well our fortune we subdue.
Fly when she frowns, and when she calls, pursue.
                                                    BARTLET.

POOR Carmichael !

He was destined to be hurled from the highest pinnacle of happiness to the lowest depths of misery.

A faithless wife and a perfidious friend not only covered him with wretchedness, but disgrace—not only blasted all the tranquillity of his future life, but drove him to become the tool and slave of an accomplished scoundrel.

He could not account for a coolness towards him which he had latterly detected on the part of his wife.

His only study had been to promote her pleasure: *her* only pleasure seemed to be the advancement of his misery.

They had just returned from a short economical trip, taken to celebrate their matrimonial felicity, when Algernon Sadgrove, a banker's clerk, was accidentally introduced to him.

He appeared so exceedingly desirous of cultivating an acquaintance with Carmichael, that, on understanding he was an especial favourite with his father-in-law the alderman, the latter unguardedly gave him an invitation to drop in at Fleet-street whenever he had a spare hour or two.

The invitation was accepted, and he became a frequent visitor.

Carmichael received him with all the frankness of cordial hospitality, little dreaming that he had been acquainted with his wife before her marriage, and that his desire to visit her under the roof of her husband was for a more sinister purpose—an opportunity of stabbing him to the heart.

On the very first day of visiting them, and when Carmichael imagined they saw each other for the first time in their lives, the husband perceived that the visitor stood uncommonly well in the opinion of his wife.

This did not disturb him much, for he attributed her partiality to a polite desire of giving a suitable welcome to the friend of her husband.

The passion of jealousy had not as yet entered his bosom ; on the contrary, had he even been capable of the dreadful suspicion, he would have remembered the preference which his Barbara had given to him over one or two suitors.

The morning after the fatal admission made by their drunken servant, and which divulged the fact that Mrs. Carmichael was carrying on a surreptitious correspondence with Sadgrove, they were sitting at breakfast with their backs to one another, and in the usual attitudes of married people after a conjugal tiff.

Carmichael was the first to break silence.

"Unless you promise me, Barbara," he said, "to break off all acquaintance with this man, I must take prompt measures to compel you."

"Well, sir, and what would you do ?"

"Acquaint your father, and be guided by his advice."

"Indeed ? Ha, ha, ha !"

"Barbara, this is no laughing matter. I do not think for one moment that there is anything criminal in your acquaintance as yet with this person; but what must the world think, if your servants report that letters have passed between him and you, unknown to your husband?"

"Pray, sir, do you never write or receive letters unknown to your wife ?"

"Never, upon my word !"

"Never ?"

"I should scorn the action."

"Recollect yourself."

"Absurd ! you have always been welcome to open any letters that may be brought into this house."

"Probably ; but have I the same privilege of inspecting those which may be sent out of it ?"

"Undoubtedly."

"You would not write a line to any person which you could wish should be kept from me ?"

"No."

"Then how comes it that you shut yourself up in the surgery almost every morning, and write with so much secrecy ?"

Carmichael slightly changed colour, and stammered out an excuse, saying that the contents of those letters merely related to an application for the repayment of some money which he owed to a friend.

"You know you are telling me a lie—a mean, despicable lie, Mr. Carmichael, and one that you ought to be ashamed of."

"Barbara, don't be jealous. I pledge my honour those letters were not to a woman."

"I did not say they were, sir."

"Well, then, take my word, and let us be friends again," said Carmichael, approaching Barbara and offering her his hand.

"Never, till I solve what I consider to be a dirty mystery; and as my name has been mentioned in the business, I will know all about it."

"Barbara, my dear !" continued Carmichael, the blood rushing up to his very temples whilst he spoke, "I regret I did not show you the contents of the last letter—the one I dare say you heard I sent off yesterday."

"Oh, but I have seen the contents of that letter, sir !"

Carmichael, in his own mind, was certain that she had not seen it, and went on confidently to say,

"That's impossible, for I sealed it before you came down to breakfast, and gave it to Penelope to post at once, that it might depart by the morning mail."

"Yes, but I was beforehand with you. I have been

determined to put a stop to this secret correspondence for a long time, and so desired my maid to watch to whom you might give the letter. Fortunately for me, you selected my confidential servant as your Mercury. The faithful creature brought it to me, and here it is."

So saying, Mrs. Carmichael took a crumpled letter from her pocket and began to read it aloud for the edification of her husband, and to refresh his memory. While she did so, Carmichael buried his head in his hands, sat down upon a chair near the table, and groaned heavily.

The letter was as follows :—

"Sir,—Nothing on earth would induce me to comply with your request, but a knowledge of what is between us, and the hope of your not cruelly divulging it to my wife. I have sent the parcel off. It will be left till called for, at the place you named in your last favour. Pray be merciful as heretofore, and be yourself very careful, or we may both get into a serious dilemma.

"Yours most gratefully,
"GEORGE CARMICHAEL."

Having read the inside, Mrs. Carmichael turned the epistle over, and repeated to her husband aloud the superscription.

It was this :
"To Colonel Dalton,
Harper's Cottage,
Llangollen,
North Wales."

"Now, will you condescend to confirm me, sir, who this Colonel Dalton is, and what transactions are between you, that I am not to know of, and why he must be so careful on his own account, lest he get into a dilemma ?"

Carmichael felt himself choking.

It was in vain he endeavoured to stammer out an an excuse.

He could not speak. After a pause.

"As you please, as you please, sir," said Mrs. Carmichael, picking up the fragments of the letter, which she had furiously torn to pieces, and, replacing them in her pocket, and looking daggers at her husband, angrily continued,—

"As you please, sir; but this goes to my dear father. He will interpret it for me, if you won't, monster !"

And so saying, the infuriated woman struck her husband a severe blow with her clenched fist on the head, as she made for the door of the apartment, which she opened quickly, going out and slamming the door violently after her.

When her unhappy husband came to reflect on what occurred, he deeply regretted that he had not disclosed the whole truth to his wife.

It was not too late to do so, and he at once determined to seek her and confess the whole.

He quitted the room to find her.

He was too late.

She had left the house.

She had darted down into the shop without cloak or bonnet, and there being a hackney stand directly opposite her own door, she was in a coach in a moment, and had driven off no one could tell whither.

With the laudable intention of giving his wife every explanation in connection with himself and the secret pertaining to his acquaintance with Colonel Dalton, he followed, as he thought, the steps of his wife to her father's.

She had not been there.

He detained the alderman nearly half the day in conversation, but Barbara came not.

He went round in despair to almost the whole of their acquaintance, but could gain no intelligence of her.

It was midnight before he gave up the fruitless search, and then it occurred to him that she might have regretted the hasty temper she had shown and had made the best of her way back to Fleet-street from very shame.

To his surprise, however, when he reached home he found that his house was in the greatest disorder, and both Ghrimes and Penelope in seeming distress.

Asking them the cause, he with much difficulty elicited from the former the fact that his wife had returned during the morning with Captain Sadgrove, who not only assisted her to carry off every article of value belonging to herself, but, as Mr. Ghrimes verily believed, bank-notes and money in gold and silver to a considerable amount.

Carmichael could not credit the information.

It appeared almost an utter impossibility either for Barbara to prove so wantonly perfidious, or for her paramour to sanction such a base act of injustice ; but the absence of both, the broken lock of his escritoire, and the damning contents of a reproachful letter which the misguided woman left behind her, too soon and too sensibly stung him into conviction.

What would he not have given for some thunderbolt to strike the guilty wretches that instant to the earth, even though he himself was engulfed at the same time !

He ran from room to room in a state of distraction, devoting the fell destroyer of his peace to far worse horrors than he was himself enduring ; uttering the most vehement and incoherent execrations, the agony of his soul became unendurable, he sank beneath the conflict, and lost himself in an unconscious flood of tears.

CHAPTER XXI.

THE OBDURATE ALDERMAN.—CARMICHAEL STANDS UPON THE BRINK OF RUIN.—IS ENGULFED.

Soft smiling Hope! thou anchor of the mind!
The only resting place the wretched find—SHAW.

ALTHOUGH Carmichael made diligent inquiry after the assassins of his peace, he was never able to obtain any tidings of them.

Some said the guilty pair had embarked for France.

Others, that they were living under assumed names in a distant part of England.

Carmichael wrote to Mr. Andrews about them, but the alderman did not take the slightest notice of him or his letter.

It was now apparent that his guilty wife had disgracefully eloped from him.

Kind friends came from all quarters, greedy to hear from his own lips the fullest particulars.

In anything but a pleasant position, the scourged and heart-broken man endeavoured to support his fate with every possible degree of fortitude.

He would, doubtless, in a short time have recovered some small share of composure, not to say of cheerfulness, but for the malignity of the world, which constantly turned his misfortunes into ridicule, and treated him with contempt instead of pity.

His wife's infidelity was everywhere mentioned with ludicrous and perverted comments on his person and conduct, and the merciless finger of scorn was pointed at him whenever he appeared in public, as if the husband was to blame because the wife had been fatally criminal.

In a word, where Carmichael ought to have found compassion he met with nothing but insult, and where he had a right to expect the soothing voice of consolation a cruel wrong was inflicted on his sensibility.

One attached friend urged him to prosecute the destroyer of his peace in a judicial way ; but what might he expect to recover from a mere banker's clerk, who had no private fortune, and but a scanty maintenance ?

Besides, had it been possible that he could have recovered the heaviest of damages, they would neither restore his repose nor render him less contemptible in the eyes of society.

Did he call the aggressor to a personal account, which was then the current mode of retaliation for injuries of the kind, he would only put it in his adversary's power to do him an additional injury. He decided to leave the unworthy man to the stings of his own conscience.

Many persons have talked in very excellent language of the perpetuity of friendship, and certainly some examples have been seen of men who have continued faithful to their earliest selection, and whose regard predominated over changes of fortune and contrariety of opinion.

Mr. Alderman Andrews was not one of them.

The ardour of his friendship for his son-in-law immediately abated when he discovered the distressing dilemma which his own daughter had brought about, and in which his son-in-law was placed by the indiscretion of the woman he had trusted.

In adding to Mr. Carmichael's misfortunes, by immediately turning his back upon him, the Alderman did it in a manner by which he escaped from any charge of criminal baseness or contemptible inconsistency.

Under pretence of keeping Carmichael to his good behaviour, as he called it, when he gave up business in his future son-in-law's favour he took a warrant of attorney from the latter as security for the goodwill and stock of the business, and bound him down to pay the full value of it within a certain number of months.

The time had expired.

Messrs. Sharp and Grably, the legal advisers of Mr. Alderman Andrews, wrote to Carmichael the day after the warrant of attorney became due, demanding instant payment of the money, and threatening to foreclose the mortgage which had been effected on his goods and chattels, if he neglected to attend to their application.

How sure is the old adage—Misfortunes never come singly!

It was impossible for Carmichael to comply with the alderman's request.

He could just as soon, and with equal ease, pay off the national debt.

All the ready money he was ever possessed of, and which he had at intervals put by from his business in order to meet this very engagement, had been purloined by his wife or her paramour on the night of her elopement.

He had even been compelled to part with, at considerably less than their real value, some original sketches done by his friend Mr. Hogarth, of Leicesterfields, and presented to him by that talented man, in return for certain sittings he had given him, when the artist elected to make him a model, in his eight famous pictures of the Idle and Industrious Apprentices.

Mr. Carmichael regretted to part with his almost priceless gems, but they went to pay the costs of his dearly-beloved mother's funeral, whose death occurred soon after his wife's flight.

In the anguish of his heart, he determined to take no notice of the lawyers' application, but to make a direct appeal to the alderman in person.

He could not but believe he would assist him, as he had never done anything himself to forfeit his good opinion.

He was confident the alderman had a good heart.

Alas! how soon does the memory of past actions fly from us, and of what little importance is the heart, where money is concerned !

Mr. Alderman Andrews thought—or he put forth his suppositions in the way of an excuse for refusing any accommodation to his son-in-law—that Mr. Carmichael had accelerated his own dishonour.

He was certain of it.

Mr. Carmichael ought to have discouraged the man's visits.

It was his duty to have kicked him out of doors at the first intimation of his libidinous intentions.

The alderman being thus prejudiced against him, Carmichael saw plainly that any endeavour to soften the asperity of his nature would be labour in vain.

Nevertheless his credit was at stake, and he would persevere.

But Alderman Andrews was obdurate.

He had no money to lend, not he.

Some men will take extraordinary pains to surmount pecuniary difficulties.

Carmichael was scarcely of their number.

"If you refuse me this request, sir, after my recent misfortune, you will appear in the eyes of the world—"

"I don't care for the world ; I despise the world. What has the world to do with me ?"

"The retention of its good opinion is surely worth a consideration."

"Pshaw ! Am I dependent upon it ?"

"You are not, sir."

"No; thank heaven, nor upon you either, Mr. Carmichael. If I was, I should be a miserable creature, indeed."

"Though I might regret the occasion of such dependency, I should rejoice in any opportunity of befriending you to the utmost of my power sir."

"Its all mighty fine to say so now, but I scarcely give you credit for your liberality."

"May I venture to hope that you will instruct your solicitors to wait a little longer for the debt, on account of which I have taken the liberty of calling upon you this morning."

"I must be guided by their advice in the matter."

"Which I know will be to enter up judgment and levy execution immediately."

"Well, it's not unlikely."

"Then I shall be a ruined man."

"You have brought it all upon yourself. I did not ask you to marry my daughter."

"I did not say you did."

"I wish to heaven you had never seen my poor Barbara."

Carmichael sighed deeply. He continued—

"I can but reiterate that wish from the bottom of my soul, sir."

"A girl so religiously brought up ! You must have sadly neglected her ! I am certain you must, or this misfortune would never have fallen upon you both."

"I was never absent from her apron strings. She cannot say that ever I neglected her."

"The world tells me that she was in part justified."

"How, sir ?" loudly exclaimed Carmichael. "Justified in what? In dishonouring her husband, and bringing her own father's grey hairs with sorrow to the grave."

"Mr. Carmichael, don't think that I mean to vindicate her conduct, or that my fondness as a father is to get the better of my principles. I know her errors; but will not, with you or your malicious friends, think that the fault she has committed is the only fault that a woman can never expiate. Let the cold, the selfish, and the worldly speak rigidly of her offences: as a father I can only feel for her distress."

"Is she in distress?" eagerly inquired poor George, with an extraordinary and accountable wish that he could instantly relieve her.

"The distress I allude to, sir, is of a mental description, not pecuniary. I trust the daughter and heiress of Alderman Andrews will never be left to want, however she may be neglected by her husband."

As he delivered these acrimonious words, Mr. Alderman Andrews drew himself up, and Carmichael, cut to the soul by this unjust assertion, resolved in his own mind to bring the interview to a speedy termination.

There is not on earth a spectacle of greater dignity than a brave man superior to his sufferings.

Carmichael was determined to endure his present

adversity, and to be proof against poverty, pain, or death itself.

He seized his hat.

"Then I am to conclude." said he, looking at the crown of his hat, "that I am to expect no mercy,"

"Well, I really cannot say what steps my lawyers will take; but I will give you a hint. You had better be prepared."

Carmichael departed.

The various ways in which misfortunes affect different minds are often so opposite, that in contemplating them we are lost in astonishment.

There are people who give way to excessive grief, and bring themselves almost to shadows through weeping.

Others are anxious to appear callous, and consign all connected with their troubles to the evil one.

Some seek to drown their cares in the glass, and make bad worse by losing their reason, in addition to their friends or property.

The sensible man adopts the most judicious way of encountering misfortunes of every kind.

He takes up a firm resolution never to shrink from them when they cannot be avoided, and endeavours, by a cheerful perseverance, to make the best of whatever may happen.

Carmichael belonged to the last class of unfortunates.

The moment he arrived in Fleet-street and got safely within his own shop, he called Ghrimes from behind the counter, and ordered him to put the shutters up instantly.

"It is not yet five o'clock, sir."

"Do as I bid you."

"You'll excuse me, sir, but Mrs. Parsons will be here at five."

"I cannot attend to Mrs. Parsons, or any other person."

"Well, sir, your permission granted, I'll endeavour to do my best with the prescription myself—it's plain sailing."

"No! I'll have no more medicine dispensed in this unlucky shop."

"Pardon me, sir, has anything happened to annoy you this morning?"

"Yes."

"What?"

"Something dreadful !"

"Indeed !"

"You won't believe me when I tell you."

"Sorry to hear you think so, sir ; but I hope it is not quite so bad after all."

"Alderman Andrews is a most unfeeling man."

"He bears a good character."

"Very ; but he's a hypocrite."

"I abhor hypocrisy."

"I never thought him so close before."

"He's fond of money, sir."

"You'll say so when you know all."

"Dear me, what has he done ?"

"I owe him a few pounds, Ghrimes."

"I am glad to hear it is but a few."

"You know how I am placed with him, Mr. Ghrimes ?"

"Not exactly, sir—but I have my suspicions.'

"Would you believe it possible, he has positively refused to lend me another shilling, although I almost went down upon my knees."

Ghrimes said he was extremely sorry to hear it, and in his heart he really was, for Ghrimes recollected that there would be half a year's salary falling due to him on the following Monday, and from present appearances he saw little prospect of obtaining it.

Notwithstanding the probability of his own loss, he commiserated with and endeavoured to console his broken-hearted employer.

"What course do you advise me to pursue in my present dilemma, Ghrimes ?"

"To pause ere you put the shutters up, sir."

"I have no strength or energy to contend against the sad difficulties which oppress me."

"A fig for them, sir ; disregard your present pecuniary troubles. When they come to the worst they must mend."

"What would you have me do ? I have no money, and am denied credit. Was ever man in such difficulties ?"

"Perseverance will sooner or later overcome all your difficulties ?"

"How do you advise ?"

"I do not recommend a stupid, insensible apathy to your distress, nor yet that listless and inactive resignation which might induce you to put your hand in your bosom, fetch a sigh, and say you bend to the will of Providence."

"What then."

"Why, look about you. Peep into your affairs rigidly. The stock of the premises must be worth something."

"Alas ! they are mortgaged."

"Well, the contents of the shop itself will fetch a good round sum."

Carmichael shook his head.

"I am certain it will. Genuine drugs bear a very high premium ever since the interdict issued from Apothecaries' Hall against the sale of adulterated ones."

Carmichael explained that the whole of his stock had been included in the security given by him to Alderman Andrews.

"Well, if it comes to the worst, a sale by auction of the furniture upstairs will enable you to meet the alderman's claim, and be independent of him and Messrs. Sharp and Grably into the bargain."

Carmichael, being determined to make a clean breast of it to his assistant, declared in confidence to him that all his furniture—nay, everything of which he was master in the world, had been assigned to his father-in-law many weeks previous to his marriage.

On hearing this latter declaration, Ghrimes shrugged up his shoulders, and observed—

"Well, then, we had better proceed to put the shutters up at once, for I now begin to see what some fellows wanted who have been in and out of the shop several times to-day asking for you, sir."

"What sort of persons ?"

"Men in top-boots—catchpole and bailiff-looking objects ; and, by Jove ! here they are again."

The words were hardly out of his mouth when an officer to the sheriffs of London and Middlesex entered, with the unpleasant though not unexpected intelligence that he was empowered to levy an execution upon the goods and chattels of George Carmichael for the sum of 300l. and upwards, at the suit of Peter Andrews.

CHAPTER. XXII.

THE MAN IN POSSESSION.—LEGAL EXTORTION.—THE APPROACH OF RUIN.

Here would we close the grief awakening tale,
And o'er the sequel cast a silken veil ;
But though our heart at every sentence bleed,
'Tis very indignation prompts us to proceed.
HARLOWE.

THE officer to the sheriffs of London and Middlesex acted at that period of our history as the generality of officers to the sheriffs of London and Middlesex do in the present day.

He had a very unpleasant duty to perform, but he would endeavour to discharge it in a manner which should put Mr. George Carmichael to as little inconvenience as possible.

Was the defendant in a position to discharge the claims of Mr. Andrews at once ?

The defendant was not.

Did the defendant think he should be able to do so on the morrow ?

The defendant declared his utter inability to do so either on the morrow or the day after.

The officer to the sheriffs of London and Middlesex declared that there was no need to make a return to the writ for at least a week, and therefore if it was any accommodation to the defendant he would leave a man for a short time in possession of the property he had seized in virtue of his warrant.

Carmichael gladly availed himself of what he designated a little breathing time, aad thanked the officer for his consideration.

"Of course," said the gentleman in question, "you will do what is usual in these matters."

"What may that be ?" asked Carmichael.

"Pay me my fee. I could commence taking an inventory directly, if I liked, and pull your place to pieces; but seeing you are a gentleman, I have no wish of the kind, and, above all, knowing that you are inclined to deal liberally with me."

"How much will satisfy you ?"

"I always prefer to leave the amount to the person I oblige."

"Well, but say what will satisfy you. What is usual ?"

"It will be a pity to destroy such a pretty shop. All those expensive fittings-up would have to come down at one fell swoop."

"Name the sum that will satisfy you for the accommodation."

"I usually have five pounds, but under the circumstances I am willing to take three."

Carmichael could not see what the precise circumstances were, but he said, "Ghrimes, what is there in the till ?"

The assistant opened the till, looked into it, shook his head, and replied,

"There's only a few shillings, sir."

"How many."

"Fifteen."

"Ghrimes, will you lend me forty-five shillings till the morning."

Whether Ghrimes wondered where the deuce the money was to come from in the morning, if his employer had it not in his power to repay him, or thought it would be a kind act upon his part not to make an addition to the number of his creditors, we cannot say, but he did not keep his master long in suspense.

"I've no money," he exclaimed, "for bailiffs—not one copper ! not the value of a hair on my head shall any bailiff get from me ! I hate bailiffs."

"Never mind your prejudices, my dear Ghrimes, but if you have the money, pray lend it to me."

"I have other uses for my money, and have worked too hard for it to throw it away upon such harpies."

The harpy looked daggers at the doctor's assistant, and his anger was doubly increased when he heard Ghrimes tell Mr. Carmichael that the demand was an imposition, and that the officer to the sheriffs of London and Middlesex could not legally enforce any demand of the kind.

That such was the case is apparent, in the simple fact that the man, finding he could not extort any more, consented to take the fifteen shillings, which were handed over to him from the till, but with great reluctance, by Ghrimes.

He did not quit the premises with a good grace.

He handed over his documents to a miserable half-clad and wretched looking individual, whom he called by the name of Jabbers.

"Now, Mr. Jabbers," said he, "you are responsible to the sheriffs of London and Middlesex for the safe custody of everything in this place. I leave you in full possession, and you must take care that nothing goes off the premises till you see me again."

"Where am I to stop, sir ?" asked Jabbers. "In the kitchen, in the shop, or in the drawing-room, please sir ?"

"Where you like, Jabbers. I shall rely on you. You have the entire range of the house."

"But, suppose they sends anything out of it by means of the private door. I can't be in two places at once, sir."

"Good, Jabbers, good ! You are no fool. Mr. Carmichael will, perhaps, lock that particular door and favour me with the key. Safe bind, safe find, that's my motto."

Carmichael did as he was asked.

Having handed the key of the private door to the officer, he sat down by the side of his counter and buried his face in his hands.

The officer to the sheriffs of London and Middlesex, seeing him so dejected, gave him a slap with his hand on the shoulder, and said—

"Come, don't be downhearted, Mr. Carmichael, these things happen every hour. You are not the first man into whose house I have been to-day; but the defendant, in the last case, paid me a fee without repining, and actually dressed up the man I left behind me in a splendid suit of livery, so that he will pass for one of his own footmen."

"That 'ere Snodgrass is in luck," said Jabber. "I wish to goodness it had a been me. Why he'll have the fat of the land whilst he's in the house, a feather-bed to sleep on, and a matter of a crown a day, possession money."

The shutters were put up now in reality, and Jabbers, in pursuance of instructions given to him, commenced the moment the bailiff's back was turned to note down with a pencil the things which appeared to be of most value in the shop.

He then proceeded to do the same in the kitchen and the upper apartments of the house, and when he had finished a task which took him upwards of four or five hours to complete, he entered the kitchen very respectfully, and inquired of Ghrimes and Penelope, "if so be the lady and gentleman would tell him where he was to sleep that night."

"Where best you can," said Penelope. "I won't have any of master's beds occupied by a bailiff's follower."

"As you please lady, I have no wish to intrude. I can sleep very well in an arm-chair here, by the fireside."

"You sleep in no arm-chair by the fireside in any kitchen of mine, man," said the inexorable Penelope.

"Well, only lend me a blanket, marm, and I'll tuck myself up under the counter—anything for a quiet life," said the meekly spoken and melancholy Jabbers.

Ghrimes felt for the man.

He had more real feeling in his composition than Penelope, and moreover he longed for the opportunity, which he now embraced, of showing her that he had more power in the house than a maid of allwork.

"My good man," said Ghrimes, "you can light yourself a fire in the surgery which adjoins the shop. There is a horsehair sofa in it, and you can sleep upon it. I'll bring you a blanket or two from off my own bed, and I dare say you'll be pretty comfortable. You don't remember me, but I knew you when you were in a respectable way of business."

"God bless you, sir," returned the grateful Jabbers, "I thank you ; people who follow my calling meet with more kicks than half-pence, I can assure you."

"I'm sorry to see you here, for two reasons; first, because its degrading to yourself, and secondly, it's a bitter pill for my employer."

"Aye, sir, I never thought the young gentleman would come to this—but let us hope that Mr. Alderman Andrews, who was his benefactor once, will advance the money for him yet."

"If the money," returned Ghrimes, "is not paid till

he advances it, the execution will never be paid out on this side of time. You might as well try to extract money from a pair of my left-off boots."

It turned out precisely as Ghrimes predicted.

The alderman left everything to Messrs. Sharp and Grably, and that highly respectable firm, having no feelings in the matter but to discharge their duty to their clients, at once entered up the judgment which Carmichael had given to the alderman, and seized upon his effects in due course of law.

CHAPTER XXIII.

THE SECRET DRAWER.—THE SKELETON HAND.—MID-NIGHT APPEARANCE OF THE GHOST.

Who can all sense of other's ills escape,
Is but a brute at best in human shape.—DRYDEN.

ON the evening of the fourth day after he had been in possession, Jabbers was ordered to prepare a minute catalogue for the auctioneer's use, employed to sell certain effects, lately the property of Mr. George Carmichael, and now to be submitted to public competition "by order of the sheriffs of London and Middlesex, under a bill of sale," &c. &c.

The work of demolition had been progressing about eight hours, and it was getting quite dark when Jabbers begged a candle to enable him proceed in the task upon which he was engaged.

Jabbers was pulling out this drawer and ransacking the other, when he heard three slight taps on the outside of the shutters.

Jabbers at first took no notice of them, thinking it might be the patrol or night watchman going their rounds, and sounding the shutters to see that they had been properly and securely fastened.

The three knocks were repeated, and the second time louder than the first.

"Oh!" exclaimed Jabbers, to himself, "I dare say it is my girl with a change of linen, but she might as well have brought it earlier ; it must be ten o'clock."

This said he approached the shop door, but before he could reach it the figure of a woman actually glided through the panels.

Jabbers trembled, his courage forsook him, and he watched his opportunity to run and call Ghrimes to his assistance.

The latter, not aware of the extraordinary visitor in the shop, entered apologising to the old man for having almost forgotten him ; but remarking blandly, "Better late than never, Mr. Jabbers ; here's your pipe and the ale. Come into the surgery, and I'll blow a cloud with you."

Jabbers was but too glad to obey Ghrimes. A companion was in reality what he most wanted.

He moved to follow him into the snuggery, when the figure which had entered the shop so abruptly, strided across the floor of it and reached the little apartment before him.

The woman took Jabbers's place on the sofa and sat beside Ghrimes.

The assistant instantly saw her ; he was dumbfounded, and far from being pleased by the close approximation of his shadowy companion.

At first he deemed it a trick or device on the part of the jocular old man in possession, and in spite of his faith in the theology of apparitions, he endeavoured to rally.

"I see—this is a trick of yours. You are his daughter, and you come to frighten us."

A dead silence ensued.

Not receiving any answer, Ghrimes was bewildered.

He called to Jabbers, but the old man could not or was afraid to leave the shop.

Ghrimes stared at the shadow, which seemed to stare at him again.

Apprehension began to deprive him of his senses, and he rose from his seat with considerable alarm.

He would have called aloud for Carmichael, but his employer was at a private lodging in the neighbourhood : he could not persuade himself to stop within that house whilst the bailiffs were in it.

By a vigorous effort Ghrimes made for a side door leading to the staircase.

The figure also rose and stood before him on the first step of the stairs.

"Who are you, woman ? and what do you want in this house ?" Ghrimes exclaimed, feeling uncommonly uncomfortable, and enduring a sensation as if all his hairs were sticking bolt upright on his head.

The shadow came nearer to him.

He rushed frantically up the entire flight of stairs.

It was still at his heels, and stood at the door of his bedroom, even before he reached it himself.

Penelope, hearing some one cry out, as she thought, seized a weapon of defence with great womanly spirit and rushed up stairs to his assistance.

She found Ghrimes groaning heavily and stretched at full length on the landing-place.

When the distracted man sufficiently recovered his senses to explain himself, he declared to Penelope that he had been followed by an unearthly being, who, at her approach, immediately stalked off and glided through the wainscot.

Penelope, although little better than a mere maid-of-all-work, was a strong-minded woman.

She ridiculed and laughed outright at her companion Ghrimes, and told him that he had been dreaming.

She was certain the broiled pork chop eaten for his supper had disagreed with him, and that he was then under the influence of what is called the nightmare.

In vain she rallied him.

He had seen an augury of something wrong.

He would go down stairs with her into the shop, and he was certain that Jabbers, who had seen the same thing, would corroborate him. The unfortunate old man, who had fallen senseless on the floor when Ghrimes and the apparition left the surgery, remained in that state till Penelope entered with a light, accompanied by Ghrimes.

The pair were partially shamed into courage by the indomitable spirit of one usually denominated the weaker sex.

Her first care was the recovery of Jabbers from that insensibility into which his fright had thrown him.

As soon as he opened his eyes, and found utterance, he looked wildly about and exclaimed, "Where is she ! Where is she ! Oh, I remember ; she flew up stairs after you, master, didn't she, sir ?"

"Something very like it," said Ghrimes.

"Now, do you think it could be a trick of my girls ?"

"I do not."

"Ah, sir! I have often laughed at the idea of ghosts, but I'm more than convinced now."

"I thank heaven that I did not see it," said Penelope.

"I dare say you do, marm, and perhaps you'll say what you think it forbodes."

"How can I say what it forbodes ? I know what it proves ?"

"What ?"

"That you are both a couple of drunken fools."

"No, no, Penelope, I am as sober as a judge," said Ghrimes, angrily.

"And as for me, marm," chimed in Jabbers, "the pot of ale which master was kind enough to bring into the surgery is still on the table untouched. Ain't it, master ?"

"It is Jabbers, and the whole affair is unaccountably mysterious."

"Can you tell me what she's like," asked Penelope.

"She was like a beautiful creature, and she was dressed magnificently, all in white satin," said Jabbers.

"What do you say, Ghrimes ?" repeated Penelope.

"She had a face like an angel," said he.

"Pshaw !"

" Don't *pshaw*, Penelope. If ever a ghost was seen on earth, we have seen one to-night !"

"I protest," said Penelope, whose patience was getting quite exhausted and her temper ruffled, " you will be as great a slave to superstition as this old idiot is. Fie, Mr. Ghrimes ! you are old enough to know better. What you have seen is the force of imagination, a kimera or something of that sort, or the effects of very strong gin-and-water indeed. I'll appeal to the bailiffs themselves, for here they come."

At this instant a knock at the door announced the arrival of the auctioneer's clerk, who called to fetch away such portion of the catalogue as Mr. Jabbers had completed.

Penelope opened the door to let him in and instantly asked, " do you think, Mr. Kettlewell, that any person could get into this shop through the shutters ?"

" No ma'am—not since Doctor Carmichael ordered them to be put up and strongly barred."

" Could any neighbour or stranger get into the shop without our knowledge ? "

" Oh, if any one were wrongfully inclined, I make no doubt with the aid of crowbars and jemmies, he could force his way in."

" That would cause a noise, and shadows don't enter places with a flourish of trumpets," said Ghrimes.

" I wish I had been in the shop at the time," said the all-important Mr. Kettlewell, " I would have proved the shadow a substance, I warrant. But come, we have no time to lose, the catalogue must be printed the first thing in the morning, and I have come to help you to make out the items."

Mr. Kettlewell soothed Jabbers and quieted his fears, by assuring him that he would pass the night in the shop with him to prevent any more of such nonsensical and unbusiness-like interruptions.

The two began to parcel out various articles into different lots, and to number them for the forthcoming catalogue.

It was far advanced into the middle of the night, and Penelope and Ghrimes were fast asleep in their beds, when Kettlewell and Jabbers were hard at their work, the former humming a tune all the while, and the other still thinking of the horrible shadow he had seen enter the shop in the earlier part of the evening.

Presently Kettlewell stopped short and asked Jabbers what sort of a person the female appeared to be who had disturbed him at his work so mysteriously.

" Awful," said Jabber, " she was just like a marble statty."

" How, like a statue ?"

" She had no appearance of breath."

" No ? "

" Not the least sign of animation."

" Quite a silent woman, then. Why, Jabbers, you would have given the world for such a wife, in your time."

" Don't talk so, for goodness sake, don't. The figger would have frightened you. I seed it but a moment— a deadly image of some person recently defunct."

" Curse this lock, how it sticks," carelessly cried Kettlewell, who had been trying to unlock, and was tugging away at a refractory draw which positively refused to leave its abiding place. " Give us a hand, will you, Jabbers?"

The man in possession tried, but he was equally unsuccessful; for after peeping twenty times into the keyhole, and blowing fifty times into the key, and thrusting it into the lock, and twisting it first one way and then another, even he failed to open it.

" It's deucedly warped," said Kettlewell.

" I'll fetch a hammer."

" Do, for we must not omit anything from the catalogue, however small the value."

Whilst Jabbers was in the surgery seeking for some instrument with which to break open the drawer,

Kettlewell determined to have another vigorous pull at it.

He held up the light to inspect it closely.

It was more like a huge chest than a drawer, and was marked on the outside " POISON " in large gilded letters, so that no mistake or calamity might ensue from the incautious use of the contents.

Whilst gazing upon the knob of the drawer, he beheld it suddenly seized by a skeleton hand, and looking up, very much alarmed, he saw the drawer itself gliding easily from its enclosure, as if pulled by magic.

" Good heavens!" he exclaimed, " what can be the meaning of all this."

He rose with a stout determination to investigate the the matter.

Kettlewell thought at the moment that somebody had intended a joke upon him, by fetching the small bones of a hand from the skeleton which stood in the surgery in a glass case. He could not but think it had been purposely placed on the knob of the drawer to intimidate him, knowing him to be rather an unbeliever on the subject of spiritual visitations.

But when he looked up again the full-grown body of a female was at the drawer, and seemingly helping herself to its contents.

She appeared to be placing handful after handful in the side pocket of her silken dress.

The time occupied in doing this afforded Kettlewell ample opportunities of looking at her ; and with a determination to stop what he could but consider an attempt on the part of somebody to take that which did not belong to them, he courageously seized hold of the arm of the intruder.

It turned round, and faced him, and smiled upon him.

" See, here—it was this," said the figure, whose peculation he thought he had arrested.

" It was what ?" bravely demanded Kettlewell, as he clutched the arm of the supposed intruder, to stop further robbery.

No response was given to his interrogatory.

A cold and chilling shudder ran through his whole frame as he beheld the arm he was holding shrink from his grasp, and witnessed the figure itself which had so mysteriously arrested his attention, gliding towards the other end of the shop.

As it retreated, he pursued it quite out of the shop into the street.

The glimmering light of the moon, which was occasionally covered with elongated black clouds, afforded him but a feeble light.

The deserted state of Fleet-street at that hour of the morning, and the exhausted oil-wicks flickering in decayed and old-fashioned iron lamps, tended rather to increase than to allay his alarm.

The mysterious being, still keeping her skeleton hand upon the pockets which contained the purloined poison, appeared to be coolly walking slowly before him.

He endeavoured to overtake it.

He did not succeed.

He lost sight of it somewhere in the Strand.

It must have descended through the iron gratings of a cellar, for a supernatural light seemed to ascend from one a short distance from him.

He did not attempt to disturb the people of the house into whose area the spectre must have vanished, but retraced his steps back again as fast as he could.

The morning was a bitter one.

Having run out without his hat he tied his pocket-handkerchief over his head to prevent catching cold, and thus whimsically attired met the gaze of Jabbers who was waiting anxiously for him at the door.

" Dear me," said Kettlewell, " what is the matter with you, Jabbers ? haven't you found the hammer yet ?"

" Yes, Mr. Kettlewell. Here it is."

THE COLONEL'S ATTACK ON MRS. SOMERS.

"Then what are you staring at so wildly? What do you see?"

"A handkerchief over your head instead of a hat, sir. Has the wind blown yours away?"

Kettlewell did not reply, but re-entered the shop, where, to his astonishment, he saw scattered about the floor the entire contents of the drawer.

Every particle of the poison was lying upon the ground, as if a handmaiden had newly strewn the floor with pounded chalk or white sand.

Whilst Kettlewell had gone on his fruitless errand to overtake the supposed lady, Jabbers found the implement he wanted, and was proceeding, on his own account, to break the drawer open.

To his surprise, he found that somebody had done it before him.

Left alone in that gloomy shop, he soon guessed that the mysterious visitor had made her re-appearance.

He looked fearfully about, but seeing nothing more to alarm him, he opened the street-door, leaned against a pillar, and waited the return of Kettlewell.

When Jabbers had sufficiently recovered from his surprise at the occurrences of the night, he said to Kettlewell—

"Now, my opinion is fully confirmed. You saw it. We cannot call it a fallacy or a deception, and therefore I'm certain——"

"What?"

"The house is haunted!"

Mr. Kettlewell—at first so incredulous that he resisted the opinion of wiser heads than his own on the subject—acknowledged himself exceedingly perplexed.

He had never in his life indulged serious contemplations of the subject, but he now took a retrospect of the previous two hours of his life.

He recollected that his approach to the shop had been announced by three mysterious knocks against the shutters.

He had a distinct remembrance of seeing some skeleton fingers upon the handle of the drawer when he was about to open it himself.

No. 6.

He had seen the hands of a woman helping herself to the poison contained within the drawer.

He had disturbed the spectral visitor, and following her into the street, had witnessed her vanish from his sight in a manner utterly impossible to one of mortal build.

As he really had seen what he imagined could never be seen, his belief, which before had wavered, was now settled and fixed.

For the rest of his natural life Mr. Kettlewell no longer doubted the existence of ghosts.

CHAPTER XXIV.

FATAL CURIOSITY—BREACH OF CONFIDENCE—MRS. SOMERS DISAPPOINTED.

How void of reason are our hopes and fears!
What in the conduct of our life appears
So well design'd, so luckily begun,
But when we have our wish, we wish undone.
DRYDEN,

How truly it is remarked that a man cannot be really happy here without a well-grounded hope of being happy hereafter.

The life of Colonel Hugh Dalton became irksome to him through the inquisitive propensities and meddling interference of Mrs. Somers.

For several consecutive days after the events narrated in the eighteenth chapter, the colonel regularly despatched a letter to London; but, with a determination to avoid the chance of the address which was written upon it being seen by the lady whose interests were deeply compromised by its contents, he never trusted it to his servants, in case they should read the superscription, but walked from Harper's Cottage to the post-office, and dropped it into the box himself.

But all his vigilance was defeated by Mrs. Somers, who, entering his study rather unexpectedly one evening, saw him busily engaged sealing one which he had just then finished.

Her sudden entrance caused him to drop the letter upon the carpet.

His mother-in-law stooped to pick it up.

Whilst handing the epistle to the colonel, she read the direction.

It was as follows :—

"Mr. George Carmichael,
Chemist and Druggist,
Fleet Street,
London."

"Dear me," said the inquisitive lady, "what on earth can you want from a chemist and druggist in London? We are very well served by Mr. Lloyd, of Beaumaris; the children are carefully attended to by him, and thrive under his clever medical treatment."

"My letter relates to money matters, madam, and therefore I beg——"

"Well, well, don't get into any of your tantrums—I don't want to know your business, or to read your letters, either."

"But I assure you, madam, there is nothing in them, even if you did."

"If there was more than you would like to divulge it would make no difference to me, sir; I only say that they ought to be shown to your wife as a mere matter of course. Mr. Somers never did such a thing in his life as to send off a letter without telling or showing me the contents."

"This will never do," said the colonel, rising from his chair with offended dignity; "I must put an end to those impertinences for the future."

The colonel left the room in anger.

During the tedious hours that too often intervene in the domestic seclusion of country life, a relief from its monotony is not unfrequently sought by those upon whom it is inflicted, by seeking out and fixing an imaginary importance upon the most commonplace things.

Mrs. Somers was exactly in this position. She felt certain that there was more than met the eye in the colonel's conduct.

Her favourite occupation, during the temporary illness of her daughter, was to sit up with her in her bedroom, reclining on a settee placed near one of the windows of the apartment and shaded by curtains and blinds, in which position she could command a prospect, without being herself observed, of the ingress and egress of all who approached or left the cottage.

Whilst Mrs. Somers was one morning opening her inquisitive eyes, in the hope of discovering some object to arouse her vacant mind, the postman crossing the road, and entering the garden before the cottage, excited her curiosity.

He was bringing, as he usually did, three times a week, the colonel's packet of letters.

This time, however, he had rather more than the regular quantity, and one amongst the number was unusually weighty and bulky.

Mrs. Somers could not resist the impulse of an intense if not laudable curiosity, to see who in the neighbourhood was going to be honoured by a letter that morning.

Colonel Dalton too was called to the residence of his friend the Rev. Mackenzie Blair, on county business, and he was likely to be detained some time by the reverend gentleman.

Mr. Blair was vicar of St. Jude's, Kent; rector of St. Bridget, Cheshire; and vicar of Little Templington, Berkshire; chaplain to Sir Morgan-ap-Shenkin-ap-Leek-ap-Buzzard, of Buzzard Hall, Carnarvonshire; librarian to the Bishop of Bothersole, at Bothersole Palace, Denbighshire; morning lecturer at St. Cosey's, Sussex; and evening lecturer at St. Grabs, near Ilchester, Somerset. So for the convenience of performing these various duties simultaneously, he purchased the house in which he permanently resided at Llanberis, and to which the Colonel that morning repaired.

There being no probability of his immediate return, his mother-in-law seized the golden opportunity, darted down the stairs and received from the hands of the village postman all the letters which were directed to the colonel.

She placed the majority of them upon his table in the library, but observing one considerably larger than the others she had an unaccountable desire to learn its contents.

It might contain bank notes.

What of that; her object was not to steal them. She would easily replace them in the letter, reseal it, and again commit the letter itself to the safe custody of the huge envelope.

Perhaps it might be a pattern of silk from a London draper, with which he meant to surprise Felicia, as the anniversary of their wedding day was fast approaching, and he usually made his wife a very elegant present on such occasions.

It might be some legal document which his lawyers had merely transmitted in order to obtain his signature, or, and this appeared to her to be the most likely conjecture of them all, was an application from some London minx—some old flame of the colonel's—importuning him for money, and detailing a long account of pecuniary difficulties.

It will not be wondered at, that with some slight feelings of indignation on her daughter's account, Mrs. Somers determined to read this epistle at her leisure, and for that purpose she secreted it in her pocket, but whilst in the act of doing so, mentally asked herself this question : "Am I doing right?"

Having asked the perplexing question, she stood motionless for some time, like Brutus, and "paused for a reply;" but as all mental questions are never known to be audibly answered, at least to mortal ear, she replied for herself, and satisfied her own conscience by exclaiming :—

"It's perfectly monstrous that the man should so perfidiously treat my beloved Felicia."

If we cannot applaud Mrs. Somers for acting on this occasion, with either delicacy or justice, we must at least admit that she displayed no inconsiderable degree of courage under the circumstances.

Had Hugh Dalton suddenly returned and caught her in the act of abstracting that identical letter, or any other one from the heap directed to him, he would have killed her on the spot. She was sure of that.

But he was far away, and Mrs. Somers was enabled to carry the packet safely up-stairs, and thence into her own room, there to read it when all was quiet and secure.

Being subject to colic and spasms, she informed the servants that she had been suddenly seized by an attack of the latter, and was compelled to lie down upon her bed for a short time, in order to recover herself.

The intelligence of her mother's indisposition was speedily conveyed to Mrs. Dalton, but as that lady's affection for her parent was rather superficial, her love only manifested itself in the slight and delicate instruction given to a servant, "to keep the poor old lady quiet, and if she got worse, to send for a doctor by all means."

But the only spasm with which Mrs. Somers was effected, was a spasmodic desire to open the letter she had in her pocket, and this she proceeded to do the moment she was left entirely to herself.

That she had some little repugnance to the mean action she was about is true, and she endeavoured to console herself by reflecting that the colonel had never been a suitable match for her daughter, that he was, in fact, in her opinion, without elegance of mien, beauty of person, or force of understanding ; who, while he courted her Felicia, would make allusions to her mother's origin, and hint that her uncle the major must have been fully aware of it, or he would never have tied up his bequest in the manner he done. His conduct, too, from the hour of his marriage, and, particularly in the matter of the alteration in the apartments underneath her, had been insufferably tyrannical ; and, therefore, she could do but little harm to such a man by taking a sly peep into one of his everyday letters.

Having thus settled the matter with her conscience, she broke the seal.

Holding the letter itself near to the window so as to obtain a better light, and in order not to lose a word of it, she read as follows :—

Fleet Street, May 13.

Dear Sir,—I am a lost and ruined man ! My father-in-law, Mr. Alderman Andrews, has seized and threatens to sell off everything I have in the world, and which, at one time, I thought was a gift or marriage portion. Not only does he refuse me assistance under my present difficulties, but he declares that the infamous elopement of his child has been accelerated by my personal neglect. You know the contrary. At this present time of writing bailiffs are in the house, and every thing is to be sold off in a day or two. What I am to do in the future, heaven only knows. I send you a larger packet of what you require than usual, because I fear it may prove the last time I may have it in my power to send you any at all. Pray be careful, for one grain administered incautiously may cause instant death.

I am, dear sir, yours, in affliction,
GEORGE CARMICHAEL,

N.B.—If you should know a druggist or apothecary requiring an assistant, perhaps you will be good enough to recommend me, as in my present wretched state of mind it will be a blessing to get out of London. G. C.

A small parcel, resembling a packet of powders, dropped from the inside of the letter, which Mrs. Somers picked up from off the floor, and carefully placed in one of the drawers belonging to her oscritoir.

There was little to astonish her in the letter itself, and having satiated her curiosity she rather regretted her imprudence than otherwise.

She inferred from the contents that the colonel had sent for some powerful medicine to administer to one of his favourite greyhounds, which had been ailing to her knowledge some time; and in her heart she commended the writer for the judicious advice he gave her son-in-law lest he might accidentally be led to use it without due caution.

The difficulty with the lady was what she should do with the correspondence itself now that she had read it.

It was impossible for her to reseal the letter, for it was impressed with Carmichael's crest and initials in wax by one of those very old-fashioned signets which were used in those days.

Any attempt to reseal it would have insured instant detection.

If she handed it and the enclosure to the colonel, with an apology that she had accidentally opened it, he was not the man to believe her, and she dreaded his anger and revenge too much to court either.

What was to be done ?

Mrs. Somers resolved to destroy it at once.

For this purpose she took a small tinder-box from a cupboard in the corner of the room, struck a light with the only means then in vogue—a flint and steel, lit a wax taper by the aid of a brimstone match, and held the troublesome letter over its flame till it was reduced to ashes.

She afterwards scattered these to the winds, and there was an end of Mr. Carmichael's communication.

CHAPTER XXV.

A PROPHETIC VISITATION OF THE GHOST FULFILLED. —MRS. DALTON DIES—APATHY OF THE COLONEL.

Fortitude and religion enable the good to support great and severe trials ; the bad, by frivolity and obtuseness, endeavour to disregard them.—YOUNG.

THE story of the spectral visitation which had been seen at Harper's Cottage during the alterations in the lower rooms, having been carried to Mrs. Dalton in an unguarded manner by a careless domestic ; that lady was most seriously alarmed, and ultimately thrown on a bed of sickness, which caused much grief to her children and her friends.

We say children and friends, because Colonel Dalton was of that apathetic constitution that no event could seriously alarm him.

During her illness he would drop into the sick-bed chamber once a day and inquire whether it was likely its inmate would get better.

In his own mind the wonder was that she had lived so long.

How came this about ? They had never openly quarrelled, and he denied her few indulgences.

In the opinion of the few who visited them, they lived happily together.

Ah ! how little can we judge of the happiness of others !

They passed their days, indeed, in ease and comfort and monotonous content, and such pleasures and amusements as the education of their three girls afforded. It must be acknowledged, too, that Colonel and Mrs. Dalton submitted to each other's wishes and desires with tame acquiescence, so that domestic jars never interrupted their domestic serenity.

It was in this dark region of commonplace serenity that Hugh Dalton first nursed his ambitious thoughts of future aggrandisement.

As ambition presided at his birth, so did it accompany his after years.

His youngest daughter, Margaret, was the adored of her father.

He determined to make her rich, and far beyond her elder sisters—Felicia and Edith ; and, come what might, they were, in the event of his demise, to be wholly dependent upon her.

On Margaret, his tenderness, like a gentle river, flowed in one soft, one uninterrupted course.

She was the sole object of his care.

In her was centred his every present joy, his one future hope.

Alas! how early was Margaret initiated into grief, and gave those manifestations of that noble spirit which never, under any circumstances, deserted her.

A spirit which alone enabled her to endure the bitter sorrow of the many trying hours she was destined to know in her maturer years.

It would really appear that all of the weaker and fairer sex, entitled by marriage to bear the name of Dalton, were destined to take up their abode in "the house appointed for all living," whilst yet the face of nature wore its loveliest smiles.

On a sunny day in bright July, the windows of a pretty chamber in Colonel Hugh Dalton's cottage at Llangollen were open, yet the rays of the god of day were carefully excluded by closely-drawn blinds. Mrs. Dalton was propped up by pillows in her bed, and Margaret, her daughter, seated by her side, was reading to her from an open volume that rested on her knees.

The mother was pale and languid, yet attentively listening to what her daughter was reading.

Suddenly, she stopped the reader and exclaimed,—

"Margaret! I am tired of that dull book; do go down into the library and bring up another."

"Have you a choice, mother dear?"

"Yes; bring up the small volume, bound in red morocco, and lettered at the back, *Secrets of the other World*, which you will find on one of the lower shelves in the centre book-case."

When Margaret returned with the volume she found her mother deadly pale, and with the tresses of her silken hair clinging to her bosom and soaked in tears.

Margaret flung herself on her knees by her mother's side, and pressing her weak and fading form to her bosom, said, "This is not a proper book for you to listen to in your present state of health, dear mother; it is all about spirits and apparitions."

Mrs Dalton took the book from the hands of her daughter and said,—

"I have seen her—I have seen her!"

"My dearest mother, you know not what you are saying; nobody has been in this room since midnight but my sister Edith. What can you mean?"

"I saw her, Margaret, as plain as I see you now."

"Who?"

"His first love, dressed in white satin, as if returned from her wedding. I saw her there at the foot of this bed—oh! so plain."

"Dearest mother! you have been dreaming."

"No—no—Margaret, it was no dream. Bring me that small wicker basket from off the wardrobe; in it is a key which may assist to unlock this mystery."

At her mother's request Margaret brought the basket. Mrs. Dalton's thin, trembling fingers undid the handles, which were tied together by a silken thread.

There was nothing in it but a small miniature.

Holding it up to the gaze of Margaret, Mrs. Dalton inquired, "Whose portrait is this, my dear child?"

"That, mother, is the likeness of a Miss Lascelles, whom my father once knew. I must say I am surprised that he should have so scrupulously preserved it."

"She has been here herself. Poor lady! She would have told me something, but Dr. Lloyd came in whilst she was speaking, and she left me before I learnt the real purpose of her visit."

Margaret, finding her mother's mind was wandering, replaced the picture in the basket, and left the bed-chamber to call up her father.

When Dr. Lloyd first entered the sick room he aggravated the alarm which the whole of the family felt, by suggesting that the Colonel, as the most fit and proper person, should be in immediate attendance upon his wife, as there were but little hopes of her surviving the next four-and-twenty hours.

Never, certainly, was a departing mother blessed wit[h] more affectionate children. Scarcely had they receive[d] the afflicting summons ere Felicia and Edith were [at] her bedside.

Margaret was already there before them. The nob[le] girl had never quitted her mother for an instant sin[ce] the discovery of her first alarming symptoms.

Margaret turned to her father as he entered th[e] apartment, and in a trembling voice and with cheek[s] suffused by tears, exclaimed,—

"Pray for her—pray for her ——"

The colonel was about to kneel in order to fulfil th[e] solemn injunction which Margaret enjoined, when th[e] devoted child proceeded,—

"Pray for her speedy restoration to all of us; d[o] dear father, do!"

The colonel uttered a few words at the bidding [of] his child, much after the fashion of those who look in[to] their hats and mutter something to themselves on fir[st] entering a church to hear divine service, but what h[e] said that night is only known to the Searcher of a[ll] hearts.

When the colonel regained the library, and whil[e] his wife was still alive, he said to Dr. Lloyd, who w[as] waiting in it,—

"Are you certain—quite certain—she will die?"

Dr. Lloyd was about to answer, when Dalton adde[d] another to his question, and before the doctor ha[d] time to reply, by hurriedly asking,—

"Is there really no hope? Let me know th[e] worst!"

"While there is life there is always hope."

The colonel bowed his head in assent.

"She may rally a little in the night."

"May she?" exclaimed the unbelieving husband, i[n] a tone indicative rather of consternation than of jo[y] "May she? For heaven's sake remain with her, f[or] fear of accident."

Dr. Lloyd consented; and the colonel, urging tha[t] the scene would be too much for his nerves, said h[e] would sit up in the library and do a little writing.

Information was brought down to him from time t[o] time by his weeping children and the domestics of hi[s] establishment as to the different changes which wer[e] taking place in the progress towards dissolution.

At midnight Edith entered the study and declare[d] that her mother "was dozing."

At two o'clock Felicia informed him that her belove[d] parent was "considerably worse."

At three a domestic who came down to fetch some[-] thing out of the library volunteered the remark tha[t] "her mistress could not possibly live through th[e] night."

At four o'clock the doctor himself sent word dow[n] that "it was all but over."

And yet, strange to narrate, as a small timepiece o[n] the colonel's mantel-shelf was striking the hour of fiv[e] the doctor entered the library with a smile upon hi[s] face.

He had hastened down stairs to acquaint the colone[l] with the welcome intelligence that in the course of th[e] last half-hour so great and wonderful an alteration ha[d] taken place that he could not resist the temptation [of] giving him hopes.

"*Hopes!*" exclaimed the colonel. "Hopes of wha[t] doctor?"

"A crisis, my dear sir. Should my patient sleep b[ut] for ten minutes such a change will have operated i[n] her system that I shall begin to anticipate her re[-] covery."

Doctor Lloyd was considered a clever man in his pro[-] fession, yet he had never been a favourite of Colon[el] Dalton's.

Instead of thanking him for the cheering informatio[n] Hugh bit his lips and said—

"We shall see."

He deliberately recommenced what he was writi[ng]

at his desk, when a loud scream from the chamber of death proved that the hopes of Dr. Lloyd were fallacious.

The patient, even whilst her physician and her husband were conversing, expired.

If there was one person more than another upon whom the blow fell with an astounding force, it was Mrs. Somers.

Her shrieks and exclamations of distracted sorrow were positive yells of misery, and she ran from room to room, clasping her hands together and invoking the blessings of heaven upon the inanimate corpse of her daughter.

One thought alone seemed to be pervading her whole soul : what was to become of that daughter's motherless children ?

So poignant was her grief that the children themselves were obliged to console her, instead of her consoling them.

The colonel spent some hours contemplating the dead.

He stood by the head of the corpse, mute, and apparently absorbed in thought, but no passionate burst of grief betrayed the anguish of a husband's heart. With great coolness he gave the necessary directions for his wife's funeral, and would have even expedited that ceremonial, but a short delay was necessary, inasmuch as his childrens' mourning had to be fetched from London.

The day after his wife died he despatched a note to his solicitors—Messrs. Edghill, Potter, and Pendril—desiring them to instruct his agent to put Dalton Hall in a fit state for immediate occupation, as, having lost the best of wives, he would for the future reside in Hampshire, his present abode in North Wales being painful to him by reason of the afflicting loss he had sustained in that part of the country.

He urged speed, as he wished to remove his family to the new abode as soon as possible.

In the interval between the death of Mrs. Dalton and her interment, the colonel made a flying visit to his brother, Sir Lionel Dalton.

He was actuated to take this trip by two reasons.

His first was that, he might in person communicate the particulars of Mrs. Dalton's illness to the baronet, and the second, that he might enjoy the envious feelings he would be sure to engender in that brother's breast, when he informed him that he had become sole possessor of upwards of fifty thousand pounds by his wife's death.

Arrived at Castle Bodmin, Hugh Dalton was soon in the presence of his elder brother.

Fearing some reproach from Sir Lionel for early irregularities, and particularly in the matter of their younger brother Reginald, as related in previous chapters, he assumed a candour and a regret foreign to his real nature.

"Lionel," said he, " I know my own faults, I have erred grievously, and am here to confess as much, and ask your pardon."

"We have both been wrong, very wrong, Hugh, in suffering such a long estrangement to take place between us You, who first threw down the gauntlet of defiance, ought to have seen your error long ago ; but you have my forgiveness cheerfully ; here is my hand.

The brothers shook hands.

"Colonel ! for I suppose I must now stand a little on old-fashioned etiquette, and address you by your military title ; who do you think I had a visit from yesterday ?"

" My nephew, perhaps."

" He is at college."

" Who then ?"

" One dearer to you than Reginald !"

" Indeed ! Who ?"

" Brother Hugh, I must tell you, and when I tell you,

you will scarcely believe me. It was no other than your wife, once Miss Felicia Somers, and the niece of my college chum and fellow student, Major Durrant."

" Oh, somebody has imposed upon you in her name."

" It was no imposter whom I saw."

" I have reasons for knowing it could not be my wife."

" What do you mean ? Do you suppose I have lost all recollection of the major's charming niece."

" I tell you it was not and could not be her."

" Why ?"

" I have left home and have posted it the whole of the way to tell you that she unfortunately died at Llangollen, in North Wales, the day before yesterday."

" You alarm and astonish me."

" It was not unexpectedly—she had been ill a long time."

" This is beyond human comprehension. Mrs. Dalton dead ! I am very sorry to hear it. What on earth will become of the dear children ?—you have three, I hear."

" I flatter myself that with their mother's fortune placed at my absolute disposal, I shall not be quite so unnatural as to neglect them, or when they arrive at marriageable ages refuse them reasonable portions."

" True, Hugh, but my unseemly visitor ?"—and here Sir Lionel's face assumed a gloomy and contemplative aspect.

He paused, evidently too agitated to proceed.

" What the deuce are you thinking about, Sir Lionel ? Surely you are not so weak as to become a convert to the old-fashioned doctrine of ghostly visitations ?" and the speaker laughed.

" You may smile, Hugh, but on the honour of a man a spirit has spoken to me in your wife's likeness."

" What on earth did she say ?" inquired the cool and disbelieving colonel, " what did she say—it is not the first time I have heard of a speaking likeness."

" My faculties are altogether so confounded by the event, that I have but an imperfect recollection of what she really did say."

" Where was it ? Where did the meeting take place ?"

" In the long walk leading to the shrubbery. I was proceeding to give some instructions to my head-gardener, when a lady emerged from an alcove near it and requested me to give her a hearing for a few minutes."

" In the form of my wife, eh ? Come, Sir Lionel, I did not travel thus far to be joked upon such a very serious subject."

" No jest is intended on my part, my dear Hugh ; far from it. But hear me. I did not recollect the lady at first, but the sun shining forth suddenly in the full power of his meridian splendour, I at once recognised the features and invited her into the castle."

" Did she accept your invitation ?"

" No ! She said she wished for my interference with you."

" With me ?"

" Yes."

" For what purpose ?"

" I could not learn that."

" Did you not ask her ?"

" I did."

" What did she say ?"

" I could not catch her words."

" Lionel, you had been dreaming."

" No !"

" Drinking ?"

" Do I not tell you it was before dinner — in the full glare of noon ? "

" You have lived so long amongst the rooks and ravens of this sequestered place as to become quite superstitious. "

"I have not a spark of superstition in my composition."

"You say it was the vision of my wife, and yet the deuce a word can you repeat of what she said to you."

"Oh! but I can."

"Oblige me, then. Out with it."

"She was serious—very."

"Pulled a long face, I suppose?"

"Don't speak so lightly of the matter."

"Well, proceed in your own way."

"She adjured me, by my fraternal regard for yourself and my duty to heaven, to beg of you to desist from your purpose."

"What purpose?"

"I cannot remember."

"Try to recollect."

"It is in vain."

"If you were to conjure me to desist from a bad purpose, I'll be bound she hinted what that purpose was."

"If, brother, it had been a good purpose," said Sir Lionel, sternly, "the spirit would not have troubled me."

Hugh coloured, but with undaunted courage, begged the baronet by all means to proceed.

"One thing which she said," replied the baronet, "is vividly impressed upon my memory."

"Aye, what is that?"

"Tell him," said she, "there is a hell!"

"Well, that's no news, we surely did not want the aid of a ghost to tell us that."

"Certainly not, Hugh, for I know it intuitively," replied Sir Lionel, gravely.

"Well, after such an important piece of information, what followed next?"

"Nothing; she walked sharply from me."

"She did not evaporate into thin air or ascend into ether, as your commonplace ghosts do."

"She never so much as deigned to look at me, but darted through a side walk and disappeared."

"How strange!"

"Very. Believing the whole thing real, I sent servants in all directions after my mysterious visitor, but no tidings could they learn of her. She was neither seen nor heard by mortal being but myself. Now what do you think of this very singular occurrence?"

"I own I am a little puzzled to reconcile circumstances, but I am convinced the whole has been a dream on your part."

"You have never done your wife a wrong whilst living, which you regret now that she is dead?"

"Never, either by thought or deed."

"Have you ever in your heart wished her dead?"

"Far from it."

"Although, by her death, you come into possession of sudden riches."

"I admit the truth of your latter observation, you sermonizer; but away with superstition. Order a good dinner and over our wine I'll tell you how I mean to dispose of her property."

During the dessert, after dinner, Sir Lionel was anxious to renew the subject of the morning's conversation, and did so, although it was evidently against the wish of his brother.

"How singular it was," said he, "I heard her words plainly enough, and saw her eyes flashing anger and indignation."

"Did you shake hands with her at parting, with your accustomed politeness?" asked the colonel, pouring out his wine from a decanter into a large tumbler, instead of the usual glass, and drinking it off hurriedly.

"Unfortunately, I did not touch her, which would have put an end to all doubt; for she did not present her hand to me, as I expected she would have done, on my nodding assent to her importunities."

After some further conversation on family matters, and an intimation on the part of Sir Lionel Dalton that he verily believed he had already made a man of little Reginald, the brothers parted for the night.

Hugh, once more left to himself, could do nothing but turn in his bed, and reflect upon what Sir Lionel had been saying, and after many cogitations he finally resolved to order a relay of horses and return to Harper's Cottage the first thing in the morning, and hurry on the funeral.

He was convinced, as far as himself was concerned, there would be no peace for him whilst the body of his wife remained above earth.

CHAPTER XXVI.

MRS. SOMERS TELLS THE COLONEL HER SUSPICIONS— THE FATAL PACKET—THE COLONEL RESOLVES ON REVENGE.

Foul deeds will rise.—SHAKSPEARE.

By this time our readers must have arrived at the real character of Colonel Hugh Dalton.

The preceding scene must have impressed some of them with an idea that he was an idiot or a madman, but such a supposition would be wrong.

Putting out of the question the ground or fabric upon which his extraordinary apathy showed itself, he was *not* a madman, neither was he an idiot.

The colonel was endowed with good, sound, practical sense.

He was a man by whose counsels many were guided in his neighbourhood, in cases of difficulty.

His learning was profound, his reading various and extensive, and his taste, if not exactly exquisite and refined, was at least polished.

Yet all these qualities and advantages were insufficient to prevent him yielding implicit obedience to the desire of gain.

He had already become the slave of avarice.

This may appear paradoxical to some persons; we will therefore abandon the figurative, and "speak by the card."

Colonel Dalton envied his wife, during her lifetime, the slightest participation in the dispensation of her wealth, and longed to possess absolute power over it.

This he knew he could not have until her death, and for her death he had waited restlessly and anxiously.

About a month after the remains of Mrs. Dalton had been deposited in their last resting-place, and when the father and his daughters were busily employed packing up various loads of furniture for the purpose of sending them to Dalton Hall, a message was brought to the colonel that Mrs. Somers desired to speak to him on particular business and in her own room.

"Hang that fidgety woman! What's in the wind now, I wonder?" said Hugh; "tell her to come down into the library, and I'll soon be with her."

A chest, in which he had been depositing plate, being carefully corded under his direction, he placed a written address upon the outside, and then walked into the library.

"Now, what is it?" said he to the lady.

"Oh, colonel, I have had such a dreadful dream again!"

"Pshaw!"

"Don't ridicule me. I have seen poor Felicia."

"Indeed! This is, I think, the twentieth morning you have told me the same thing since it pleased Providence to take her from us."

"But I never saw her so plainly before as I did last night."

"Well, don't detain me. I wish to send off the plate chest by the waggon to-night. It starts at eight."

"She looked so white and so mysterious, that I could not sleep in my bed."

"This unintelligible jargon is out of place here, and if you have nothing more important to communicate, you must excuse me listening to you."

"Don't go just yet."

"Why?"

"She told me a secret."

"I dare say—what was it?"

"She said she had been foully dealt with."

"What do you mean?"

"There was something wrong in my poor girl's death."

"If you persist in giving utterance to such a falsehood I shall procure you a lodging where you least expect."

"You may threaten me, colonel, but the long and the short of the matter is, I am dissatisfied with your wife's death."

"Because of the disposition of her property?"

"No, sir, not as regards her property, but her person. Why was not my Felicia opened?"

"What can induce you to ask such a question?"

"Do you insist on my reasons for asking it?"

"I insist on hearing them."

"Then what will you say when I tell you that last night she informed me that she had been——"

"What? out with it."

"Murdered!"

The colonel grew as pale as death; but whether from fear or rage it was hard to tell.

"Woman!" he exclaimed, "you are mad—raving mad, and for the peace and happiness of myself and my motherless children you must be placed in a lunatic asylum, if you persist in giving credit to such diabolical statements."

"Colonel, since you force me to divulge my suspicions, I beg to tell you that I shall get the dear child's body exhumed for the purpose of examination by a London surgeon. I mean to do it, and I will, the very first opportunity."

"If you or anybody else disturb the sanctuary of the grave," said the colonel, violently, "or with your unhallowed and sacrilegious curiosity dare to meddle with my wife's revered remains, I'll shoot you, for an officious fool, through the head. I will, by ——!"

Mrs. Somers, who was naturally a weak woman, verily believing the colonel would carry his sanguinary threat into execution, began to repent of what she had been saying, and meekly observed, "Well, my dear sir, I was told all this in my dream; but what are your commands?"

"That you let this scandalous calumny proceed no further, but go yourself directly and help the girls to pack up in the morning."

"I will, colonel—I will."

"Of course you will, if you would value your own advantage."

But Mrs. Somers could not let the matter entirely rest. That night, as the colonel was going to bed, and passing her chamber door on his way to his own room, she called him in and locked the door.

"What mare's nest, now?" said the colonel, as he placed his candle on her mantel-shelf.

"Nothing particular—only I don't like to have anything on my mind."

"Disburden it, then, can't you?"

"I can."

"Do."

"You wish me?"

"Of course I do."

"I may, then?"

"Quickly, if you please. I want to go to bed."

"Colonel, have you been in the habit of receiving similar packets to these?"

Mrs. Somers pulled out of her drawer a small packet, and held it up to the gaze of the astonished colonel.

It was the identical packet of powders she had abstracted from Carmichael's letter.

Had a thunderbolt fallen from the zenith and struck him on the head at that moment, he could not have been more astounded or electrified.

Quick as lightning he snatched the packet from the hands of Mrs. Somers, and trembling in every joint like an aspen leaf, he exclaimed, "How got you this?"

Mrs. Somers was silent.

"If you don't tell me, woman, I'll throttle you, I will."

Sharp was the word and quick the action with the colonel.

He sprang towards her, and clutching the affrighted creature by the throat, she implored his mercy, and said she would tell him all about it, how she got it, an when she got it.

Mrs. Somers then narrated the way in which she had intercepted the letter from Carmichael, and gave from memory its contents, not omitting, however, by way of embellishment, to add certain accusations against him, which were not exactly in the letter itself.

The colonel was infuriated to madness.

He shook the poor creature violently against her own hard mahogany bed-posts, swore at her for a wicked interfering devil, and called on the heavens above to bear him witness, that if she ever dared to mention such a lie to any third person he would annihilate her.

The reader will bear in mind that he could do this with perfect impunity, as Mrs. Somers, in one and the same breath, admitted that she had burnt the letter itself.

Releasing his hold of the frightened woman, the colonel placed the packet he had forced out of her hands in his own pocket.

Thrusting her from him, he said, "I will talk seriously to you in the morning, madam, for I see we must part company. The woman who confesses herself a thief is no fit companion for my daughters."

The colonel left the room, slamming the door violently after him.

Mrs. Somers got into bed.

In vain she tried to sleep.

Before she dropped into the arms of nature's sweet restorer, she had made up her mind what course to pursue.

Since it had come to the worst, she would declare her suspicions in the face of the whole world, and drag somebody to justice, that she would.

Colonel Dalton, though a bold, bad man, was but mortal.

His nerves had received such a shock by what had fallen from the lips of Mrs. Somers in her disclosures to him, that he resolved in his own mind to prevent any recurrence to the subject on her part in the future.

He thought it possible that his foolish mother-in-law might succeed with some of her acquaintance in getting up what he deemed an absurd and disgraceful investigation in the village, even before he was fairly out of it.

She must be got rid of.

But in what way?

That is shown in the ensuing chapter.

CHAPTER XXVII.

THE DISINTERMENT—DISCOVERY OF POISON IN THE BODY OF MRS. SOMERS—MAGISTERIAL INQUIRY.

If you have tears, prepare to shed them now.—HENRY VI.

THE very first thing which the colonel did the next morning was to send off an express to Dr. Lloyd, to say that his immediate attendance was required at the cottage.

The doctor returned with the messenger in the post-chaise sent to fetch him.

The colonel and the doctor were long closeted together.

"I am sorry to be again required here," said the latter; "what am I now sent for?"

"Is Miss Felicia ill?"

"No."

"Miss Edith has a return of her old complaint?"

"No."

"Poor little Margaret caught cold during the late severe weather?"

"Nothing of the kind."

"Glad to hear you say so."

"I wish you to be candid and free with me, doctor."

"I trust I always am."

"I mean, that you will really tell me the disease of which my wife died."

"Consumption, my dear colonel—rapid consumption. I endorsed the certificate of her death to that effect."

"And you are certain it was of consumption?"

"I pledge my professional skill. But why do you ask such a superfluous question?"

"Because there are unpleasant rumours in the village."

"Indeed!"

"Very unpleasant."

"Of what kind?"

"Horrible!"

"Dear me!"

"Yes, they even go so far as to say my beloved wife was poisoned!"

"Scandalous—infamous!"

"Nevertheless they do say so, and I want to set the matter at rest."

"Colonel, you may command me in any way you please. What do you wish?"

"That her body may be exhumed and examined."

"That, my dear colonel, is unnecessary. There is my certificate to disprove the allegations; and, besides ——"

"What besides?"

"The process will be tedious and expensive."

"I care not for the expense."

"We must obtain permission of the proper authorities."

"Do you think you can obtain it?"

"In my professional capacity I have a right to demand it, and, sanctioned by your wish, being the husband of the deceased, I think the application would be attended with success."

"Without the necessity of a coroner's inquest?"

"Or any such painful and distressing alternative."

"Pray lose no time in carrying my wish into immediate execution."

"I shall require the aid and assistance of an eminent surgeon."

"Can you obtain one?"

"Yes, from London."

"Who?"

"Dr. Blennerhasset."

"He is truly well known and eminent. Engage him by all means."

"It will cost you upwards of a hundred pounds."

"I care not if it cost me two hundred; it must be done."

"Very well, my dear colonel, I will go by the mail to London this very night."

"Not a word to any one of what we are about to do."

"Secresy, my dear colonel, is the very essence of my calling."

They separated.

Within a week of this conversation, the villagers, great and small, residing in the vicinity of Llangollen, congregated at an early hour one fine morning, to witness the lifting up of Mrs. Dalton's coffin from its grave.

Headed by a bevy of surgeons and a constable, empowered by a local magistrate's warrant, the coffin was removed to an appointed place, where the body was duly examined by Dr. Lloyd and others.

The result of a long and careful investigation, ended in a manner which caused the greatest fright and alarm to all who witnessed it.

Dr. Blennerhasset discovered some grains of arsenic in the intestines of the unfortunate lady.

Sufficient, in his opinion, to have killed half-a-dozen people.

The clamour against her unknown destroyer arose all at once into a tumult impossible to check, every one declaring aloud that he or she would subscribe to a reward for the detection of the monster.

The crime was not to be tolerated, and everybody rallied round the colonel, giving him consolation and assurance of aid and co-operation, in any steps he might take to detect and punish the authors of it.

Nothing could exceed the consternation of everybody at the painful discovery.

The news fled rapidly, and half of the Principality was up in arms at the dark and mysterious event.

Colonel Dalton issued a bill offering a reward of five hundred pounds for the discovery of the perpetrators of such an atrocious crime, and a proportionate sum for any information giving a clue which might fix suspicion on the implicated.

Occupation and labour were at a stand.

The barber stood gaping with his razor, whilst the lather on the chin of his customer cooled and congealed; the farrier held the red-hot horse-shoe so long in his hand, that the strokes of his heavy hammer fell powerless; and even the village blacksmith discoursed so long and so feelingly on the horrible event, that his fire went out and his bellows became useless.

Every new comment upon the transaction was stronger than the last; and there was but one question bandied from door to door.

That question was "Who is the murderer?"

Ultimately the outcry of the people became so loud that the magistrates of the district were compelled to take notice of it, and the last gathering of any importance which was held in Harper's Cottage was a meeting of gentlemen in the commission of the peace, who did their duty as magistrates, and constituted themselves into a court of inquiry, which lasted an entire day.

The whole of the domestics who had attended upon the poor lady were examined, but nothing was elicited from their evidence tending to elucidate the affair or throw the smallest ray of light upon it.

At last Colonel Dalton arose from a chair on which he had been sitting, narrowly watching the proceedings, and in a calm and impressive manner begged to be permitted to address a few serious words to the assembled magistrates.

Apparently deeply moved, he passed his handkerchief to his eyes, as if he was in the act of wiping away some tears which impeded his utterance. He proceeded:

"Gentlemen, I have long struggled against wounded feelings, but in this instance near and dear ties must give way to justice—consanguinity must be sacrificed to appease an offended God. In accusing the person I am about to charge with this foul, and as you will find in the sequel, most unnatural murder, you will have no reason to fear my being influenced to neglect my duty by tenderness or compassion, or that the remorse, the anguish, and despair of the wretched being I mean to accuse shall melt my zeal for justice into pity."

So smooth and insinuating a prelude created a remarkable sensation in the room, but it had but little effect upon Sir George Alvers, a venerable and respected magistrate, unanimously voted chairman of the investigation.

He never liked Colonel Dalton, and therefore cut his pathetic address quite short, remarking, "If you desire to be esteemed and honoured by your fellow men, Colonel Dalton, you have adopted a proper course. Pray whom do you suspect?"

"I have good reasons for suspecting one person."

"We beseech you, in the name of justice, at once to say upon whom your suspicions fall."

MR. PYBUS INFORMS MRS SOMERS OF THE NOTICE IN THE PAPER.

It is not mere suspicion. I have in my own proper
[per]son the power of bringing it home to the guilty
[cri]minal."

A buzz of surprise ran through the room.

"Name him or her."

As the colonel hesitated and seemed at a momentary
[l]ittle whether and what he should answer, one of the
[presi]ding magistrates observed—

"We can respect your feelings Colonel Dalton, if
[you] are about to implicate any of your own family.
[So] take your time and be composed."

"It is a stern necessity, gentlemen, but I publicly
[char]ge my own mother-in-law, Hannah Somers, with
[the] wilful murder of her daughter, and if she is within
[the] house I demand that she be taken into custody."

"We must first have substantial proof of her guilt
[be]fore we proceed to such extremes," said Sir George
[Som]ers. "Can you produce anything likely to bring such a
[shocking], not to say inhuman charge, home to her?"

"I can, Mr. Chairman."

"Do it without further circumlocution."

"You are all aware that myself and family are re-
moving to Dalton Hall, Hampshire."

"Your removal can have little to do with this serious
charge."

"It has much."

"How?"

"I have personally superintended the packing up of
every bit of furniture in the house."

"What induced you?"

"A desire to see that nothing was wantonly broken
or destroyed."

"Before the witness proceeds further, Jackson,'
said the chairman to his clerk, who was taking his
evidence down at a table, " you will have the goodness
to swear him."

The testament was placed in his hand.

The oath was administered to him, and he solemnly

swore in that room to speak the truth, the whole truth and nothing but the truth, so help him God !

"You can now proceed, sir," said the chairman.

"I happened to pull out and open a drawer which belonged to an old chest in Mrs. Somers's room."

"Well ?"

"In that drawer I discovered this packet."

"What is it ?"

"Dr. Lloyd will tell you, gentlemen. He has analysed it. It contains the deadliest of all poisons."

He placed the paper before the astonished bench, and stood firm and erect whilst they carefully examined it.

The contents were pronounced arsenic, as a thrill of horror ran through the densely packed and ill-ventilated apartment.

"Some portions of this, or a similar packet, were administered to the unfortunate deceased by her own mother ?"

"I think so."

"Do you believe so ?"

"I regret to say I do."

"What motive could induce the wretched woman to attempt the life of her own child ?"

"She was always quarrelling."

"About what ?"

"Trivial things ; on the last occasion it was concerning an alleged apparition which Mrs. Somers declared she had seen in the lower apartments of the cottage."

"Did she ever threaten the life of your wife ?"

"I have heard her repeatedly."

"Was she addicted to drinking ?"

"You will excuse me, Mr. Chairman, but we are not called upon in this place to investigate her domestic habits."

"It is material to the case, in my opinion. Did your wife ever ask for drink and take it from the hands of her mother ?"

"Many times."

"What sort of drink ?"

"Spirituous liquors, which were secretly given to her, against my express commands."

"Did you ever see the suspected person so overcome by drink as not be aware of what she was doing?"

"Often."

"Did you remonstrate?"

"No."

"What were your reasons for that ?"

"I have a mortal antipathy to the approximation of inebriated persons—especially women."

"What did you do when Mrs. Somers came to herself ?"

"How do you mean?"

"When she was sober."

"I did what I thought most proper under circumstances of such provocation."

"What might that be ?"

"There are private reasons for my not stating. I assure you, gentlemen, there are some things connected with this dreadful tragedy which I am bound in honour not to reveal. I hope you will not compel me to divulge them at present."

"You are bound by a solemn oath, Colonel Dalton, which is the highest of all obligations, and for the expedition of common justice it would be better for you to tell all you know about this matter without the necessity of question and answer."

"I shall, with your permission, reserve what else I have to say until the day of this woman's trial, if you think there is sufficient evidence before you to commit her."

"Of that we are the best judges, sir," said the chairman.

"We will, gentlemen, with your concurrence, call in the medical men and examine them," and so saying,

he turned to the other magistrates, who signified their approval.

The examination of Drs. Lloyd and Blennerhasset materially tended to confirm the allegations directed against Mrs. Somers, and, at the conclusion of Dr. Blennerhasset's evidence the unhappy woman was ordered to be taken into custody.

A diligent search was made in every part of the house for her, but strange to relate she was nowhere to be found.

Scouts were sent about in every direction, but with no better result.

It was evident that the guilty party had fled to avoid the consequences of her atrocity.

Her sudden flight predisposed the whole of the assembled magistrates against her ; and the chairman, before quitting the court, signed a warrant for the apprehension of Hannah Somers, on a charge of "Wilful murder."

CHAPTER XXVIII.

THE FLIGHT TO LONDON—MRS. SOMERS SEEKS REFUGE IN THE HOUSE OF MR. PYBUS—A KIND LAWYER.

At length arrived the fatal morn,
    When trembling, too, with anxious fear,
Off from her bed she rose forlorn,
    And vainly tried to stem a tear.—SHENSTONE.

THE dreadful termination of the previous day's proceedings was carefully concealed from his daughters by Colonel Dalton ; and the sweet girls, in total ignorance of what had really occurred, were sent off, before it was possible for the officers of justice to execute their warrant, to their father's new residence, Dalton Hall.

The servants sent with them to conduct them safely through their journey received strict injunctions not to allude to the dreadful proceedings which had just terminated.

They arrived in Hampshire in total ignorance of the extraordinary prosecution their parent had instituted against the unhappy mother of the being to whom they themselves were indebted for life.

At Dalton Hall we will leave them for the present, to follow the footsteps of Mrs. Somers, who, immediately after her quarrel with her son-in-law, set off from Llangollen in the common stage-wagon for London, with the sole intention of consulting the only lawyer she knew in the world—a Mr. Cyrus Pybus—on the difficulty in which she was placed by circumstances, but more particularly as to her dark suspicions of the colonel.

Her reasons for not acquainting the family with her intention were palpable.

She knew that the colonel would have taken some pains to prevent her flight.

Poor Mrs. Somers ! She little imagined, during the time she sat in the inside of the stage-coach, pursuing her long and miserable journey — for it took an entire week to reach the metropolis from any part of North Wales in those days and in such a conveyance— that the walls of the chief towns in the Principality, and through which she passed, were actually covered with bills offering a reward for her apprehension, and describing her person.

Notwithstanding this peril it pleased a protecting Providence to allow the unfortunate creature to alight from the vehicle, in which she had travelled safely, at the door of the George and Blue Boar, in the Oxford Road, where it stopped after performing its tedious and wearisome journey to the metropolis.

Mrs. Somers partook of no refreshments at the hostelry, but desiring a sedan chair to be fetched, entered it.

When Prince Charles, afterwards Charles I., returned from his faithless wooing of the daughter of Phillip

IV., he brought with him three chairs of the description Mrs. Somers now selected to be carried in as far Gerrard-street, Soho. Previous to Charles's time, such a mode of conveyance was unknown in England or to the English. They had seen the fair and the feeble carried in a box, supported by a horse before and a horse behind, but they felt, therefore, something like what we have felt at the sight of an election rabble harnessed to the wheels of a popular candidate—they felt that men were degraded, when the favourite of James and Charles—Buckingham—first moved into the streets of London, borne in his sedan on men's shoulders.

In time this prejudice wore away, and no more notice was taken of Mrs. Somers' mode of conveyance, than if she had called a cab from off its rank in the present day. "Where to, ma'am?" said the principal pole-bearer.

"To Mr. Pybus, the lawyer's in Gerrard-street, Soho," answered the lady, popping her head out of the sedan, and promising the men extra gratuities if they were quick.

"All right, ma'am; we knows Mr. Pybus, and a main good man he be," said the chief pole-bearer, as he and his companion set off in a brisk trot to their destination.

A good man, indeed, was Mr. Pybus at heart, but although happily free from any organic impediment in his composition, there was one word in his mother tongue which he could scarcely ever be brought to pronounce.

That word was the monosyllable "no."

He faltered to ejaculate it even in the days of his boyhood.

If a school-fellow begged his marbles, he could never say "no" to the application.

If a bigger boy than himself asked for a clear half of the nice plum cake, forwarded to the academy in which he boarded by his fond and affectionate parents, it was at once cut in two and fairly divided; but he was not coerced to the act, for if a lesser boy had made a similar request for the remaining half it would have been unhesitatingly handed over to him.

Arrived at man's estate, the annoyance created by his infirmity was immense.

There was not a distressed cousin in his family or a poor poet of his acquaintance who wanted a couple of pounds, but if he made an application got an affirmative reply by return of post or a messenger, whom the kind soul paid out of his own pocket, to be the almoner of his good bounty.

Such good nature was a terrible bar to great success in his avocation as a lawyer.

He never had the heart to thrust a poor family out of their homes, though he was often desired to do so by clients, and final judgment was the very last thing he resorted to in his legal capacity.

Innumerable were the scrapes in which he was involved by his reluctance to give utterance to a denial, and more than twenty times in the course of his professional career he had handed over to the plaintiff the full amount of debt and costs, because he could not say "no" to the poor wretches who applied to him from time to time for a little grace or permission to pay off their liabilities by easy instalments.

He was for ever being solicited to enrol his name on the lists of subscribers to the public hospitals; and there was scarcely an institution of the kind in London but boasted of his patronage as an annual or life subscriber.

Such was the man who, on seeing the sedan stop at his door, rushed out from his little back parlour and handed in Mrs. Somers as she alighted from the sedan.

"Good heavens! is it you, my dear Mrs. Somers? Why it must be thirty years since we last met."

"Full that."

"I recollect; it was the very night before your brother the major, then Captain Durrant, departed for India. I recollect it well. I could not say no to the invitation he gave me to meet you and him at your father's house in Queen-square, Westminster."

"What a memory you have, Mr. Pybus!"

"Yes, and I recollect you a very fine young creature, too."

Mrs. Somers held up her head.

"Aye, not only a very fine creature, but a very beautiful one into the bargain."

Mrs. Somers smiled, evidently pleased that his memory had not failed him in that respect.

"But time has worked a sad alteration. Who would ever think I am now looking upon the once beautiful little Hannah!"

"I suppose, Mr. Pybus, I appear a perfect fright!"

Alas! the spell, from the fatal power of which he suffered so much all his life, still had its influence over the old lawyer.

He could not say "No."

After a conversation of some thirty minutes in the back parlour about old friends, old times, and old associations, Mr. Pybus got more than usually hospitable, and would insist that his early friend should take up her abode with him whilst she remained in the metropolis.

He would not hear of her putting up at the "George and Blue Boar," but sent a proper messenger to the inn to fetch her box to Gerrard-street.

A thousand important things had occurred since they last met. Hannah herself had married; a daughter by that espousal had also been united in wedlock to somebody, and the once elegant Hannah was metamorphosed into a grandmother of sixty and upwards.

Nevertheless the warm-hearted Mr. Pybus was glad to see her, and proved the sincerity of his welcome by giving instant instructions to his housekeeper to secure her every comfort during her stay.

Vast changes had taken place in Mr. Pybus's affairs during the long period of a score and ten years.

He had not been so enamoured of a bachelor's life as to say "No" when a friend asked him to take his daughter in marriage, and gave him a few thousands with the friendly proposal.

But his connubial happiness was destined to be of short duration.

Mrs. Pybus did not live above three years, and as he really loved the woman to whom he gave his hand, he evinced the sincerity of that love by remaining a widower for the residue of his life.

After the fatigue of her journey had worn off, and in about three days subsequent to her arrival, Mrs. Somers made her legal adviser acquainted with all the particulars which we have related in previous chapters, excepting only that as yet she had no knowledge of the horrible advantage which Colonel Dalton had taken of the secret imparted to him by her to him.

It was a ticklish case for Mr. Pybus, for he had a very great aversion to interfere with what he deemed family quarrels.

He soothed the lady as well as he could, and threw out a hint that if she remained passive the colonel's anger might possibly blow over.

One thing he positively refused to do—namely, to write to the colonel, demanding a proper settlement for his mother-in-law, which that lady thought she had a right to, and wished him to demand accordingly.

"An ounce of oil, my dear madam, is better than a gallon of vinegar. We will ask what you require as a favour. In that shape I don't think your son-in-law will say 'no' to my application."

Mrs. Somers did not see it in that light, and was for instituting a lawsuit on the instant. She was surprised at Mr. Pybus's hesitation.

"A word of advice," said Mr. Pybus, "may be of service to some ladies in directing their thoughts to that which they cannot comprehend, but I never can expect that you should see exactly as I do. It is one thing to make a woman turn her head, and another to make her see with a legal eye. I am sorry to say, as to any enforcement of this claim, you have not a leg to stand upon."

The subject dropped for that day.

At breakfast the following morning, and as the good lawyer was reading the newspaper, the printed sheet fell from his hands, and he exclaimed—

"Oh, good God! Can it be? What is the meaning of this!"

Mrs. Somers, alarmed, put down her cup of coffee and said—

"Dear me! What distresses you, Mr. Pybus?"

"Shocking! Dreadful!"

"Some accident? Pray read it to me, if you please."

"Worse than any fatality in the world!"

"Indeed! Pray tell me. Does it relate to yourself?"

There is not a more insignificant word, both as to sight and sound, nor in the whole vocabulary of the English language, than the one which Mr. Pybus uttered in answer to the interrogatory, and which upon all other occasions he had a difficulty in bringing forth.

In this instance it was out before Mrs. Somers had half finished her question.

"No."

"To whom, then, does it refer?"

"You."

"Me?"

"Yes."

"Bless me! how could I get into the paper? A poor weak creature like me, not worth a penny in the world."

"Excuse me. You are at this moment worth one hundred pounds to anybody."

"Explain."

"There is in this newspaper an advertisement offering a reward for finding you, to that amount."

"For me?"

"Yes, for you."

"Dear me! Perhaps there's more money in India belonging to my poor dear brother, the major, and his representatives are seeking to find its lawful owner. I knew there was luck in store for me, my dear Mr. Pybus, because, you see, I saw a white-and brown horse standing at your door the very morning I entered it."

Mr. Pybus shook his head. He knew it was a horse of another colour.

He shook his head.

"Well, don't keep me in suspense; what does the paper say?"

The kind-hearted man would have crumpled the paper up and put it into his pocket, but Mrs. Somers, seeing his intention, exclaimed: "Don't keep all the good news to yourself, dear Mr. Pybus, but enlighten a poor lone body."

Thus directly appealed to, he said:

"I am certain there must be some dreadful mistake here. My dear Mrs. Somers, they are offering a reward for your apprehension on a charge of murder."

"Gracious heavens! Murder—Mr. Pybus? Murder of whom, in God's name?"

"Your own daughter."

Mrs. Somers could not speak; she fairly gasped for breath, and faintly articulated, "Who has done this?"

"It don't say. All I can tell you is that you are accurately described, even to the dress upon your back, and the advertisement goes on to state that you left North Wales suddenly, and are supposed to be concealed somewhere in London at this very moment."

"Oh God!" said Mrs. Somers, falling upon her knees and clasping her hands together in an attitude of prayer, "support me under my affliction! You know that I am innocent. Merciful heaven, what will become of me?"

A flood of passionate tears succeeded to this pathetic appeal, but the blow was too much for her.

She sank senseless upon the floor and Mr. Pybus was occupied a full hour in endeavouring to restore the poor creature to a state of consciousness.

He at last succeeded in bringing Mrs. Somers somewhat to herself, and he endeavoured by all the soothing endearments in his power to allay her alarm.

For reasons which did equal credit to his head and heart, Mr. Pybus called up nobody to his assistance but performed all the offices of resuscitation himself.

He burnt brown paper and held it under her nose.

He bathed her temples with vinegar.

He rubbed her hands patiently for ten minutes at a time, and adopted all the conventional and usual remedies in cases of hysterical fits.

When thoroughly restored and able to comprehend what was said to her, he hugged and kissed her like a maniac, endeavouring to assure the trembling creature by every means in his power that he thought her quite incapable of slaying a worm, much less killing one of her own flesh and blood.

"This is—dreadful—shock—ing," sobbed Mrs. Somers, who was terribly alarmed.

"It is, indeed; but what had we better do under the circumstances?"

"I know what I am resolved to do," said Mrs. Somers very composedly, and as if she was making up her mind to an ordinary inclination.

"What is that, my dear madam?"

"You do not—you cannot believe me such a fiend in human shape?"

"I do not, I never did," said Mr. Pybus, blandly.

"Oh, you know not how I loved that girl!"

"I can believe it."

"To be accused of killing her—oh, it is terrible!"

"It is—very terrible!"

"I will disprove it to the whole world."

"You shall in due course; but you must first take my advice, and——"

"I appreciate your good, kind, Christian-like intentions, but I must and will give myself up to the officers of justice at once and have my innocence proved on the instant. This is the cruel colonel's doings. He said—he would—break—my heart—and—he has done —it."

Mrs. Somers sobbed so loud and so bitterly that she really alarmed her generous friend.

Mr. Pybus had again recourse to the stimulants, and Mrs. Somers being once more restored to a comparative state of calm, he proceeded, "Give yourself up! You must do nothing of the kind. Why, it is only the month of October; you would have to lie in gaol till the spring assizes. They won't be on till next April; you would be half dead before you could be tried. Five months in a county prison! No, no! I won't hear of such a thing."

"Oh, they would never send a poor innocent creature like me to gaol upon mere suspicion."

"They will if they catch you, my dear Mrs. Somers There is no bail in such cases, or on such a charge, o I would be one myself and get fifty of my neighbours to be the others; but they won't hear of it, and, therefore——"

"I must be thrown into gaol."

"I don't say that."

"How is it possible to save me?"

"I have it."

"Almighty heaven bless and preserve you!"

"We must play at hide-and-seek. You must be concealed somewhere till within a few days of the assizes, and then I'll defend you."

"You will?"

"Yes, for I see there is some hellish plot against you, which I must foil."

"Oh, how shall I ever repay you! I never can, but heaven will."

"We'll talk about squaring the account when I send in my bill. For the present you must go upstairs, feign sudden and alarming illness, and keep in your bed until I am cool enough to decide what I mean to do with you. For the present I shall call you by the name of Mrs. Martin to my servants, and by that name alone you must answer whilst you continue under this roof."

The good old lawyer urged his wishes with an eloquence peculiarly his own. To have said "No" to his commands would have been ungrateful and impolitic, and under circumstances which presented themselves acquiescence on Mrs. Somers' part was the safest course she could pursue.

CHAPTER XXIX.

THE ASSIZE WEEK—MRS. SOMERS SURRENDERS TO TAKE HER TRIAL—MR. JUSTICE FERRET AND MR. BARON BLOOD.

Man's inhumanity to man, makes countless millions mourn.
POPE.

MRS. SOMERS had scarcely been ensconced in her new lodging in Vauxhall, near to the once famous gardens which bore that name, a fortnight, than the locality she had quitted—Gerrard-street—was frightened from its propriety by a report that the house of Mr. Pybus in that street had been searched by Bow-street runners, in blue coats and scarlet waistcoats, properly armed with warrants, for the apprehension of a person charged with the revolting crime of murder.

It was early in the evening of an autumnal day in the month of October, just as the soft twilight had faded into a serene night, when the loud and furious knocking of a patrol and a posse of constables alarmed Mr. Pybus, who was quietly reading in his arm-chair by the fireside of his neat little office.

"Dear me, what is the matter?" said he to his housekeeper, who had put the chain up on the inside of the street door, to keep out intruders.

"There's a whole regiment of catchpoles outside, sir, who want to get in. Harkye to what they are saying, sir?"

"We will break the door down if you don't open it," was exactly what they were saying.

"What do you want, my good people?" meekly inquired Mr. Pybus from the inside.

"Why there's a reward of one hundred pounds offered for the apprehension of a woman charged with murder, and we suspect you are hiding of her."

"Martha, open the door to the gentlemen," said Pybus; "let them in, by all means."

"Oh, for goodness sake, don't let me do that, sir!" said the housekeeper. "We shall all be dragged out of our beds and put in prison. I won't unlock the door to a thief-taker."

The opposition produced its natural result—an increase of violence on the part of the besiegers, until the door itself was smashed to pieces.

In rushed at least a dozen people.

Finding the constables in the passage, Mr. Pybus demanded what right they had there? what they wanted? and how they dared to break into his house in such a violent manner?

They demanded to search every nook and corner in it.

Their roughness and threats worked so effectually on the fears of the imbecile Martha, that she yielded an acknowledgment that Mrs. Somers had been residing with her master, but had left the house ten days previously. She was gone, but where to, Martha did not know.

The officers did not believe her.

A search was made in every room—not a corner, not a cellar, not a cupboard was overlooked—but all to no purpose.

No fugitive could be found.

At last Mr. Pybus said—

"I myself represent the laws, and I am bound to respect them. The person you are in search of, I admit, was staying with me for a day or two a fortnight since, but she has left my house and has gone I know not whither."

The lawyer was too well known and too much respected for his word to be long doubted, and—after peeping into the letter-box attached to the street door, and the candle-box behind the kitchen one—the Bow-street runners offered an apology and departed.

Each succeeding day made the kind lawyer feel still more forcibly that his consideration and humanity subjected him to a very disagreeable kind of espionage.

His footsteps were dodged, his clerks followed wherever they went to, and every letter he sent by post minutely inspected as far as their addresses were concerned, before his messengers could be permitted to drop them into the post-office.

Despite all this surveillance the bloodhounds were defeated.

The whereabouts of Mrs. Somers remained undiscovered till the period arrived for her transit into the country to meet her accusers.

Hercules plying his distaff could not be more out of his element than was Mrs. Somers, in the character of a Mrs. Martin, taking in needle-work, apparently for the means of existence.

Such was the avocation she followed in the obscure lodging which her friend and adviser secured for her.

Pybus was proud of his secret.

The lonely place he resorted to when the laxity of his watchers offered him the opportunity, brought him visions of Christianity.

He had a soul to save—something to extricate from an abyss of misery—and come what might or come what would, he was resolved to succeed or perish in the attempt.

Chivalric Pybus, how heartily do we wish that you may succeed.

At the spring assizes for tha Principality, held at Beaumeris, in the early part of April, the Honourable Mr. Justice Ferret and Mr. Baron Blood having been selected for the Welsh circuit, took their places in the shire-hall, there to despatch the business which had been accumulating for six months previously, the former holding his sittings in the Nisi Prius Court, and the latter presiding for the trial of graver offences in the shire-hall.

On taking his seat on the judicial bench, Mr. Baron Blood called the attention of the grand jury to the state of the calendar before him, which, he regretted to say, was anything but satisfactory in a moral point of view. He was happy to announce to them, however, that the county in which they resided had been placed under a new commission, by which means the North Wales district would be guarded and protected by a most respectable and powerful magistracy, which was the most sure and certain safeguard for its inhabitants, at a time when the utmost exertions of wise, able, and upright men were wanting, to suppress the commission of those notorious crimes which had so long and loudly called for the particular attention and interference of the supreme legislature. He could not dismiss them to their several duties without directing their attention to a very remarkable bill which would be brought before them—no less than an indictment against a woman for the murder of her daughter, by administering poison, but whose apprehension, he regretted to observe, had been thwarted and prevented by friends, or accomplices in the crime; and, although large rewards had been offered by the prosecutors in the matter, as well as by His Majesty's Government, the apprehension of the criminal party had not been effected. A great flourish had been made throughout the country, and it was boldly asserted that the suspected person only kept out of the way to avoid the long imprisonment which would take place after commitment—a period exceeding five months. But in his own mind he could not believe that any sane individual, knowing herself to be really innocent, would deem such a very short incarceration as other than a feather in the scale as opposed to their own innocence, and the salvation of their soul. Whoever advised the wretched being to take the course she had done, was an enemy to his country, an offender in the eye of heaven, and, if belonging to the legal fraternity, a disgrace to the rolls upon which his name appeared. He (his Lordship) would only now add to this opinion an intimation that if the grand jurors did their duty, he would perform his; and in the case of a true bill being returned by them, the court would issue bench warrants and take effectual means for arresting the principal, and also the whole of the persons suspected of harbouring or concealing her.

The grand jury having retired for deliberation, returned into court in about two hours, finding a true bill of indictment against Hannah Somers for the wilful murder of Felicia Dalton, her daughter.

The result of their deliberation did not surprise Mr. Baron Blood.

His lordship had every reliance they would arrive at a proper conclusion, from the facts brought before them, and he begged to observe that they would have grossly failed in their duty if they had ignored that bill.

If Mr. Baron Blood was not surprised at an every-day course of proceeding on the part of the grand jury, his lordship must have been much more so at the extraordinary scene which followed their presentment.

An elderly gentleman, who had been seated under the bench beneath the learned baron, rose, and calling the attention of his lordship to a female in deep mourning, who sat beside him, said : "My lord, Hannah Somers is here to surrender herself into the custody of this court. The unfortunate woman sitting by my side courts the fullest inquiry into her life and conduct."

Every eye in court was immediately directed towards the trembling creature.

A sad alteration was perceived in her appearance by all who had previously known her.

She was literally wasted to a mere skeleton, and her once black hair was completely turned to a silvery white.

It was not surprising that she was unrecognised, for if the thick lace veil in which her features had been wrapped had fallen off, there remained in those features no outward resemblance to the once happy mother.

The stern and unbending dispenser of the law—Mr. Baron Blood—indulged in a long, not to say indecent stare at the female, and then exclaimed, "Let the prisoner take her proper place within that dock, by the side of the gaoler."

The poor, tottering woman was dragged to the bar, and was only prevented fainting when within it by clutching hold of one of the iron spikes.

Scarcely knowing what she was about, she kept smelling a small piece of the rue which she picked from a board before her, and on which a quantity was strewn to renovate all prisoners.

Mr. Pybus—for it was no other than the humane lawyer, who had come from London on purpose to surrender her—seeing that she was likely to fall down in the dock from fright and acute agony of mind, rose and addressed the bench.

"I hope your lordship will allow the unfortunate creature at the bar to be accommodated with a chair."

"If the prisoner can produce a medical certificate that she is ill, or suffering from ill-health, why——"

"She is really so, my lord ; there is no time to procure a certificate—perhaps your lordship will dispense with the necessity for one in this case ?"

"I cannot depart from the usual course; but if the prisoner makes a short affidavit as to her indisposition, you may hand it up to the bench, and we will consider of it."

During this short colloquy, Mrs. Somers really fainted; and then, but not till then, Mr. Baron Blood said the gaoler might accommodate her with a seat.

One was fetched.

Upon this seat she remained, totally insensible to what was passing in the court, and in the whole of which she was so materially concerned.

"Does your lordship purpose to try this indictment at once ?" asked Mr. Pybus.

"Certainly not. Neither the prosecutor nor his witnesses have received any notice of the prisoner's surrender."

"When will it please your lordship to try it ?"

"Let me see," said Mr. Baron Blood, looking at the calendar; "we have three important cases of sheep-stealing, one of burglary, two of highway robbery, and not less than sixteen indictments for passing forged notes. I will try the prisoner on Friday. I name this day, being enabled to do so by the humanity of the law. However, as she is now before us, we may as well see what she pleads to the indictment. Ask her, Mr. Hopkins."

The clerk of the arraigns put the usual question, and Mrs. Somers, in the wildest state of excitement, answered with a solemnity of tone and an apparent sincerity which went home to the hearts of three-fourths of the assembled multitude, "Not guilty, my lord—not guilty ! I call upon my Saviour to bear me witness."

"Gaoler, remove your prisoner to a place of safety. Let no one have access to her but her professional adviser."

"Any other instructions, my lord ?" asked the gaoler, who placed his hands on her shoulder.

"Handcuff her, by all means. The ends of justice must not be frustrated by any attempt to do herself violence."

The gaoler did as he was bid, and the wretched prisoner was removed from the bar in a state bordering on distraction.

Her shrieks, as she was borne through the intricate underground passage of the court-house, were so long and so piercing, that Mr. Justice Ferret was disturbed in his summing-up of a case—Jones v. Smith—and he asked what the noise meant.

"It's only a murderess being taken to her cell from the other court," answered the usher of his own.

But no murderess ever received the kind and generous attention which Mr. Pybus paid to the accused.

He was early and late in the prison, consoling and comforting her.

As the regulations of the gaol permitted persons committed thereto to provide for themselves or be provided for previously to trial, he was constantly sending or bringing her little delicacies, such as her system required, and of which, if she had been debarred, fatal consequences might have ensued to a naturally tender constitution, weakened and broken down under pressure of unmerited misfortune.

Poor Pybus ! He was like a fish out of water when excluded from the prison on the arrival of the hour for locking out strangers.

But for the fact of its being assize week, the town of Beaumeris would have appeared little better than a desert to him.

As it was, he took but very little notice of the busy scene before him.

It was the very first time in the course of his long and honourable career that he had ever been called upon to act on behalf of any one under a criminal charge, and especially of such a dreadful nature as that of murder.

The attorneys and counsel engaged in the prosecution were civil to him, but one and all declared that he had undertaken a very hopeless defence—his unhappy client would be sure to be found guilty.

Indeed, such a sensation was created by the dreadful nature of the crime, that illibral persons brought it home to the unfortunate creature in their minds, and said she was sure to be hanged.

Others had the heartlessness, not to say indecency, to wager on the certainty of such an ultimatum.

Three days intervened between the committal and the trial, and these days were spent in the usual apathetic manner such days are spent in an assize week.

There was a dinner given by the high sheriff to Mr. Baron Blood and the Honourable Mr. Justice Ferret, on the eve of that dreadful morrow which was to decide the fate of Hannah Somers.

The gentlemen of the long robe who went the circuit with the judges, were invited together with the usual notable persons on such occasions.

After the cloth was removed the bottle passed briskly round the table, and almost everyone said, or attempted to say, something smart on the occasion.

Mr. Vokins, a junior counsel, who had never spoken in public before, was rather anxious, as the lrwyers would say, to make an *incipite*, and he asked Mr. Justice Ferret if his lordship had seen a great curiosity then exhibiting in the town.

"What is it, brother Vokins?"

The learned counsel had achieved a triumph.

He had positively been called brother by the Honourable Mr. Justice Ferret in the hearing of all the practising barristers present. He (Vokins) who had never been entrusted with a brief or asked a question of a witness in his life.

He bowed to the judicial interrogatory, and in reply said, "The elephant, my lord; it arrived on Monday last."

"And brought his trunk with him, I suppose," observed the facetious Mr. Justice Ferret; at which the whole bevy of barristers set up a loud laugh, and signified their high approval of the forensic wit by tapping on the mahogany with the end of their taper glasses.

The learned judge, encouraged by such a very successful defeat, essayed a second appearance.

"Seriously, my dear Vokins, I have not seen the wonderful animal," said the judge; "but, as we both travel with a flourish of trumpets, I believe we stand upon ceremony—the ceremony—of who shall make the first visi."

This was irresistible.

The whole room rang with applabse, and Mr. Sorjeant Grogblossom got up and declared it waf the most brilliant piece of wit he had heard in the whole course of his life.

The routine of passing from the judges' lodgings to the shirehall, or court-house, greatly amused Mr. Pybus, who, unable to sleep, took an early stroll round the town to see what was to be admired, and what was doing in it.

At nine o'clock the trumpets sounded in the High Street.

Ladies in full dress flocked to the windows to see or be seen.

The high sheriff bows politely to them as he passed in his carriage, and, fearing that he is rather behind time, asks the Honourable Mr. Justice Ferret, who is with him, in a most earnest way and with a serious countenance, "Has the last trumpet sounded?"

The answer of the learned judge was, "I hope in God not, Mr. Sheriff, for I am by no means prepared;" and wound up his witjicism by declaring that he was doubtful "whether Mr. Baron Blood, the barristers, nay, the whole court, are not in the same predicament."

Arrived at the Nisi Prius Court, Mr. Justice Ferret took his seat in a room scarce big enough to contain, with any degree of comfort. half the number of suitors crammed into it.

On taking his seat, he bowed to the assembled barristers, who all rose and mysteriously shook their wigs at him, by way of returning the compliment.

There were about twenty barristers, many of whom Pybus was informed had never spoken, and about as many more who were never likely to speak, that is to say, to the purpose, in his opinion.

The real business of the circuit was confined to about three favoured individuals.

To a man of such quiet habits as Mr. Pybus, the entire court presented one scene of general confusion.

Counsel opened without being heard, and when the crier, by violent exercise of his lungs, succeeded in obtaining him a hearing, in calling the attention of the jury to the pleadings in an action for ejectment, he gravely declared that he had not read a word of his brief, yet proceeded very deliberately to inform the jury of what he was himself entirely ignorant.

The action for ejectment having been decided suddenly in a most off-handed manner by Mr. Justice Ferret without going to the jury, a juror being withdrawn, he hurriedly got through squabbles about cattle trespassing where no grass grew, settled contemptible slanders between parties who never had any character to lose, and disposed of endless litigations about titles where no title ever existed, in such a talismanic manner that Pybus said to himself on quitting the court—"That man will be Lord Chancellor before long."

On the Thursday he dropped into the Crown side, and found crowds paying homage to the presiding deity, in the person of Mr. Baron Blood, who was occupied in trying fallen beings, once as innocent as himself or any of the spectators.

Here he was hurt to see idle curiosity get the better of humanity, the pride of human nature rising superior to compassion, and none in that Court, not even Mr. Bason Blood, disposed to make Christian or charitable allowance for the frailties of their fellow men.

Mr. Pybus himself could, and did, make allowances for wrong education, pressing necessity, strong passions, and painful temptations, which, in most cases, rendered the miserable creatures before him objects of compassion; but Mr, Baron Blood in almost every case urged the jury to convict, and when they had convicted seemed to feel an actual pleasure in sentencing the offenders, some to long imprisonment and others to transportation for the rest of their natural lives.

Pybus shuddered when he withdrew from that court, and reflected that before such a prejudiced judge, on the very next day, an innocent woman was to be placed upon trial for a charge which affected her life.

CHAPTER XXX.

THE GHOST HOVERS OVER THE GAOL—TRIAL FOR MURDER—THE GHOST IS SEEN BY A JURYMAN—VERDICT—A DISAPPOINTED JUDGE.

> The ways of heaven, though dark, are just,
> And oft some guardian attends unseen to save
> The innocent.—BLAIR.

AT seven o'clock all the lights were extinguished in the gaol, and Hannah Somers, in a cell by herself, was contemplating the horrors of the next morning.

Her handcuffs had been removed by order of the high sheriff, a most humane man, who set at nought the commands of the judge in this instance, he being in the eyes of the law the only one who was really responsible for the safe custody of his unfortunate prisoner,

She was just rising from an old piece of matting, on which she had been kneeling in an attitude of prayer, when she was aware of the presence of somebody, who came hastily towards her.

The mysterious intruder was a supernatural being, or how could she have gotten entrance into the interior of Hannah's cell?

It was barred and bolted securely.

In addition to the common bolts which fastened it on the outer side, a huge padlock, affixed to a heavy ponderous chain, trebly secured it, and the rattling of the chain itself gave trueful notice to the solitary inmate of the entrance of the gaoler, the chaplain, or any other person.

The figure had a face scarcely like that of a human creature, for it was careworn and sorrowful; but it was. nevertheless, far from repulsive to look at, and was sensible in speech.

It bade the prisoner be of good courage, and said it came to bring her tidings of happiness.

Hannah Somers answered,

"I shall never enjoy happiness on this side the grave again."

"What is your wish?"

"Alas! why should you ask my wishes? They are nothing now to any one."

"Had you not a fair and beautiful daughter?" asked the spirit.

"It is a heart-rending question; but on her account I am confined in this gloomy dungeon."

"What became of her?"

Hannah shook her head, turned round, and would have hid herself from her ghostly interrogator, for it was a theme that her heart could not brook. She only articulated, "Oh, my poor Felicia! my dear lost, murdered child!"

There was a hopelessness in her grief that would have moved a heart of stone.

"Despair not," said the spirit, "for in doing so you are not acting according to the dictates of reason or religion."

Hannah could not reply from very grief.

Her deep, heavy sobs resounded through the dark avenues and passages of the dreary gaol.

"What are you that you should fret, or any woman that she should repine, under the chastening hand of her Maker?"

Hannah buried her face in her hands, for a sudden light revealed the face of her questioner.

It was no other than the same face and figure which had given her warning of a coming evil in Harper's Cottage, whilst that place was being altered and repaired.

The affrighted prisoner stood trembling and clasping her hands in an excess of mental agony which the spirit perceived and proceeded.

The voice which spoke was that of an ordinary person, and it said—

"No subtleties! I demand, as I did before, what became of your child?"

"Ask the Father of her spirit and the Framer of her body!" said its mother, quite calmly, and as if inspired by the holy visitation itself. "Ask him into whose hands the murderer plunged her in the ripe vigour of her womanhood. He alone knows the secret—I do not."

"You still grieve for her?"

"With a fond but broken heart. Be thou a spirit of evil or of good, I tell you that."

"And still will mourn?"

"Yes; and I will even place my foot upon the scaffold, if that I am to die upon it, mourning for my child, the comfort of my age, and my heart's earliest affection."

A smile was radiant on the face of the spirit.

"Oh, thou unearthly moniter, knowest thou aught concerning the fate of my child? If thou dost, have pity on me and reveal it!"

"You will be happy yet!"

"Yes, when I am permitted to rejoin her in the realms above."

"No; you will yet be happy on earth. Be firm and place your trust in Him."

The ghost pointed upwards as it spoke; and when

Hannah turned to give assurance of her faith and belief in another and a better world, it had vanished.

The miserable prisoner was again in darkness.

Tears now rushed from her eyes like fountains, and dropped from her sorrow-worn cheeks on the cold flag-stones of the prison cell, and then, kneeling at the side of her solitary mattress, she poured out her soul in thanksgiving to her Maker, for what she could not but consider an augury of speedy emancipation from all worldly suffering.

But she had many severe ones to undergo before she could anchor her bark in such a desired haven.

Precisely as the clock struck nine the next mooning, Hannah Somers was placed at the bar, and her trial proceeded.

The court was densely crowded.

It resembled one of the triennal gatherings at the musical festivals which, by a strange perversity of taste, were usually held in the same place once in three years.

As much as a guinea was demanded and willingly paid by morbid sightseers for a place inside the court, from which they could get even a glimpse of the wretched prisoner.

The intense curiosity extended even to the family of the judge, and with these, it is recorded, the lady of Mr. Baron Blood sat at the back of the judgment-seat, near her husband, and surrounded by a long train of relations and aristocratic friends, having procured the judge's permission to peep at what has not been inaptly described as a human raree-show.

The preliminary business commenced. The names of the jurors were called over, and when they had taken their seats in a box and were duly sworn the trial proceeded.

The indictment charged the prisoner with the murder of Felicia Dalton by the administration of poison.

The counsel for the prosecution stated the particulars of the case, which he said would be proved by the testimony of credible witnesses.

He was occupied more than two hours and a-half in addressing the court. He called especial attention to the fact that the prisoner at the bar had lived for many months in open rupture with the deceased, that they had been heard in violent altercation by their servants on various occasions; that no one attended upon the deceased during her last illness but her mother—prisoner at the bar; that the only medicine she ever took was administered to her by her mother; that after the death of the deceased arsenic was found in a drawer belonging to the prisoner, and that on a *post mortem* examination of her victim, particles of the deadly poison were discovered in her body corresponding with that contained in a packet, the contents of which would be produced in evidence, and from partaking of which, no doubt, the unfortunate victim had died.

Counsel then proceeded to call evidence.

The first witness, William Blennerhasset, deposed to finding poison in the body of the murdered woman after that body was opened, and nothwithstanding the body itself was in a state of rapid decomposition.

In answer to a question from Mr. Baron Blood, the witness gave it as his opinion that the poison had been administered at long intervals, and in quantities infinitisimally small at a time.

Dr. Lloyd was called to prove that his patient never took her medicine unless given to her by her mother.

On cross examination this witness affirmed that he could not bring himself to imagine the prisoner guilty of any such detestable crime. She appeared to be very fond of her daughter, was in a state of madness when she died, and had no motive, that he could conceive, for the act.

Mr. Baron Blood: "That may be your opinion. The motive will come out anon. Call the prosecutor."

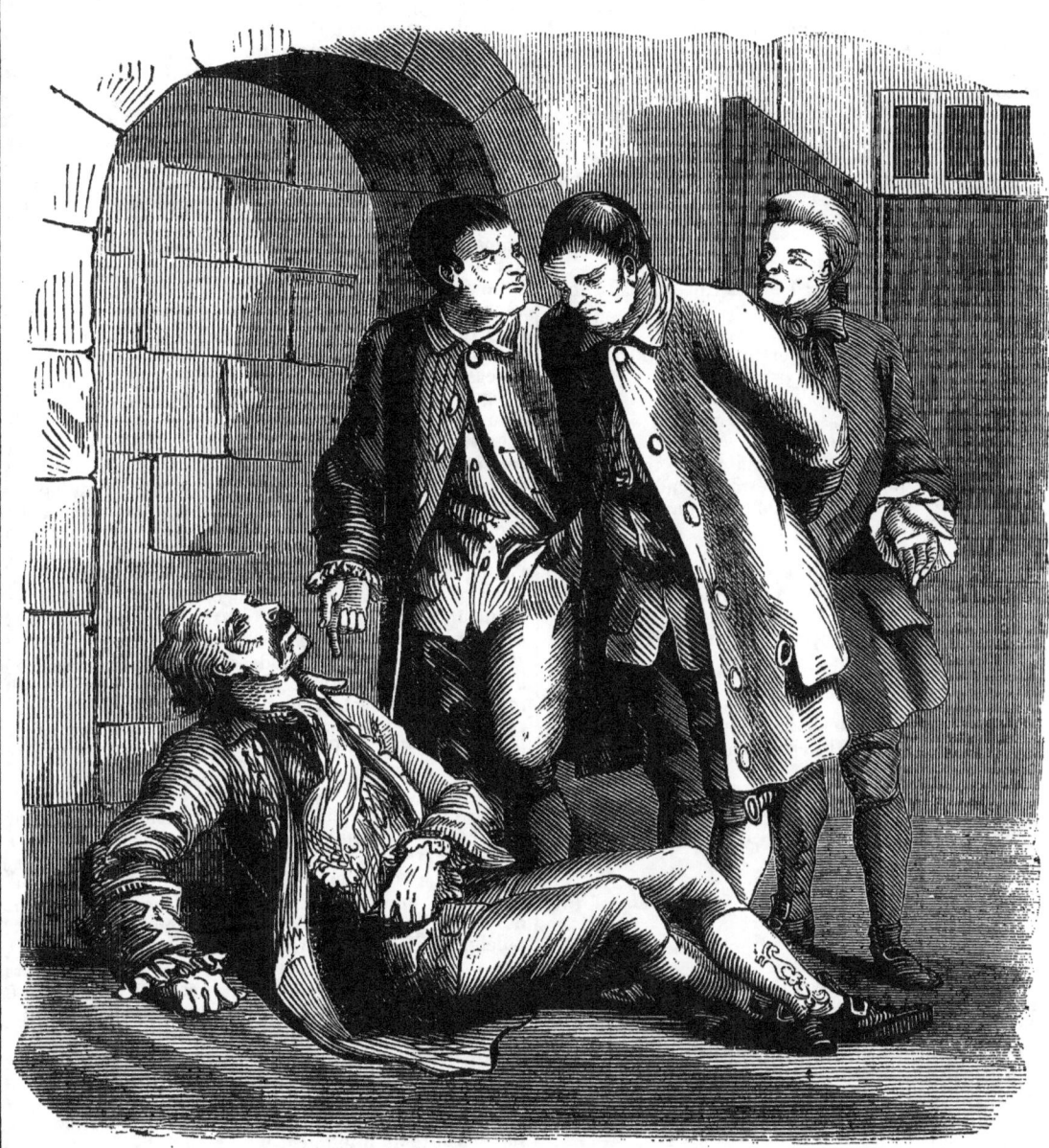

THE DEATH OF COLONEL DALTON.

Hereupon Colonel Dalton stepped into the witness.

He deposed to an inordinate fondness for his wife the mother of his children, and appeared to exhibit much agitation and reluctance in the matter, that Court begged him to compose himself for a short e.

After a pause, in which affection and duty seemed be struggling for the mastery, he proceeded.

His statements were not extorted from him by examination.

He volunteered every one of them.

His evidence appeared to bring the crime home to unfortunate prisoner at the bar.

He had found a packet containing poison in a drawer onging to her; and she had very reluctantly consed to him that it belonged to her.

" Had she any motive for the crime ?"

" She was always at variance with her daughter, and s continually quarrelling with his wife from morning o night."

" Did he know from whence the arsenic had been obtained ?"

" No : he had caused the most minute inquiries to be made, but fruitlessly. It was not sold in any of the shops belonging to the adjacent towns, and must have been procured by the prisoner from London."

" What cause existed for the prisoner's enmity towards her daughter?"

" It was known to her that if the daughter died, the prisoner would be wholly dependent upon the witness"

These were the chief points elicited from the evidence of Colonel Dalton, but some of his servants deposed to the unhappy state in which the mother and and daughter lived for a long time; and one of them, a woman, named Sarah Chernock, swore that she heard the prisoner, in a terrible passion one day, say " she should be glad when it was all over ;" but whether she alluded to she illness of her mistress, or the improvements then going on in her master's house, she would not undertake to swear.

The evidence for the prosecution being closed, the unhappy prisoner was called upon for her defence.

Scarcely knowing what she was about, she declared her total innocence of the crime imputed to her, and beseechingly implored the learned judge to let her go.

Mr. Baron Blood: "Woman, we cannot part with you just yet. How do you reconcile the possession of a deadly poison with these protestations of innocence? How did you come possessed of arsenic?"

"I will tell you, my lord. It was sent in a letter to my son-in-law."

"To Colonel Dalton?"

"Yes."

"How did you know that?"

"I intercepted the letter; I broke the seal and took out the contents."

"What were the contents?"

"The small packet of powders produced in court this morning."

"Who wrote that letter?"

"My memory is failing me fast, my lord; I cannot recollect the writer's name."

"On such a charge as this, and when the writer's name is of paramount importance to the ends of justice, do you mean to tell the bench that you have really forgotten the name?"

"I have, my lord."

Mr. Baron Blood shook his head, but proceeded in the course of examination he was pursuing, and which appeared to produce a great sensation.

"Prisoner, produce the letter you are speaking of."

"I cannot, my lord."

"Cannot. Why not?"

"I burnt it, my lord."

Mr. Baron Blood again shook his head disbelievingly, but took a note of the prisoner's reply; and having entered it in his book, asked,—

"To whom was the letter, which you say you destroyed, directed?"

"Oh, *that* will never be effaced from my memory."

"To whom?"

"To Colonel Hugh Dalton."

"Was he in the habit of receiving packets of this description, and in a similar way?"

"Frequently, my lord."

"You are sure of it?"

"Yes, as I hope to be saved, my lord."

"Did you ever open his letters before?"

"Never, my lord; I was culpable in doing so then."

Colonel Dalton was called and re-examined by Mr. Baron Blood.

"Were you in the habit of receiving any sealed packets of this description from London?"

"No, my lord."

"You swear it?"

"I do, my lord."

"Then it is a wicked fabrication of the prisoner?"

"It is, my lord."

"You can stand down, witness, we will not trouble you further on this painful subject."

"Has the prisoner any witnesses to character?" asked the inexorable Baron, as if determined in his own mind that nothing they could adduce should alter his opinion.

Cyrus Pybus deposed that he had known the prisoner for the long period of fifty years.

He represented her as a kindly disposed woman, but admitted, on cross-examination, that he had lost sight of her during the last thirty years.

Mr. Baron Blood: "It is wasting the time of the Court in listening to such testimony."

At this moment all eyes were directed to the prisoner, who had sunk from sheer exhaustion, and the matron and gaoler were busy in chafing her temples and endeavouring to restore her to a state of consciousness.

While yet the eyes of the spectators were thus strained, and some of their hearts melting with tenderness and pity, Mr. Baron Blood charged the jury.

In his summing up he began by a conventional dissertation on the serious nature of the charge for which the female prisoner was arraigned at the bar, deeming it alike detestable in the eyes of God and man. It was not for him to dilate upon the wickedness of those who committed such crimes; they were mostly sure of detection in this world and of everlasting punishment in the world to come. He did not wish to add one additional pang to the pains which the unhappy wretch must be enduring at the bar, if she had committed the foul crime which she would be called upon to answer with her life, but he should ill discharge his duty to society if he did not point out to the gentlemen of the jury the very grave suspicions which were attached to her. In very rare instances was the crime of murder brought directly home to the perpetrator, and certainly never in cases of poisoning. They were obliged chiefly to trust circumstantial evidence, and in that position the Court were placed with respect to the miserable creature then in the dock. He had his own idea of her guilt or innocence, but it was no part of his painful duty to prejudice the case by an avowal of what that opinion was. They must be guided by the evidence before them and by that alone. What was the evidence? In his eyes and in that of many persons there in Court, it was most damning. Poison of the same description as that of which the murdered lady died was found in the actual keeping of the prisoner, and when she was asked to account for its possession she declared she had opened a letter addressed to a third party and extracted it therefrom. Who sent that letter? Her memory was treacherous. She could not even recollect the name of the writer. What had become of the letter itself? She had destroyed it after perusal. Such were the excuses which the prisoner put forth, but it stood to reason that these excuses were a palpable deviation from the line of truth. If such a letter had ever been received and opened by her, why was not the postman of the district called to prove its delivery? He at least could have sworn to the date, the size, the direction, and the person into whose hands he had delivered it. It was obvious from the absence of such official testimony no such letter had been received by her. Where, then, could she have procured the poison? Nobody could be so wicked as to suppose for a single moment that her son-in-law, Colonel Hugh Dalton, the husband of her victim, a man of undoubted character and of the highest integrity, and whom she evidently wished to impugn in the matter, was a participator in her crime. He did not give the slightest attention to such a diabolical suspicion, and he was sure an intelligent jury would disregard it. His lordship then proceeded to probe the motive which led to the horrible crime. It was proved, he thought, by the evidence of respectable and responsible witnesses that both mother and daughter frequently disagreed. The subject upon which they were at variance was of no consequence, but the words "She would be glad when it was all over," deposed to by a witness, presented a very remarkable feature in the case. Did the prisoner wish her daughter dead, and had she a guilty knowledge that she would die? This was a secret known only to her own breast; but, blessed with an ordinary share of common sense, he could put but one construction on it. He shuddered to name it to the jury, but doubtless it would leave the same impression on their minds. Then, after the discovery of the poison in her own bed-chamber, did she act like an innocent person? He was sorry to say quite the contrary. For reasons which he could not but say, were palpably evident, she took to flight, and this he was bound to remark almost rivetted the suspicions attached to her. The jury would also take notice that, although she had lived with the prosecutor and his amiable family since the colonel was united to his wife, and had herself assisted in the bringing up of their three daughters—not one of them had been called that day to speak on her behalf. No; the only person who had dared to give the prisoner a character, and had ventured to depose to a knowledge of her natural disposition, was an imbecile man, almost in his second childhood; who, on cross-examination, admitted that, until within a few weeks of the present investigation, he had not even seen or heard of the prisoner for the space of thirty years. He was not, therefore, in a position to say, to whether she was accustomed to retire to meditate mischief and to exasperate her own rage, nor whether, as was too often the case with revengeful people—particularly women— her latent thoughts were employed on means of retaliation for real or imaginary oppression. He knew nothing about her, and for the good he had done the prisoner at the bar, he might just as well have stopped at home. Finally, Mr. Baron Blood declared many persons had been executed on less than half such strong grounds of suspicion. The facts already proved in evidence demanded the most serious attention of the jury, though in dismissing them to the consideration of their verdict he was bound to tell them 'that if any doubts arose in their minds as to the prisoner's guilt or innocence, she was entitled to the benefit of them.

It being now nearly six o'clock, candles and oil lamps were lighted in the court, and the jury withdrew.

One hour passed and the jury returned not.

Another terrible hour of suspense convinced the anxious spectators that the jury were not unanimous as to the verdict they were required to give.

Mr. Baron Blood got fidgetty.

The unhappy prisoner had been removed from the dock at the same time the jurors retired.

She was to be brought up when they delivered a verdict which would either consign her to the gallows or restore her to liberty.

At nine o'clock, Mr. Baron Blood, who was one of those judges who would "hang the guiltless rather than eat his mutton cold," sent to know whether it was likely the jury would soon agree.

Word was brought the learned Baron that such a course was exceedingly unlikely.

"Bring the whole of them before me," roared the impatient and angry judge.

The twelve men stood before him all of a row.

"Now, you fellows, are you not agreed in this matter?"

Mr. Adam Strong, the foreman, said that eleven out of the twelve had made up their minds, but the twelfth was an obstinate man, and so strictly conscientious, that he required longer time for deliberation before he could make up his mind to give in his adhesion.

"The case is as plain as a pike-staff," roared the disappointed judge. "Twelve mere in'ants would have seen it before this. Take them back, usher, and let them be locked up in a room without fire, or candle, or victuals, or drink. Don't let any person have access to men so obstinate; and when they are all agreed come you to my lodgings and I will return with you and take their verdict. I am not going to inhale the pestilential atmosphere of this black-hole all night. The court is therefore now adjourned till the jury are prepared to return their verdict."

So saying, Mr. Baron Blood rose and quitted the bench.

The jury returned to the scene of their cogitations and were locked in.

The only light admitted into the apartment, which was a large one, and generally used as a card-room on the nights of public assemblies, came through its windows, and was afforded by the moon.

The moment the obstinate juryman re-entered the place he betook himself to an obscure corner of it, and prepared to make himself pretty comfortable by the aid of chairs and the damask curtains of the window to lay his head upon.

"Once for all, John Stubberly," said Adam Strong, the foreman, "are you still of the same opinion in this very dreadful case?"

"Just as I was at the beginning, am now, and ever shall be."

"You still think the poor creature administered the poison?"

"What I think I have said, and I mean to stick by."

"It's a thousand pities, neighbour," said one of the jurors to the last speaker, "it's a thousand pities that the law does not empower a judge to take a majority of opinions in these cases."

He was a meek old gentleman, who terribly missed his supper and comfortable warm bed.

"Not at all, Mr. Lamb," said the obstinate juror; "that would be almost as bad as making a lottery of it. It would only require seven men, instead of twelve, to decide the guilt or innocence of any party."

"If you have a doubt upon the matter, my dear friend Stubberly, recollect what his lordship said. We are bound to give the prisoner the benefit of it."

"But I have no doubts in the case," returned the other, "so don't bother me."

Hearing this the whole eleven waxed exceedingly wrathful, and were for pitching Mr. Stubberly out of the window, but it was so exceedingly dark that they could not get at him very easily, and could only imagine where he was located by the sound of his voice.

One by one the unfortunate jurors dropped off to sleep. Some with their heads resting in their hands and their elbows on the tables.

Others stretched at full length upon the carpet.

When all were fast locked in sleep, Stubberly began to think that he had held out too long, and that it might be possible the eleven were right and that he was wrong.

The recommendation given him to consider well what he was about, and to give the benefit of his doubts, if he had any, to the miserable wretch whose fate depended on his single voice, somewhat startled him.

He had children of his own, and what would be said of him by them if he was instrumental to the hanging of an innocent person?

His determination began to waver, and it is possible that he would have given in before the morning, but he was coerced to do so at once by an irresistible power.

At various periods of the world grave sages have been much alarmed at the idea of man's aspiring too much. In ancient days there were grave persons who thought it sinful to have anything to do with fire. Prometheus, who probably first discovered the means of striking a light, was said to have stolen fire from heaven.

In the third book of Horace we read that the effects of this were very serious. Fevers, unknown till then, afflicted mankind, and Death found half his work done to his hand through the impious labours of the person we have named.

At a later period it was considered a dreadfully wicked thing to raise the devil. It was believed to be possible, and all the abominable murders perpetrated under the laws against witchcraft may be regarded as the fruit of this notion.

In various other instances men were supposed to possess powers which it was unlawful to exercise. Stones and bones were forbidden in a wager of battle to be worn as charms by the combatants, who, before they fought, were required to swear that they had nothing of the kind about them.

These things, once so awful, are now laughed to scorn; and the only thing which remains to shake the credulity of man, is the visitation of ghosts, and especially those who are commissioned to bring to light crimes which the laxity or supineness of the age cannot discover.

Suddenly a dim unearthly light fluttered through the window, and lighted up the carpet on which reposed so many of his tired and worn-out neighbours.

A strange commotion shook the building.

In the alarmed and highly excited state of his imagination, he heard voices exclaim "Better to let ninety-nine guilty persons escape than hang one innocent! Save her! Save her!"

He looked up.

A gibbet was suspended over the head of every juryman, and above the gibbet appeared on it, in bright, fiery letters, the name of Hannah Somers, the wretched prisoner they had that day been trying, and whom he was for condemning.

Stupified with horror, he saw plainly that a number of skeletons appeared to seize him, and that he was immediately surrounded by all the ghastly characteristics of death—skulls, cross-bones, worms, and reptiles.

He was in the act of shrinking from their loathsome embraces, when he suddenly turned and beheld before him the figure of a woman kneeling by his side, as if in the act of prayer.

She arose, and with a sweet and most expressive smile placed her finger upon his shoulder, and said to him in accents of peculiar softness, "You will, I know you will!"

"Wh–a–t?" stammered out the terribly alarmed juror.

"Save her!"

"Who?"

"She who is unjustly accused."

"The prisoner?"

"Yes."

"Do you know her?"

"She is my mother. Remember, we may meet again."

The spectral visitor looked fondly in his face, as if anticipating compliance, and proceeded—

"Wilt thou promise?"

"I will."

"Swear by your belief in heaven."

He swore as dictated, and then, in a whisper which curdled his blood, she breathed in his ear the words, "Thy soul is now unstained!" and vanished.

The most discordant yells now proceeded from Mr. Stubberly. So long and loud indeed were they, that he awakened every man in the room by his screams.

"Oh, such a dream!" said he to the first who approached him.

"Hang your dreams, Mr. Stubberly. Are you wiser than when you fell asleep? Do you agree with us?"

"I do! I do!" said the alarmed Stubberly.

Hereupon the whole eleven crowded round him, and such a shaking of hands took place as was never seen between jurymen in that room before.

Bells were rung, and the usher instantly summoned to the door.

"Are you all agreed, gentlemen?" said the usher.

"We are!" shouted several at once. "Send for the judge immediately."

On returning into court, the jury found to their amazement that it was still nearly filled with well-dressed people, who, having paid for admission to the tragedy, were determined to wait for the end.

It was now five o'clock in the morning of Saturday.

At ten minutes past five, Mr. Baron Blood again took his seat upon the bench in the midst of a death-like silence.

He ordered the prisoner to be placed at the bar immediately.

Hannah, more dead than alive, assumed her former place in that horrible dock.

The whole of the jurymen having re-entered the court,

the clerk of the arraigns broke the death-like stillness which prevailed by demanding, in the usual way—

"How say you, gentlemen—do you find the prisoner 'Guilty' or 'Not Guilty?'"

The foreman answered—

"NOT GUILTY."

The words were no sooner pronounced than there was a loud attempt at applause, which Mr. Baron Blood could scarcely silence, even under a threat of commitment.

"Well, gentlemen," said that astonished judge, "this is your verdict, not mine, thank God!"

Such an exclamation, at such a time, and in such a place, acted as a thunderbolt upon the astonished jurymen; but, nevertheless, they knew that they had conscientiously discharged their duty, and the foreman, in the name of the others, asked his lordship if he had expected any other verdict.

"Certainly, assuredly. After the evidence," said Mr. Baron Blood, "I consider the verdict infamous."

The choler of Mr. Strong rose as the judge uttered these words.

Strong was an honest and a sensible yeoman, and determined not to be brow-beaten by the bench, he thus addressed the judge:

"My lord, we hear your lordship's extraordinary language of reproof, but we do not accept it as properly or warrantably applying to us. It is true, my lord, that we ourselves, individually considered, in our private capacities, may be poor insignificant men; therefore, in that light, we claim nothing, out of this box, above the common regards of our humble but honest station; but, my lord, assembled here as a jury, we cannot be insensible to the great and awful importance of the department we now fill, and we form, as a jury, the barrier of the people against the passion, prejudice, or malignity of the bench. We do not in this verdict presume to offer you disrespect, much less insult; we pay you the respect one tribunal should pay another, for the common honour of both. Still, my lord, we cannot blot from our minds the words of our school-books, nor erase the early inscriptions written on the first pages of our intellects and memories. Hence, we are mindful that judges are but fallible mortals, and that the sanctuary of justice has been polluted by a Tressilian and a Jeffries."

Mr. Baron Blood was astonished to hear such words from the lips of a man, who, though he acted throughout the trial in the capacity of foreman of the jury, he regarded in his own mind in a light little better than a clown.

He stammered out a few words about his duty and his knowledge of the law, and that the jury had much to answer for in the eyes of the murdered woman's surviving relations.

He was cut short in his harangue by the intrepid Strong, who said, "We took our seats here, my lord, yesterday morning, sworn to give a verdict according to our consciences, on the evidence before us. We have fearlessly done that duty. If we have erred, we are answerable, not to your lordship, nor the bench upon which you are placed, nor to the king himself, who placed you there, but to a higher Power, the King of kings. We now claim our discharge."

Mr. Blood was dumb, the few barristers who remained to hear the issue were silent, but a murmur of astonishment ran throughout the court.

At the end of this extraordinary scene Pybus felt somebody embracing his knees, and, on looking down, he beheld Hannah Somers kneeling at his feet.

The good-hearted old man uttered a loud hysterical scream of joy, and clasped her to his bosom, while the grateful creature hung upon his neck and wept.

Mr. Pybus raised her tenderly from the ground, and supported her to the inn where he was stopping; but she was unconscious of all around, and looked wildly upon the good lawyer.

There is a time when the fountains of the human heart are dry, when tears refuse relief to the over-burdened heart.

It was thus with Pybus and his client.

Now that Mrs. Somers had fairly escaped the danger to which she had been exposed she looked and shuddered at the awful brink upon which Colonel Dalton had placed her.

Tears of joy and gratitude gushed forth, and when she was congratulated by her legal adviser the flood-gates of her feelings could no longer withstand his kindness, and she wept from very joy.

What a thrill shot through the breast of old Pybus when he heard the magic words—"Not Guilty:" they touched the most sensitive chords of his heart, and gave new-birth to happy days of old.

And as for Mrs. Somers, she was, indeed, alive again.

The two old friends flew into each other's arms.

"Guardian! preserver!" exclaimed the overjoyed woman; "my past has gone like a dream, my present is happiness unspeakable, my future shall be devoted to prove my gratitude to you."

"Nay, my dear soul," said Pybus, "if any thanks are due let them be paid to Heaven alone. Let us think no more of last night; the remembrance of it—of that dreadful scene—curdles my blood with horror."

After awhile, and when Mrs. Somers had somewhat recovered her fortitude, Mr. Pybus asked what course they had better pursue with regard to the prosecutor in the trial just finished.

"Oh!" returned Mrs. Somers, "I will heap no re-proaches upon his head, my voice would fall unheeded; but there is a voice within his own breast which will shock him far more than my weak upbraidings—a voice whose echo will only be silenced when the spirit returns to Him who gave it."

"Still, my dear madam," continued Pybus, "he ought to be punished."

"And should, but for the disgrace it would bring upon his children, the daughters, recollect, of my own dear, murdered Felicia."

"True; I had forgotten the poor girls; God help them!" and the lawyer sighed.

"I will not think of their father too harshly, for fallible indeed is man's judgment. We will leave him in the hands of our present Advocate, our future Judge. If there be a fatal stain upon his soul, oh! may it, ere that last day dawns, be washed white as snow!"

Mr. Pybus used every Christian artifice to cheer and console Mrs. Somers, and he partially succeeded.

She would, however, break forth afresh whenever she reflected upon her trial.

"What matters?" she would say, "what comfort is left for me on this side of the grave? she has been taken from me, my all, my only treasure."

But at times, when her heart would fain repine, and her spirit bow too deeply beneath her grief, a strong hand was ever ready to support her, a ministering voice was near her to whisper words of comfort and encouragement, and bid her to remain firm to her Father above, and that voice was ever on the threshold of the lips of Pybus.

When Mrs. Somers returned to Llangollen she was often seen, in the stillness of the evening, treading with slow steps the winding path that led to her daughter's resting-place; there would she stand, with her grey hairs waving in the breeze, and feast upon associations linked with her that lay beneath.

Calm as the scenery around was the heart of Mrs. Somers; when the twilight came on its shadows did not affright her; a ray of hope cheered the forlorn widow, resignation supported her, and faith, from its inmost sanctuary, guided her onward course.

It was broad day-light before a quarter of the people present throughout the trial had departed from the interior of the court-house on that eventful morning.

CHAPTER XXXI.

THE SECRET DIVULGED.

Now anxious cares his pensive soul opprest,
Sleep fled his eyes, and peace forsook his breast.
POPE.

THE termination of the trial gave universal satisfaction throughout the country, and those who were doubtful before now asked themselves this question—"Could any other conclusion be expected?"

Immediately after the issue the colonel removed to Dalton Hall, and, with a liberality which was wholly involved in mystery, established Mr. George Carmichael in a large way of business in the neighbourhood.

But he was not destined long to set at naught the commands of his Creator and the dictates of his own conscience.

The painful proceedings against Mrs. Somers were almost forgotten, when one morning, during their breakfast, Hugh addressed his daughters as follows—

"Well, my dear girls, it is true we are at last delightfully and comfortably settled. It must, however, be dull and solitary for you to be buried alive in the country, without a companion or friend during the long winter months. I therefore propose we invite my nephew Reginald to spend a few days with us. What say you?"

"Do, dear father!" said Margaret. "I hear that he is a kind-hearted young creature, and I quite long to see him."

"Shall we have him here, Edith?" observed the colonel to his second daughter.

"Oh, by all means!" returned the young lady, "for I see my madcap sister is already in love with her cousin."

"Sister Edith!" observed Felicia, "we must allow the colonel to do as he pleases in the matter; our likes and dislikes are nothing to him. As master of Dalton Hall, he is the best judge of his own guests."

The colonel hemmed, stammered, and uttered some kind of expressions in return, while he looked down, as if doubting in his own mind whether the words of his daughter were a compliment or a sarcasm.

The colonel's invitation was accepted, as narrated in our first chapter, and in due course the handsome young Reginald arrived.

Colonel Dalton's style of living, and occasionally his manner of talking, contributed to perpetuate an error, by which he hoped to profit in the establishment of his daughters.

But the gentry of the county were wise in their generation; and, although his fair girls were in great repute, and their fortunes were said to be large, and Dalton Hall was never without a reasonable supply of visitors—still they came to drink the colonel's wine and not to woo; and postponed their declarations until such time as his character could be cleared on a material point which remained as yet unelucidated.

Reginald had been on a visit to his uncle about a fortnight when the event occurred mentioned in the opening chapter, and which ended in his proposal to marry Margaret.

The lovers arranged that a private marriage should be solemnised between them, and to which no person was to be privy but Edith, who was to be entrusted with the secret upon peril of forfeiting their future love and friendship if she divulged it to any living soul.

From the moment that Margaret agreed to become the wife of Reginald, the terrors of the ghostly visitation had been banished from his mind.

His soul was wrapped up in the living—the dead had but little, if any, influence over his actions.

He gazed on the lofty yet angelic features of his beloved—her bright eyes, which indicated an ingenuous truth—that glow, like as of the morning, which seemed to beam from out her heart through her transparent skin—all conspired to make him idolise his choice and hasten the consummation of his happiness.

To accomplish this Reginald had to overcome many difficulties; for singular to relate, the colonel, who had ever been anxious for the match, no sooner heard that it was likely to take place than he appeared discontented and annoyed.

After Edith had intimated to him her suspicions that the event was coming off, he was more than ever capricious and unreasonable.

He was discontented with himself; and when a man is ill pleased with himself he is seldom well pleased with others.

He seemed altogether left to the influence of the evil one, running about in a rage, finding fault with everything and every person, and cursing bitterly where there appeared no occasion.

It was evident to the servants that Dalton Hall, which used to be a scene of hilarity, was then, or about to be, turned into one of gloom and dissatisfaction.

In the midst of this uncertainty, Reginald and Margaret stole away and were united.

It had been arranged between them that the marriage was to be strictly private, and that immediately after the performance of the ceremony Reginald was to set off to inform his uncle, Sir Lionel, and then return to claim his bride and prepare an establishment of his own.

But this arrangement was nearly frustrated.

On entering the hall after their return home from church the happy pair separated for a few minutes. Margaret to attire herself in walking costume, and Reginald to write a letter to his uncle, apprising him of what had taken place that morning.

Whilst writing he looked up from his desk, and for a third time in his life his mother stood before him.

He was less awed than usual, and made an effort calmly to address her.

"Is your presence here an augury of good, or does it forbode evil, mother?"

The spirit pointed with its hand upward and said—

"Reginald! Reginald! You promised to avenge me!"

"I did, mother, and I will. Of whom do you complain?"

"Of him who basely murdered me!"

"His name?"

"You have this day wedded his child!"

Reginald started. He leant upon the back of his chair for support, and had scarcely strength enough to articulate—

"Colonel Dalton?"

"Even so. He is the poisoner. I have long wished you to know it. Will you now keep your oath?"

"Mother, I will."

"I am satisfied!" and so saying, the spirit disappeared, as Margaret ran laughing into the apartment, and threw her arms playfully about the neck of her husband.

We will pass over the harrowing struggles, between love and filial duty which agitated the breast of Reginald. It will suffice to state that they expected his journey to Castle Bodmin in the full determination to explain everything to his uncle, Sir Lionel, and to abide by his advice.

With this intention he took a hasty leave of Margaret and departed, as had been previously arranged between the lovers.

We must now recur to events which transpired after the judicial proceedings against Mrs. Somers.

Notwithstanding her sufferings, the unfortunate lady conducted herself with great fortitude, and aided by the counsel and advice of her kind friend Mr. Pybus, she made no attempt at reprisal, but left the retributive to an offended Deity.

For many months after her acquittal she was urged to take steps against Colonel Dalton, to render her pecuniary compensation for the wrong his false accusation had done her, but she refused all solicitors of the kind.

Mrs. Somers, who had endured such cruel persecution with a calm, unruffled temper, was yet to be avenged; and thus it came about.

Mrs. Carmichael reading in the newspapers a report containing the trial of Hannah Somers for the murder of Mrs. Dalton, felt assured that Carmichael, from whom she had separated some time, knew something about that dread affair, if he was not actually implicated in the murder.

Mrs. Carmichael had long been anxious to find an ostensible reason for flying from the society of her husband in the disgraceful way she had done.

She recollected the letter she had intercepted between George Carmichael and the colonel.

The fragments were still in her possession, and, with the assistance of her paramour, Sadgrove, these fragments were carefully pasted together on a sheet of paper, and acted upon.

The first step taken was to consult her father, the alderman, and that upright man was but too glad to clutch at any proposal which seemed likely to end in the trial, conviction, and execution of his son-in-law.

A second time it seemed likely that an innocent person would be implicated in an unfounded charge of murder; and most likely this would have been the case but for the sagacity and foresight of Mr. Pybus, who, being asked to take up the affair, and required to state whether or not he did not think George Carmichael had a guilty knowledge of the murder, to this interrogatory the good lawyer found no difficulty this time in saying "No."

Mr. Sadgrove and Mrs. Carmichael had been commissioned by Mr. Alderman Andrews to consult him upon the subject, and he very quickly pointed out the mistake under which they were all labouring.

If any person was open to the serious charge compromised in the accusation it was the colonel himself, and he thus commented upon the written document.

"You see, madam, the letter commences thus— 'Nothing on earth would induce me to comply with your request but a knowledge of what is between us ——.'"

"Well, Mr. Pybus, but he does comply, and evidently sends the poison down."

"Yes; but we must not infer from the fact of sending it down that he had a guilty knowledge of the purpose to which it would be appropriated; on the contrary, he cautions the colonel to be very careful of its use, or else they might both get into trouble."

"You, then, decline to take the matter in hand, so far as relates to my husband?" said the infuriated Mrs. Carmichael.

"I certainly do, madam, for I believe he is innocent of this crime, whatever his other faults may be."

"You will not undertake to prosecute him?"

"Certainly not," continued the kind lawyer. "I could not sleep in my bed if I undertook such a case."

"Never mind, Messrs. Sharp and Grably will do quite as well, and are better men" and so saying, the alderman's daughter seized the arm of Mr. Sadgrove and bounced out of the office.

A fortnight after this interview, all Hampshire was thrown into a state of consternation by an incident which occurred at Dalton Hall.

The colonel was sitting at his library table one evening, in the company of his daughters, Felicia and Edith, hurling terrible anathemas against Margaret for the steps she had taken in marrying young Reginald so secretly, when their neighbour, Mr. Jeremiah Hardcastle, was announced as waiting to see Colonel Dalton on very particular business.

"I never liked that man," said Hugh, "I wonder

what he wants with me. Say I am engaged—will you, Walter?—and cannot be disturbed."

"That is impolite, dear father," said Edith; "he is our neighbour, and. we have so few acquaintances of his standing that to cut him thus short would be unwise and impolitic."

"Besides," said Felicia, taking up the thread of her sister's observation, "he is a bachelor and unmarried."

"Well, show him in; he can't eat me," drily returned Hugh.

The ladies prepared to receive Mr. Hardcastle with smiles and a kind welcome.

But the colonel rose haughtily on his entrance, and demanded his pleasure.

"Would it were a pleasure," said Mr. Hardcastle; "yet it is important, and I must speak with you alone, sir."

"I have no secrets from my children, sir. You will be good enough to say what you have to say in their presence," replied the indomitable colonel.

"Excuse me, but I decline to do so. What I have to communicate is not exactly fitted for the ears of the young ladies."

Felicia, who always affected great prudery, now rose, and looking at her sister, beckoned that young lady out of the apartment, saying, "Neither myself nor my sister, Mr. Hardcastle, desire to remain under such circumstances, and, therefore, we take our leave for the present."

The young ladies withdrew.

When alone, Mr. Hardcastle looked at the colonel very gravely, and said, "I presume you know that I am a magistrate?"

"Yes; I am told that you are in the commission of the peace. What then?"

"By virtue of my office I regret to say I have been compelled to issue a warrant against you."

"Against me. For what?"

"The most horrible of crimes."

Libeller! How dare you have the effrontery to enter my house and say as much to my face? Of what am I accused?"

"Murder."

"Murder?"

"Yes, double murder. First by administering poison to the late wife of your brother Reginald, and secondly, in committing the same crime upon the daughter of Hannah Somers, whom you basely slew to enjoy uninterrupted possession of her fortune."

The colonel looked round the room as if to seize upon some deadly weapon, but the magistrate was beforehand with him.

He stamped his foot upon the ground, and in a moment the apartment was filled with a posse of constables.

"Seize that man," said Mr. Hardcastle.

Despite the most desperate struggles the colonel was seized and handcuffed.

That night the colonel was lodged in Winchester gaol.

CHAPTER XXXI.

THE DOUBLE SUICIDE.

Last scene of all, which ends this strange, eventful history.
SHAKSPEARE.

It ended at length—that long, long career of horror.

At the instigation of Messrs. Sharp and Grably, George Carmichael was apprehended upon a warrant charging him with the murder of Mary Dalton.

He was arrested on returning from one of his usual visits to Colonel Dalton; and the poor wretch was so astounded by his capture that he had no opportunity of eluding the vigilance of the officers of justice.

On learning the nature of the accusation upon which he was taken, he raved incoherently, and in his parox-

ysms of madness openly accused Hugh Dalton as the demon who had brought him into his present trouble.

He became, too, so alarmingly ill, that the officer who had the warrant for his apprehension allowed him to sleep in his own residence for the single night, but never quitted him whilst life remained in his body.

The torments of a guilty conscience punished him sufficiently on this earth; let it be hoped that the mercy of heaven was subsequently shown to a truly repentant sinner.

In the morning he was found dead in his bed; but he confessed to the officer who held him in charge the atrocious share he took in the first murder, yet stoutly denied—as was the fact—that he had any participation in or knowledge of the second.

A phial was found at his bed-side the morning after his death, which but too plainly told the story that he had died by his own hands.

Whilst this tragedy was being enacted in the neighbourhood of Dalton Hall, a similar scene was performed in the county goal at Winchester.

When the turnkey unlocked the door of the cell in which Colonel Dalton was confined, they were shocked and surprised by the discovery of his body, cold and inanimate, lying undressed near the miserable pallet on which he had been placed overnight.

Gaolers are matter-of-fact people, and Beddowes, the Winchester gaoler, merely called to his aid another turnkey to assist him to lift up the colonel, and to surmise as to the cause of his death.

These men deserve particular mention.

The first had a broad, full face, curiously mottled with red, as if the blood had been forced by hard feeding into every vessel of his skin.

It is certain he was swelled into ugly and revolting dimensions by frequent potations of that very liquor the introduction of which into the gaol itself was accompanied by a threat of fine or three months imprisonment, if we were to believe a black board with white letters upon it, stating such to be the penalty for surreptitiously conveying the contraband articles into the interior of the gaol.

Beddowes wore a broad-brimmed, low-crowned hat, and rattled a huge bunch of keys in his hand, and always carried in summer-time an equally large bouquet of flowers in his button-hole.

His waistcoat was of a bright scarlet colour, and his small-clothes extended far below his knees to meet a pair of top boots which reached about half-way up his legs.

Yet, notwithstanding the seeming grossness of his appearance, there was still discernible that neatness and propriety of person which is singularly inherent in the English gaoler.

Bagshawe was of even greater consideration in the gaol.

He enjoyed frequent conferences with the governor of the place, who looked upon him as a man of great trust and dependance, and he contrived to keep up a good understanding with the prisoners — especially with those before trial, and said to be well-to-do in the world.

He enjoyed an enviable notoriety for recommending the felons before trial to make over all they had in the world to some friend or relation, in case things might take an unfavourable turn with them, and what they possessed became forfeited to the Crown.

In such cases he had a lawyer at hand, ready to make the legal assignment, and with whom he was sure to go snacks in the plunder.

Bagshawe was a great character in his way, he was.

During assizes he was entrusted with the custody of great criminals from the county goal to the shire-hall.

The moment he handed over his prisoner to the dock of the criminal court he was at liberty to stroll into the courtyard and amuse himself by relating anecdotes of the accused to impatient listeners.

The moment he was off duty his hands were thrust into the pockets of his great coat, and he rolled about the avenues of the court with an air of the most absolute lordliness.

Here he was generally surrounded by an admiring throng of barbers, old women, shoe-blacks, and those nameless hangers-on, who usually infest the environs of a law court at assize time.

These all looked up to Bagshawe as an oracle, and if he said that the prisoner under his charge would be acquitted, acquitted he invariably was.

Such were the two men who, on entering the colonel's cell, found that the unhappy prisoner had cheated Justice of her due.

"It must have been very sudden," said Bagshawe, the second turnkey, "to leave no mark. Has he strangled hisself?"

"Perhaps he has only poisoned himself," said the other; "many prisoners have died that way."

"That's duberous," said Bagshawe, giving the dead body an inglorious kick to turn it over, "for in that 'ere case his skin would have been covered with dark green spots."

"Your chirurgical study, my fine fellow, is very limited," said the gaol-surgeon, who now entered the cell, "if it leaves you in ignorance that many violent deaths may be inflicted without leaving any wounds or signs upon the body at all."

"How long will it remain here?" asked the first gaoler of the surgeon.

"Only till the coroner's 'quest has sat upon it. Perhaps till nightfall, and then it will be buried."

"Not in 'secrated ground?" observed Bagshawe.

"Certainly not," answered the surgeon, "it's a clear case of *felo de se*, and he will be thrown into a hole dug in the road."

Saying this, he departed to summons an inquest.

Subsequently, a small bottle which had contained poison, now emptied of its contents, but firmly grasped in the colonel's hand, proved the dreadful alternative which the unhappy man had taken to avert his fate, when he found himself openly accused of the horrible crimes he had committed.

Exactly at the same hour, and within a few miles of each other, the bodies of two men were committed to the earth without a ritual of any kind.

It was midnight in both cases, and the cross-road which received their dead remains also witnessed the revolting ceremony of driving stakes through their bodies by torchlight.

The first was the remains of Colonel Hugh Dalton.

The second was that of George Carmichael, his victim and accomplice.

Little remains to be told to complete the present history.

Sir Lionel died of a broken heart, caused by the odium cast upon the Dalton family through the atrocities of one of its members.

There was one person to whom his death caused unmitigated and real sorrow.

That person was no other than his niece Edith.

She had long and secretly loved him,

How many bright eyes grow dim—how many soft cheeks grow pale—how many lovely forms fade away into the tomb, and none can tell the cause that blighted their loveliness! As the dove will clasp its wings to its side, and cover and conceal the arrow that is preying on its vitals, so is it the nature of woman to hide from the world the pangs of wounded affection.

The love of a delicate woman is always silent, even when fortunate. She scarcely breathes it to herself; but when, as was the case with Edith, it is otherwise, she buries it in the recesses of her bosom, and there lets it cower and brood among the ruins of her peace.

Our tale is nearly told; the death of Edith soon followed that of Sir Lionel.

Reginald succeeded to the baronetcy, and, as Sir Reginald Dalton, obliterated all traces of the foul crime committed within the Hall in days bygone by razing it to the ground; nor would he consent to rebuild a dwelling of any kind on the original site.

So endeth the chronicle of the Daltons and the revelations of the "Ghost's Secret."

BOY'S MISCELLANY

Vol. II.—No. 29.]   LONDON, SATURDAY, SEPTEMBER 19, 1863.   [Price One Penny.

THE BARGAIN ON HAMPSTEAD HEATH.

SIXTEEN-STRING JACK;

THE DARING HIGHWAYMAN.

HIS SINGULAR EXPLOITS AND MIRACULOUS ESCAPES.

CHAPTER I.

THE MEETING ON THE HEATH.

THE night was dark, and dismal, heavy clouds shrouded the heavens, and fitful gusts of wind swept on with a spitefulness indicative of the coming storm.

It was towards the end of autumn, and the scene of our opening chapter was the famous Hampstead-heath—the resort of many evil-disposed persons and the dread of every traveller journeying to or from the metropolis.

It was night, and, save the sound of the rising wind, nothing was heard in the neighbourhood of the heath.

The hour of midnight had chimed as a well-mounted horseman dashed on the heath from the London-road.

He rode some little distance, and then drew his steed away from the beaten track and listened attentively.

This horseman was a well-formed, well-dressed young fellow,

ANOTHER NEW TALE OF THRILLING INTEREST

BY A POPULAR AUTHOR,

In No. 37 of the BOY'S MISCELLANY, Price One Penny, will be commenced and continued weekly until completed,

MAZEPPA;

OR, THE DWARF'S REVENGE.

A ROMANCE OF THE WILD HORSE OF TARTARY.

For exciting incidents and powerful character-painting this Story has never been equalled In order to give due effect to the opening chapters of the Tale, the Proprietor has determined on presenting his subscribers with a splendid engraving, on tinted paper, the subject chosen being

"MAZEPPA PURSUED BY THE WOLVES."

OFFICE: 1, CRANE COURT, FLEET STREET.

SIXTEEN-STRING JACK,

THE DARING HIGHWAYMAN.

HIS SINGULAR EXPLOITS AND MIRACULOUS ESCAPES.

Commenced in No. 29 of the BOY'S MISCELLANY, One Penny Weekly.

With this Number was GIVEN AWAY a magnificent Engraving of the celebrated Picture,

"THE SHIPWRECKED SAILOR BOY TELLING HIS STORY,"

This glorious work of art is produced on fine tinted plate paper.

OFFICE: 1, CRANE COURT, FLEET STREET, LONDON, AND ALL BOOKSELLERS

NOW READY, POST FREE 14 STAMPS,

SHILLING ILLUSTRATED BOXIANA,

CONTAINING

PORTRAITS OF THE GREAT BOXERS OF THE DAY.

The History of Pugilism—Lives of the Champions of England—Famous Prize Battles —The Science of Modern Boxing—New Rules of the Prize Ring, &c.

The Portraits are printed on tinted plate paper.

OFFICE: 1, CRANE COURT, FLEET STREET, LONDON, AND ALL BOOKSELLERS.